Everfree

"Sagan's mind-blowing postapocalyptic trilogy comes to a satisfying, terrifying conclusion. . . . He brings the story to its end with a refreshing grace and palpable sadness rare in fantasy of this kind. A powerful plea for sensible human cooperation delivered via a knockout story."
—*Kirkus Reviews*

"A compelling work that will appeal to fans of speculative fiction and apocalyptic thrillers. . . . Readers will admire those trying to live as they refuse to allow humanity to become extinct even when the odds are overwhelmingly against them."
—Alternate Worlds

"A great story . . . nicely rounds off an amazing trilogy."
—BookLore.co.uk

Edenborn

"I believe that *Edenborn* is the finest book that I have read this year. . . . It's one of those few books that I literally could not put down. . . . Sagan's mantelpiece deserves to be heaving with shiny metallic awards and I certainly do not think it would be wrong to mention the word 'Hugo'. . . . Sagan is an adrenaline shot straight into the heart of SF. Do yourself a favor—don't miss these books."
—SF Crowsnest

"*Edenborn* is one of the best postapocalyptic novels you will ever read. . . . The story itself is one that has been thought out and rehashed so many times that to experience such an exciting and original take on it is breathtaking. With a rumbling urgency throughout, *Edenborn* is tough to put down without finishing, whilst Sagan's depiction of a fragile, fallible race will bring people back to this book time and time again. It's not often authors like Nick Sagan crop up, and it's a crying shame they don't."
—*SFX Magazine* (5 star review)

continued . . .

"In his riveting first novel, Nick Sagan both embraces and contests his famous father's vision of the universe." —*Popular Science*

"A dark, twisted carnival of oddities and slippery reality . . . beautiful . . . an extraordinary ride." —*Ithaca Times*

"A landmark new voice. . . . Part thriller, part action-adventure, Nick Sagan's debut is a wake-up call . . . brilliantly executed." —*Books Quarterly*

"The tension is palpable from the first page. . . . Sagan captures perfectly the voice and actions of a rebellious, extremely intelligent teenager . . . mesmerizing." —*Booklist*

"Sagan may have more imagination than he knows what to do with—a wonderful thing in a new author." —*Kirkus Reviews* (starred review)

"Aimed at the audiences of *The Matrix* and *Minority Report* and fans of Neil Gaiman, Orson Scott Card, and Mark Danielewski, Sagan's novel . . . is a fine debut . . . and fans of those same authors will enjoy this." —*Library Journal*

"This is an absolutely stunning novel and a great entry for Sagan onto the scene. The text is packed full of dark humor and wonderfully evoked settings. . . . It is rare for an SF novel to pack so much into so little space. It's what you'd get if you took all the best bits of *Buffy* and stirred in a healthy dose of philosophy and seasoned it with some Grade-A postapocalyptic pepper." —*SF Crowsnest*

"Fusing elements of cyberpunk with the high-tech crime novel, *Idlewild* is taut, edgy SF." —*SFX Magazine*

"[Nick Sagan] captures a disturbingly paranoid tone and delivers a mystery that gathers pace nicely as the pages turn and his alternate realities mess with your mind . . . a very promising literary debut that hints of wonders to come." —*Starburst*

"Sagan seems to delight in changing the rules just when you think you've got the hang of them. There's plenty to confound the reader's expectations, and all of it is couched in engaging, well-paced prose. . . . As a novel, this is one of the best I've read all year. As a debut, it's utterly astonishing." —*Infinity Plus*

everfree

·

NICK SAGAN

New American Library

New American Library
Published by New American Library, a division of
Penguin Group (USA) Inc., 375 Hudson Street,
New York, New York 10014, USA
Penguin Group (Canada), 90 Eglinton Avenue East, Suite 700, Toronto,
Ontario M4P 2Y3, Canada (a division of Pearson Penguin Canada Inc.)
Penguin Books Ltd., 80 Strand, London WC2R 0RL, England
Penguin Ireland, 25 St. Stephen's Green, Dublin 2,
Ireland (a division of Penguin Books Ltd.)
Penguin Group (Australia), 250 Camberwell Road, Camberwell, Victoria 3124,
Australia (a division of Pearson Australia Group Pty. Ltd.)
Penguin Books India Pvt. Ltd., 11 Community Centre, Panchsheel Park,
New Delhi—110 017, India
Penguin Group (NZ), cnr Airborne and Rosedale Roads, Albany,
Auckland 1310, New Zealand (a division of Pearson New Zealand Ltd.)
Penguin Books (South Africa) (Pty.) Ltd., 24 Sturdee Avenue,
Rosebank, Johannesburg 2196, South Africa

Penguin Books Ltd., Registered Offices:
80 Strand, London WC2R 0RL, England

Published by New American Library, a division of Penguin Group (USA) Inc.
Previously published in a G. P. Putnam's Sons edition.

First New American Library Printing, April 2007
10 9 8 7 6 5 4 3 2 1

Grateful acknowledgment is made for permission to include copyright material from
"Scarred but Smarter" by drivin' n' cryin'.

[NAL] REGISTERED TRADEMARK—MARCA REGISTRADA

New American Library Trade Paperback ISBN: 978-0-451-22043-1

The Library of Congress has cataloged the hardcover edition of this title as follows:
Sagan, Nick.
Everfree / Nick Sagan.
p.   cm.
ISBN 0-399-15276-8
I. Title.
PS3619.A36E84   2006   2005056478
813'.6—dc22

Designed by Gretchen Achilles

Printed in the United States of America

for my father

Nobody said it would be fair

They warned you before you went out there

There's always a chance to get restarted

To a new world, new life

Scarred but smarter

drivin' n' cryin', *"Scarred but Smarter"*

PART ONE

victory city

·

(to reign in hell)

Nothing in the sky with nothing. No moon, no stars. Just a canopy of black swallowing the light. Lucky break for the fox. Tough break for the hounds.

Scentless, this fox. Normally, there's a subdermal transmitter. You implant it—it lasts for about a month, then dissolves harmlessly in the bloodstream. A month is a decent observation period to make sure there's no dementia. That's procedure.

Procedure hadn't been followed.

The crisp October wind swept against me as I cut in and out of Quincy and Prescott. Deserted streets. No thermals. A serious fuckup, this, a potential disaster.

Voices crackled in my ear. Slow Bridge reporting equal success.

"History of heart problems," I said. "Well documented. Now he's running. He's scared. We have to find him before he drops."

"Maybe we should back off?" said Bridge.

"Yeah, let him calm down on his own?" said Slow.

"Not in his right mind, wandering off, a threat to himself and others? No thanks," I said. "And that's on you, Slow, because you botched the protocols. You spooked him. You took your eyes off him. If he gets hurt, it's on you."

"Okay, I get it," she said. "Yell at me later."

We made the rounds. Silence on the channel until Bridge called out: "He's here—he's past the Fogg!" And then: "He's doubling back!"

But she lost him, and called his name fruitlessly until I caught up.

"He's quick for an old Popsicle," she apologized, panting hard, hair in her eyes. "Army trained, right?"

"Marine."

"Took me to school. Vanished. It's like he owns the campus."

"He went here," I reminded her.

She sighed. "Why can't he be a Yalie?"

We stood under the Statue of Three Lies, a slumping, seated figure with the inscription: John Harvard, Founder, 1638. Wrong person, wrong founder, wrong year. But it was Harvard University, nevertheless, where I'd dreamed of going to medical school back when I was young and naive about the world. Tourists used to touch the statue's foot for luck. That's what Bridge was doing now.

I pulled up a schematic and tried to ignore Slow's voice on the channel. Something about how it shouldn't matter how trained or skilled he is because he's just a human being, a classic, while we three stood a cut above on the evolutionary tree.

"Sloane, we've lost home-turf advantage," Bridge said. "He's the farmer." I'd once told them that the best soldiers in the world are tactically disadvantaged if they don't know the terrain they're fighting in—and any farmer who knows the ins and outs of his farm could outwit or get the drop on those soldiers if they weren't careful. Good to know they'd been paying attention.

"So think like he's thinking. You know the area. You're being chased. Where's the best place to lose someone?"

"Down?"

"Down."

Into the tunnels went my hounds. Harvard was built atop a vast network of infrastructure—a labyrinthine underworld of steam lines, boilers, electrical relays and such—and as the school ran out of room to expand above ground, it continued to build below. An excellent place to hide.

A flurry of comm chatter as they found him. They tried to calm him but he ran, so I had them herd him up to where I was waiting, syringe in hand. He was a bear of a man, white-haired, square-jawed, with a face that inspired confidence. But sallow now, haunted, confused. He'd spent decades in cold storage, revived only now that we'd found a cure for the microbes that nearly put an end to the entire human race. We'd cut the disease out of him, but the last stages of it had left their mark. I could see it in his eyes. Was I an enemy soldier to him? What combat flashback was he reliving? It was as if we'd turned the flood back, but the water damage remained.

He wanted past me and I wouldn't move, so he lunged and I caught his punch with my ribs. Clinched him long enough. He let out a cry like a wounded animal, staggered off a little ways, and fell. He lay on the grass, sprawled out, staring wild-eyed up at us, clutching his arm where I'd pricked him. I nodded as the sedative took hold, trying to look as reassuring as I could. Sobbing, he curled into a tight fetal ball. In my pocket I found my stethoscope, and I put it on to listen to his heart.

"Relax, Mr. President," I told him. "It's going to be okay."

I didn't know the man. Didn't vote for him. Didn't particularly care for him, but then I didn't much care for his opponent, either. In fairness, I don't have a very high opinion of most politicians. I agree with the man who said, "Politics is the art of looking for trouble, finding it everywhere, diagnosing it incorrectly, and applying the wrong remedies." That would be Marx.

Groucho, not Karl.

Left to my own devices, I'd never have thawed the POTUS out. Hell, I'd never have thawed out anyone. I was born to be a doctor (*designed* to be one, really), but I never took the Hippocratic oath. Even if I had, the few thousand cryopreserved humans secreted throughout the world weren't my patients. Not in my book. No, they'd cooled their heels for forty years; they could stay frosty for a little longer.

It hadn't been my call. I'd been outvoted, four to one. Just because we had the ability to bring people out didn't mean that we should. My argument. But, ethically speaking, it wasn't right to leave them frozen. So my friends said. And though I'd been tempted to pick up and go—old habits die hard—I stayed to help.

One friend in particular: Naomi d'Oliveira, better known as Pandora. She was, I'd come to realize, the best of us. Because she didn't want to be. Vashti, Isaac and Champagne had won my friendship, but they were hypocrites with enormous egos. And the same could be said for me. But Pandora had a quiet strength, and she was undeterred. Not untouched by the grief of the world—not dead inside, as I'd been for so many years—but simply unwilling to let it stop her. Indomitable. She'd believed in me long after anyone ever should have. She gave up her sight for me. More than a friend, Pandora, much more than that now.

While my security team and I escorted the POTUS to New Cambridge Hospital for tests and observation, she was trying to restore life. No mean feat. It's very easy to annihilate someone you're trying to revive.

You have to get the metabolism going again, but carefully. You'd better protect the brain with everything you've got, because normal circulation can really fuck it up. Free radicals and metabolites can do major cerebral damage during "reboot," so you can't be too quick, but you can't be slow, either, because you're up against the process of cellular decay. The dreaded "I," *ischemia,* the fast track to the brain withering, because it isn't getting the oxygen and other nutrients it needs. It's a balancing act to flush out the cryoprotectant and then flood the body with molecular scissors—Vashti's special blend—the ones that can cleave Black Ep from the genome like chaff from wheat. That "turns back the flood," but there's still all the "water damage" to repair, all the myriad degeneration the plague did during its stay. More often than not, some of the patient's major organs are shot, which means accelerated therapeutic cloning is required. If the new organs play nice in the old body, it's time to shock the heart and fire up the brain, and cross your fingers the ultrastructural damage isn't too bad.

To see Pandora work, you'd never know she was blind. Malachi helped guide her—our old pal, Mal, an artificial intelligence who could serve as her eyes via cameras in the lab, and even as a force beyond her eyes via biodegradable microcameras injected into the patient's capillaries. But Mal could only do so much. As a computer program, he lacked intuition—and that was where Pandora excelled.

"She goes against the odds and wins," he told me. "Not always, but enough to make me wonder what she understands that I don't."

"Power of the subconscious," I shrugged.

On that night, everything was going wrong. Touch and go. It had been a risky attempt to begin with, this patient suffering from a degree of cellular necrosis just at the borderline of what we feel comfortable trying to save.

ICBA, Mal predicted. Irreversible cessation of brain activity. Vashti joined the operation and reluctantly agreed with Mal. But Pandora wouldn't hear of it.

"He's a fighter," she said. "He wants to live."

In the end they saved him. She came home, pale and exhausted. I took her to bed, rubbed the tension from her shoulders and told her she couldn't keep working these hours. I said she was risking her health. She kissed my cheek and told me not to worry. She knew her limits.

I doubted it.

But we could talk about it later, I supposed, in one of the rare windows of time when neither of us had anything immediate to do. I'd watched those windows shrink over the past year. Sometimes I felt like I was in a lightless room.

Okay, so you can bring a person back to life. But you can't just thaw and run. The thawed have questions. It's a confusing time for them. Even the ones without dementia. First of all, they don't know how long they've slept. Most are prepared for a year or two. Tell them it's been over forty, and their worldview curdles. It's a big hit to take. It helps to put it in context.

For Rip van Winkle was old and gray,
And twenty summers had passed away—
Yes, twenty winters of snow and frost
Had he in his mountain slumber lost.

So it's the double plus Rip van Winkle coma, or 2RVW+, which sounds like the far side of forever. Fortunately, there are mitigating factors. For one thing, cryopreservation puts a bullet in the natural aging process—the thawed are no older nor grayer than they were at the moment they were frozen. Vanity mitigates. For another, the time they lost—all the summers and winters I spent and they didn't—well, they didn't really miss anything. Just all the struggles my friends and I went through—but who were we, right? Everyone they knew—friends, enemies, rivals, politicians, newsmakers and trendsetters—well, they were either dead or in cryonic stasis like them. Envy mitigates.

Hey, you haven't lost your looks, and you really haven't lost any time, so you can save your mourning for the dead. Which, in fairness, they did. The thawed had lost more than any generation before them, more than any generation in human history. It's awful hard to mitigate a dead family. And that was always one of the first questions they'd ask. *What about my loved ones? What happened to them?*

To which you have to be absolutely direct, because anything else is cruel.

Other questions include: *Where am I?*

New Cambridge Hospital.

New Cambridge?

That's what we call Cambridge now. Cambridge, Massachusetts. Do you remember being frozen? You're just a mile from where that procedure took place.

Am I going to live?

Yes. You are no longer infected. Our medical staff is monitoring your condition closely and will work to repair any lasting damage the plague may have caused.

What's it like out there?

It's a new day. Black Ep was the biggest threat humankind has ever faced, but we've beaten it at last.

How many survivors?

No human beings survived the plague. It emptied the world, claiming every last man, woman and child.

Then how are we still here?

Posthumans.

Like on the news?

Right. Genetically engineered offspring with redundant organs and enhanced immune systems. Designed by the biotech company Gedaechtnis in the darkest days of the plague. Posthumans, PH. You're looking at one now.

So you saved us?

Not me personally, but yes. It took decades to find a cure. That was the first step, "Response." This is the next step, "Recovery." New Cambridge has the largest collection of cryopreserved individuals anywhere in the world. We are conducting triage here, disaster relief. Those who can be revived will be revived. Our goal is the continued eradication of Black Ep and the resuscitation and treatment of infected peoples. To that end, we have established an ad hoc government, as was proposed by the Emergency Plague Powers Act back in 42 BR.

What's 42 BR?

The year you were frozen. Forty-two years "Before Recovery." I'm afraid the old calendars have changed.

What's going to happen to me?

That's the magic question. Once they ask you that, you know they're starting to look forward instead of back. So you reassure them that their options are wide open so long as they don't do anything criminal or crazy. As soon as they're given a clean bill of health, they're free to go anywhere in the world they want. Not much civilization beyond our fence, admittedly, but that's what pioneers are for. Godspeed. That said, here you give them the Invitation, encouraging them to stick around and help rebuild the promise of the future.

This is Year One of the New World and you're smack dab in the center of it: New Cambridge, Victory City. Here beats the heart of the Recovery, and it's beating strong. You have a golden opportunity to live in the latest, greatest city on planet Earth. Be a part of it. Pitch in. Why struggle for food and shelter when we have gourmet dining and luxury apartments? All you have to do is contribute. We have many jobs available. We have farming, construction, renovation, acquisition, counseling and service positions, and if you lack training it will be provided free of charge. You've lost family and friends—we have counselors here who can help you through your pain. You're not alone. We've thawed out over a thousand people—you'll make friends here. You can renew yourself. And here you give them the Doctrine. You pass on a philosophy, something solid for them to push against. This world is collective. This is it right now and we're all in it together. Let's find a new way of living where we all look out for each other. The future is big and bright and full of opportunity—let's explore it together.

That's what a Greeter does. It's an important job because you're the first person they get to talk to, and what you do sets the tone for the rest of their stay. I'd tried it for the first three weeks of the Recovery, but didn't have the temperament for it. Just not my bag. The last straw came when, after I explained the situation to this one guy, he kept asking me if it was a joke. *Are you kidding me? Is this a practical joke?* Nine times he asked me. I said yes. God, yes. I sat back and told him that he was dead, I was the motherfucking devil, this was Hell, and welcome to it.

"Same as any other business. Build your brand with the right team around you, a strong team, empowering them. Then it's a question of understanding the market, taking initiative, outthinking your competition and leveraging your strengths. Same deal. I'd never trade it, but it isn't, you know, magical. When you're a kid and you grow up in the family business you think maybe it might be, but no. It isn't Willy Wonka."

Mars had a first name, but I've forgotten it. He was a twitchy, chatty sort, friendly enough, but damaged in the way that so many of them were—overwhelmed by the feelings that crop up from a brush with oblivion and determined not to drown in them. Just another absurd, privileged, self-deluded, guilt-ridden human being, thrilled to be alive.

"And it's more than just chocolate. Many people don't realize that. We've got vending management systems, information technology, not to mention coffee, pet foods, Uncle Ben's Rice. We're diversified."

The royal *we*. Bad habit with the CEOs. *We* have this and *we* have that. Right. Who's *we*? Black Ep had annihilated billions. Mars was alone in the world. A couple thousand tycoons had been lucky enough to finagle cryonic suspension, but their management teams had not. To say nothing of their labor forces. You can own anything you like on paper, but who's going to run the factories? Who's going to sell the merchandise? Let alone buy it?

Capitalist existentialism—"How do I prove my wealth and status now that the world's been destroyed?"—had given rise to a collector culture. With so many abandoned possessions available for the taking, many thawed would establish a pecking order based on who had the most cars, jewelry, gadgets, olive forks and so on. With the economy in shambles, they competed to see who had the rarest of the rare, who had a complete set, etc. Useless pastime as far as I was concerned, but I pointed out the flea market as we passed it by.

Mars wanted to know if we'd thawed anyone from Hershey or Nestlé. Scoping the competition. One of the first questions he asked.

"I don't know how anyone's supposed to come back from a disaster like this," he said, as if surfing my thoughts. "But we sure as hell have to try."

"Sure as hell," I agreed. "Assuming you're talking about civilization in general and not just your candy empire."

He arched an eyebrow. "The one doesn't preclude the other?"

I interrupted my tour of our little utopia to look at him, eye to eye, because I wanted him to understand. "It just might," I said. "Do you want some free advice?"

"As long as it's free."

"Mr. Mars, the past is gone. You can't return to the status quo. You can't chase a fantasy. When you do, you waste everyone's valuable time, and worse than that you disrespect the sacrifices we've all had to make. Maybe someday you'll have a chance at reclaiming everything you've lost, but right now it's adapt or die. So embrace the Doctrine."

He was listening. I watched the wheels turn.

"In the meantime," I told him, "if I find any unemployed Oompa Loompas wandering about, I'll be sure to let you know."

"Is that your role in this?"

"To look for Oompa Loompas?"

"To push the Doctrine?"

Overhead, geese winged their way south. Follow the leader. I tracked the V with my eyes.

"No. You can do what you want. It's your life. Live in the past. Live stupidly. I won't push. I won't interfere at all unless you cause trouble. But trust me, you'll be a lot happier if you live in the now. Hence the Doctrine, hence the advice."

Mars didn't seem like he'd be trouble and he wasn't obsessed with *what's the best part of town* and *what's in fashion,* so I answered all his questions and made a point of introducing him to all the good apples I could find. Good apples make a huge difference. Wake up with so little left and you might be desperate to bond—so we tried to get the newly thawed to bond with our supporters, the ones who believed in what we were trying to do.

Handshakes, business cards, link numbers—all the rituals and buzzwords, all the trappings of corporate culture. They found it comforting, and I couldn't argue with it, though I couldn't relate to it, either. One dog sniffs another—*Who's the alpha, you or me?*

I'm not big on hierarchies. Don't like groups. Don't play well with others. But I can't isolate myself anymore. Not when I have responsibilities and—like the old poem goes—promises to keep.

Because Mars was new, he served as a lightning rod for the regulars. As the ultra-rich tended to socialize only within their circle, many already knew him from before the plague. Those who hadn't wanted to greet him and take his measure, which meant I could trot him out in front of me and duck most of the questions about the President. Word had traveled, but rumor had traveled farther.

"He's fine," I assured them. "Resting comfortably. Prognosis is good; I'm sure he'll be up and running the free world again before you know it."

Everything's lovely. Everything's better than perfect. Shut up. Trust me, this is the best of all possible worlds.

"You make people nervous," said Mars, once I'd moved us on.

"Do I?"

"Well, there's something unsettling about the lot of you. The different genes—the whole 'not quite human' thing. But there's something about you specifically, if you don't mind my saying. The bright orange hair, maybe."

"Never trust a redhead."

"I've heard that before," he said. "The mark of Cain. Also Judas, I remember. My family's Christian, but I broke from the faith a long time ago."

Cain, Judas and the Egyptian murder god, Set. Thank you, exotic gene for red hair, MC1R. Not terribly long ago, they burned redheads as witches. In Egypt they buried them alive. I'd been buried alive once. Didn't care for it. Had yet to be burned.

Mars had picked up on something, but it had less to do with hair color and more with a growing feeling among the thawed that

I was not their greatest friend, that I did not love them unconditionally, and that any who wanted to gum up the wheels of progress might not like what I'd do in return.

I'd made myself the one PH who wouldn't budge. No, I'd done more than that. I had been keeping a very close watch on the bad apples, and while my day job consisted largely of solving their disputes with kindness and understanding, I'd been moonlighting as a hammer. As a trip wire. As a poison pill.

Someone who'd even think of threatening the people I cared about, or the fragile peace they'd achieved—well, that poor misguided prick had to understand that the cost would far outweigh the benefits. He had to know it, so I made sure he knew it. By putting fear in his heart. Because no one else would. Because it had to be done.

Another reason why I'd embarked on my campaign of intimidation: it made me visible. I'd come to the conclusion: *If I find the troublemakers and make myself the flashpoint for their anger, this will insulate my friends.* And so it had, but only to a degree.

"White Crane Spreads Wings," Mars said. He'd taken sight of a line of men and women making slow, steady movements on the lawn of the Harvard Square Hotel, each maneuver flowing smoothly into the next.

"You do tai chi?"

"It's how I relax."

"Beginner or expert?"

He shrugged. "I put in eight years."

"Can you fight?"

"Fight? Never tried. To me, it's just for relieving stress. When I got sick, it was practically the only thing that helped me. I'm good on the forms, but still can't meditate for shit."

"That's Getty," I said, indicating the graceful, white-haired instructor. "He never turns away a student, and if you're interested in doing more than that, I know he's looking for someone to teach a beginners' class."

I made introductions. When called upon, the candy mogul demonstrated decent technique—despite protestations of rust—and promptly won himself the job.

He seemed willing to integrate with the community, meet people, get involved, pitch in—positive indicators that Mars would in fact be one of the good ones, neither obsessed with fortunes lost nor so overwhelmed by grief as to be unable to participate in the Recovery. One less person to worry about made my job that much easier.

"Tai chi chuan," he told me. "I guess that's one reason to get up in the morning. Now I just have to find a few others."

He was on his way.

When the Roman Empire would set out for war, a consul would go to a temple of Mars and chant, *"Mars, vigila!"* Mars, awaken! Then he'd shake the sacred lances, the ones that had been consecrated in the war god's name. I had to shake the sacred lance myself about then, so I made a pit stop at Grendel's.

Grendel's Den had been an infamous Cambridge hangout, catering to Harvard students, faculty and alumni. A subterranean monster-themed restaurant/bar I might have frequented had I actually gone to school here. We'd pegged it as a good place for the thawed to relax, and had prioritized its renewal over all the other bars and clubs in the neighborhood. Since then the Planning Commission had reopened a sports bar, a meat market, a cigar club and a serious drinker's bar. Alcohol could sometimes make patrons aggressive—I'd found that out firsthand—but it also played a big part in placating the masses. It was a drinker's culture. Facing the future was hard enough, but without martini lunches and brandy snifters—or at the very least, AA—that was unthinkable.

Out of the bathroom, I found Mars telling his story to one of the bartenders—"unofficial grief counselors," some called them, though we had retrained a number of the thawed to serve as official ones as well. Everyone wanted to talk about what they'd lost. Only natural. Human nature. But I'd gotten pretty tired of it. I'd lost my fair share and then some, but didn't see the point in broadcasting my woes to every new person I met. Why bother? To bond over shared tragedies? How could they even share?

Hi, I'm Gabriel.

Hi, Gabriel!

Right, well, it's Halloween now. Long story. Everyone calls me Hal.

Hi, Hal!

Right. So. I'm a genetically engineered experiment, optimized to survive the Black Ep plague. There were only nine others like me in the world and four of them are dead. My parents are a witches' brew of genetic material—which is to say, I never met them—and the two people who went around calling themselves my parents were actually computer programs. That's because I spent the first eighteen years of my life in a virtual simulation, one where the painful truth about Black Ep was hidden from me. You had to watch billions die slowly from the disease, sure, but I had to absorb that knowledge all at once and nearly went mad from it. One of my friends went on a murderous rampage. My first love committed suicide. So did my son. I've killed and I've buried. I don't even have my idyllic childhood to measure it all against, because that part of my memory's been zapped, and after twenty-five years of trying to recover it, all I have are scraps. Everything I've been through is for a good cause, of course, your cause, you people who wouldn't give in, who wanted to triumph over non-existence. That's where we come in. And so here I am with them, the posthumans, the only ones who can understand what I've been through. And only one of them really does. We've defeated Black Ep and worked to bring you back from the brink of death, and some of you are grateful and some of you are asshats. Would you be shocked to discover that I feel just a wee bit alienated from each and every one of you?

How could they relate to that?

It's not like I had an ax to grind. I didn't. I just didn't feel warm and fuzzy with these people. They weren't my tribe.

God knows it could have been different. When we got out— when we learned what was real and what wasn't—we found letters. Letters from elementary school classes, kids from all over the world wishing us well, drawing pictures, telling us about their families, praying for us to someday beat the plague.

And yet *they* weren't frozen. They weren't lucky enough. Rich enough. Well-connected enough. So they're gone. They don't get to come back. But the CEO of Nike? Here. So were the top execs of Pfizer and Fannie Mae. Just like the Sultan of Brunei, the last big Oscar winner and the chairman of the RNC.

Did I have sympathy for these people? Some. Could I treat them fairly and well? Of course. But a zookeeper doesn't have to love his animals. He only has to take care of them. And not turn his back on the carnivores.

"Just listen," said one of Las Vegas's wealthiest casino owners, a spiffily dressed hulking mass of futility.

"We've been through this."

He blocked my path when I tried to move past him.

"Twenty percent. That's a killing. And just for doing your job."

I shook him off me. Everyone wanted something.

By the pool tables in the back I found Grendel's proprietor, the former majority shareholder of Eastman Kodak. I'd nicknamed him Kody. He'd nicknamed me Thursday—no explanation why.

His real name was Suchart Shinawatra. A reclusive Thai national who'd made billions over the years, Kody was the sole exception to my rule—he'd won me over early on, being the one captain of industry who could consistently make me smile.

"Ho, Thursday. Is it President season already?"

"You heard about that, did you?"

"Talk of the town."

He offered a quick game of 9-ball, which I refused, as he knew I would. He didn't really want me to play. When you rack up, the 1-ball goes in the head spot, the 9 goes in the center, and the other balls make random parts of the diamond. Not so random when Kody did it—the 5-ball at the right corner meant he had intelligence for me, and the 8-ball touching the 5 meant it wasn't safe to tell it now. Kody was the eyes and ears of the town, my most useful source of strategic information by far. We had to talk obliquely and walk a fine line—he couldn't be seen as my spy. Since first meeting him, I'd been trying to use him as a buffer between his fellow thawed and myself. For a multibillionaire, he was remarkably unassuming about himself—even better, he was a natural mediator, someone who could inspire reason and tractability.

"Rumors are flying," he told me, keeping up the harmless, less clandestine talk about the President. "If you have the man, you have to bring him out. Show people he's unhurt."

"Working on it."

"Twenty-five," Vegas rudely interrupted. "It's proprietary software. You know I'm getting screwed."

He had a stake in Mammon, a popular casino system played through the links. Thawed matched skill and luck throughout town; a table of Kody's patrons were in mid–craps game as we spoke. Vast sums of virtual money were won and lost, and the real-money subscription fees were supposed to trickle into Vegas's pocket. Not any longer, thanks to a recent exploit in the payment subroutine.

"It's all worthless anyway. This is a postapocalyptic barter economy, or did that somehow escape your attention?"

"Then they should damn well barter for it," he said, steering me away from Kody. "Gold, my man, is disaster-proof. Always keeps its value."

I shook my head. No one knew what was valuable anymore.

"Look around and what do we see? Solid-gold watches, platinum rings, diamond cuff links. I set a barter price, you enforce the law and take your cut. Or don't you think I should be compensated for providing a service?"

"Don't much care, honestly. Even if I did, I don't have the time or manpower to enforce pre-Recovery commercial law. Try petitioning the Assembly."

"I want *you* to help me," he pressed, voice loud enough to draw a few curious stares. "I know you won't screw me over."

"You know that, huh?"

"You're an honorable man."

"I don't have time for this."

"Shit, neither do I! I'm tired of not getting what's rightfully mine. And I need it for leverage."

"Take your hands off me," I said, but he only gripped my jacket tighter.

"Aren't you here to help me? How much do you want, thirty? Forty?"

"You can't buy me, so take your hands—"

"I can't buy you, huh? Motherfucking People's Republic of Cambridge! You miserable socialist piece of—"

He was screaming in my face. I could smell his breakfast and feel flecks of his spit on my cheek. And he wouldn't give up my jacket. So I took his wrist and twisted it. Not enough for the bone to snap, just enough to persuade him to let go. Restraint. He took a knee and an expression of anguish. Then came the yelp. Louder than I'd expected. At once, everyone in the bar was gawping at me, as skittish and silent as deer. Not just the bad apples—the good ones, too. Even Kody had lost his voice and his nerve, suddenly unable to look me in the eye.

I left before anyone thought to start broadcasting. Outside, Mars wouldn't say much to me, and what he did say was so soft, it drowned in the autumn wind.

Was I wrong to use physical force?

In principle, no, I decided.

Did the pros outweigh the cons?

I didn't know.

What I did know was the situation was getting more and more fragile as days went by, and my temper kept getting shorter. If I wasn't careful, the whole thing could collapse. And I realized, reluctantly, that we were a lot closer to that than I'd feared.

1AA: New Cambridge Restaurant Reviews

HARVEST

44 Brattle Street, Harvard Square, New Cambridge, link: "Harvest"

M–Sa 12pm–10 pm, Su 11am–3pm

⊕ New Cambridge's first Recovery-age restaurant is also its best, thanks to the inspired *vive cuisine* creations of celebrity chef Francisco Fierro. Whether you're nestled in the warm-wooded interior or in the verdant splendor of the outdoor garden café, Harvest offers the finest upscale dining experience available today. Though the service is notoriously spotty, the crystal is always shining, and the vegetarian and near-vegetarian meals are as healthy as they are delightful. A globe-spanning wine list is sure to please all but the most exacting oenophile, and patrons unanimously adore Fierro's signature desserts. The honey-and-vanilla-drizzled *panna cotta* alone is worth coming out of hibernation for.

"A poor substitute for Pandora."

"You're not my favorite dinner companion, either," Isaac replied, taking a seat opposite me at the outdoor table. Over the past few years he'd eliminated his goatee, cultivating a clean, bland, professional look. His clove brown head remained as bald as a marble egg.

"She double-shifting again?"

"You know how it is."

"Oh, sure. A physician's work is never done."

"She's putting in a lot of hours," he admitted. "The cost of trying to get back on schedule. Now if we brought more doctors out, or gave more responsibility to the ones we have, the situation might be different. Of course, Vashti thinks that's dangerous."

"With good reason."

"With some supporting evidence, yes," he said, qualifying it, conflicted as ever about giving up the secret we'd kept from the thawed. "Anyway, Pan's dear to me, too. You know I keep an eye on her. Try to set your mind at ease."

My lips curved into not quite a smile. He stared wanly at me.

Isaac and I had never been particularly chummy. We'd put our differences aside because we'd bonded over one thing: children. He'd lost his and I'd lost mine. So to hear the man telling me not to worry about Pandora—it was a nice gesture, but useless. He knew it. But what else could he say?

"Good to see you again, Mr. Abdelrazek, Mr. Hall," said the waitress, and from her body language I decided she meant it in Isaac's case. She was a headliner, a young and radiant ingénue who'd made quite a name for herself despite—or perhaps because of—an enigmatic blankness that made her look vulnerable and slightly stupid. There's an old adage about actors and waiters, but this one had never waited tables in her life until we assigned her to Harvest. We had an unofficial but tacitly agreed-upon policy of putting the thawed to work in the food-service industry as a first job. It helped kill the idea that anyone was too good for hard, honest labor, though not everyone could make the transition smoothly. To help her along, I'd suggested she view it as research for a role. I'd pointed out that, at the height of his success, Andy Kaufman had worked as a busboy to keep in touch with the common man, but she'd had no idea who he was. Way before her time. Mine, too, but I was a dogged fan of surreal, anarchic humor. Given my fucked-up past, there's no way I couldn't be.

She took our drink orders. Isaac flirted with her. Lonely bastard. Among the thawed, he wielded a charm that was as effective as it was empty. He could have enticed the blank beauty into his bed—surely, for after saving so many lives, we were celebrities even to celebrities—and yet I knew that he would not. He wouldn't entangle himself. Too focused on his work. But it meant something to know that he could.

I watched the other tables to see who was watching us. A fraction of the construction team had clustered around a nearby space heater. Two members of the Yacht Club were keeping tabs. And a table of phobes decked out in full antimicrobial gear, fear-flecked eyes peeking out from behind their masks. Good luck trying to eat in those things. Phobes were a minority, albeit a sizable one, a nuisance about town with all their linkspam and graffiti. Slogans like "How safe is 'safe'?" typified the movement. All day long you could tell them that Black Ep was under control now, a nightmare they didn't have to worry about anymore. Not once would they listen. A persistent reminder that we were, above all else, a plague culture—damage had been done.

"Nice crowd," said Isaac, and whether he meant temperament

or numbers didn't matter much to me. He wanted something and was stalling.

"What?" I asked him. "You want to talk about the President's dementia? Or how Sloane let him run off? I already spoke to her."

"I want to talk about you."

"Have at it."

"Grendel's," he said. "The arm twisting."

"Oh, that. It's nothing."

"Of course it is."

"He put his hands on me. Bad precedent."

"You tore a ligament."

"And?"

"And it's the kind of act that builds resentment."

"There's already resentment."

"Admittedly. Hal, I see it every day, and I deal with it every day. What I don't do is exacerbate it. You're using too much force. Period. I need you to cool it."

"And you think that's best?"

"I think it would make my job easier."

The drinks came. After the waitress left again I said, "Who's asking me, Isaac? You or the Assembly?"

"Ideally, I'd like to keep this out of the Assembly. For your sake."

"Well, if this is an unofficial request—just you and me—I'll think about it."

He studied me from behind his wineglass. "You have to think about not using excessive force? How much contemplation do you suppose it merits?"

"You're not seeing the whole picture," I said, "and frankly I'm not sure you can."

"Why not?"

"Blinded by your job."

"Oh? I'm the smile and you're the teeth?"

"You approach this from a 'how can I make everybody happy' perspective. You want everyone to like you. I approach it from a security perspective. Threat assessment, that's my role in this. And this nice-looking crowd we have—most respect us, some revere us, but there's a growing number who are conspiring against us, hoping to marginalize us, eliminate us if they possibly can."

He made a steeple of his fingers, dark eyes looking thoughtful and concerned. "Let's turn it around. Is it possible that you've become blinded by *your* job? Could you be seeing imaginary wolves among the sheep and phantom foxes in the henhouse?"

"Isaac, even if you think I'm paranoid—" I began.

"It doesn't mean they're not after you," he finished, smiling.

"So you say. But this casino owner was after us how exactly? And hurting him accomplished what?"

"It sent a message."

"The wrong one."

"For the past week here at Harvest," I said, "a busboy has been preserving all the glasses and cutlery we touch. I suspect he's collecting fingerprints. Not sure why. The phobes at the table to your left are spreading a whispering campaign—how we're not bringing enough doctors and scientists out, how we're putting our personal interests ahead of their welfare. The smug fellow behind you has been quietly conducting a poll, asking the rank and file if they're happy with the way things are being run here, or would they support—and I quote—*a reorganization.*"

"There's reason to be concerned," he admitted, "but you're talking about a small number of malcontents—"

"Only takes one."

"—most of whom we can expect to be mollified by the President."

"Assuming we can make the man healthy, sane and willing to play ball."

"Vashti assures me we can. In any case, the malcontents—do you think we're looking at doers or talkers? Are they just venting?"

"Plotting."

"Hard evidence?"

"Not yet."

"When you have evidence, bring it to the Assembly. Until then, don't forget that the vast majority approves of what we're doing. As they should—we're a democracy, not a tyranny. We're not oppressing anyone, we're not depriving anyone of his rights and we're not keeping anyone against his will. We might not be fully transparent, but we take pains to be as open as possible. We've drawn up the Victory Doctrine, and many have embraced it as a new ideology—with any luck, they'll hold on to it when they go back to running things on their own."

"And when's that?"

"Soon."

"Soon?"

"You know we can't give a hard date yet," he scowled. "Not after the last estimate we gave. But everyone knows the day isn't far off—we're a *temporary* government."

"Not temporary enough. Frustration's building."

"That's why you should be wiping noses instead of spraining wrists. Look, I'm not saying there aren't times when you might have to use force. I'm saying it's too much force. And this isn't the first time you've done it."

Three weeks earlier, I'd put Parker through a window.

Parker was Parker—if I knew what he did, I'd have given him a nickname, but the son of a bitch was tightlipped. There was a certain amount of "quiet wealth" in the world, and he apparently had a piece of it. In any event, he was still in the hospital recuperating.

Concussion, lacerations and multiple fractures—he'd walk funny the rest of his life. But there was a good reason for it, and her name was Izzy.

Like all my nieces, Izzy was smart and pretty, but unlike Brigit and Sloane, she was one of those rare individuals who could get along well with anyone. Izzy was short for Isabel, and her mothers named her after Isaac, but let's not hold that against her. Slender and dark, with an exotic Nigerian–Sri Lankan heritage informing her genome, she cut the figure of a leggy supermodel, though a surprisingly unassuming and disarming one. She'd come of age without male companionship, and had only recently become aware of the kind of effect she had on men. Most of the time, she knew how to take care of herself. Not when she was drinking.

Beyond Grendel's, there were four bars of note. The Cellar was a serious drinker's bar, nothing fancy, just a place to unwind. The Druid was an Irish pub–slash–sports bar, Celtics memorabilia on the walls. Oasis was the place to pick someone up or get picked up—our dance club, our meat market. All three served a useful purpose; they let our populace feel more human, social and alive. Like things might almost be normal—if you squinted and pretended real hard. I made the rounds as part of my security detail and very rarely would anyone give me trouble. The alcohol flowed freely, but the bars were good about policing their patrons when anyone got belligerent. And it didn't hurt that I had informants scattered throughout.

But the fourth bar gave me trouble. Once a highly acclaimed Mediterranean restaurant, it had found new life as a cigar club, a power bar, a watering hole for those who mourned their lost glamour and privilege. To me it would always be known as the Cigar Club, but technically, it was called the Casablanca, and as in the old movie, most knew it as Rick's. That was in no small part due to the new proprietor's name—Richard Ning, the legendary corporate raider. As in the film, the patrons saw themselves as a heroic Resistance, and we who presented the Doctrine could only be cast as Nazis.

Perverse, but even the worst villains like to play at being heroes.

So I made a point of showing up there as often as I could. *Kick the hornets' nest.* They didn't have to like me, but they had to know they couldn't control me.

"You're like a bad taste that won't go away no matter how many times I swallow," the doorman told me when I approached.

"Now now, Fitch, Hal is an *acquired* taste," Ning suavely corrected him.

"That's right, Fitch, I'll grow on you," I promised. "You'll come to associate me with sweetness and laughter. One day I won't be in your life anymore and you'll realize how desperately you miss me, and what a void in your heart I've left behind. Now fuck off."

He did. My host welcomed me in. Ning could be gracious, and always made a point of offering me amenities—this time a carton of clove cigarettes, which I refused.

"Truly? I heard you still smoked these atrocious things," he said.

"Not in years."

"And here I thought I knew something personal about you," he said with a frown.

"Sorry."

"I daresay you're the most mysterious of all the PH. Part of the job description, hey? When someone writes your unauthorized biography, I hope you'll let me know."

He used PH not for posthumans but "placeholders." As in, "We call you placeholders because you did an excellent job minding the store while we were sleeping, but we're back now, so the graceful thing for you to do would be to step aside and let us get on with business." Often followed by, "That's really the only problem I have with you people."

At heart an optimist, Ning tried to sway me to his side every time he saw me. "You obviously don't believe in the touchy-feely tripe your comrades are peddling any more than I do," he'd typically say. "Everyone's unhappy, you most of all. Why not end this foolishness and tell me what I want to know?"

Always tempting, but never would I do so. He was a poor Prometheus, the last I'd trust with Vashti's secret. His disciples—a mosaic of me-firsters, moral relativists and Strangelove patriots—had to be watched carefully for fear of the damage they'd do.

So I told him no, like usual. But on that night he intimated that I wasn't the only PH being pursued at the Cigar Club.

I found Izzy with Parker and Parker's friends all crowded around a table near the back, laughing and carrying on. More often than not, my nieces served as liaisons between the Assembly and the various teams to which they'd been assigned—power, transportation, agriculture, and so on. In Izzy's case it was construction, the borders of our city slowly expanding, lost infrastructure reclaimed piece by piece from decades of neglect. That was how she knew Parker—he'd been working construction jobs ever since leaving Harvest.

They were teaching her how to blow smoke rings. They were throwing back shots. Parker had an arm around her—fine, she was a big girl, and I'd no interest in sitting in judgment of her dates—but something in my intuition sent up a red flag. Was this an evolution of Ning's strategy? To have his supporters buddy up to the younger generation and turn them against us? I couldn't say for sure, but I'd caught a bad feeling, so I took Izzy aside and told her so.

She huffed. Shot daggers. Rolled those daggers skyward. She said, "No offense, Hal, but you're probably the last person I'd take fatherly advice from."

I'd no snappy comeback. What could I say? My son had committed suicide.

So I left the Cigar Club's effluvium and stepped back out into the cold night air. Back to my rounds.

Later that evening, she linked me. Briefly. Unintelligibly. She was completely smashed, crying or both.

This was no particular plan of Ning's—I'd overcomplicated what was going on. Parker had simply gotten her drunk, and then invited her to an unfinished apartment under pretext of scouting it for the next day's work. But when she got there, he trapped her, all kisses and coercion—her *I'm not ready* struggling against his *Oh, honey, yes, you are, you just don't know it yet.*

Too drunk to protect herself, she'd still had enough presence of mind to link me. When I found them, he was atop her, holding her arms down, using his weight as an advantage—and she was half-conscious, her clothes half off.

I dragged him up by his elbow and he slipped free, slick with sweat. He locked eyes with me. He was grinning. That didn't really bother me—I've been known to smile inappropriately sometimes myself. Nerves and all. What bothered me was the appeal for sympathy. A look in his eyes that said, *Oh, this is awkward, but you know how it is, right?* Then he spied the door. As he tried to edge past me, he said, "Look, I've been frozen for a really long time."

For some reason, I remember thinking, *Some people won't see the light of day even if you throw them through a window.* Even though it was pitch-black outside, that's what came to mind.

• • •

"I hit you?"

"Yes, sir. Gave me a good shot to the ribs," I said.

"I don't remember that at all."

"Well, you weren't yourself that night."

"No hard feelings, then."

"Not on this end," I said.

He nodded, rubbing the ache from his temple with the heel of his palm. "And the sickness is to blame? I wasn't just out drinking?"

"Not to my knowledge."

"Thank sweet Jesus for that," he muttered, chasing the pills we'd given him with a tall glass of water. He wasn't nearly as presidential as the virtual program of him I'd been exposed to while growing up. Or rather, that program had been modeled after the man at the height of his confidence and power, while this sad, bedridden fellow in a bathrobe had since been unhinged by the collapse of civilization. You don't want a leader who's constantly on the verge of tears. On the plus side, Vashti had restored his sanity—by her prediction, buoyancy and self-assurance would follow.

But not before we made a deal with him. Because when you're looking to negotiate with a former world leader, there are few positions more advantageous than having him completely traumatized and thanking you for bringing him back from the dead.

"You know I bet against you?" he said. "Bet against all the contingency plans. Not publicly, of course. For the cameras, I did what I had to do to keep hope in people's hearts. But in my heart, I just didn't think anything would work."

"Happy to prove you wrong," said Vashti with a self-satisfied smile.

"It just boggles the mind to think of what you've achieved," he said. "For your ingenuity and heroism, extraordinary heroism, this country owes you one hell of a debt. And as President, I hope to find many opportunities to repay that debt. Whatever's in my power to give you," he added, "I'd like you to have."

"Well, thank you, sir, and of course, we're delighted you feel that way," she said, after flashing me a *so far so good* look. "Right now, what we need most is your endorsement. Also, your patience as we try to finish the work we started."

"Reminds me of Jakarta," he mused. "I was right about Jakarta. Everyone wanted to rush us through there, but wars take time. Why should a war against a disease be any different?"

"It shouldn't."

"And I can't imagine many people opposing *this* war. They're frustrated with your timetable? Are you being especially slow?"

"Cautious," I said.

"Is this the low-hanging fruit thing you told me about? You're doing the easier extractions first and saving the more damaged patients for later?"

"That's part of it," Vashti explained.

She told him about one of the first human beings we'd thawed out, an eccentric media mogul who begged us to bring his nearest and dearest out next. They'd apparently been tucked away in another cryonic facility, one that we hadn't yet discovered. We'd heard of a number of "off the map" labs, privately constructed and well hidden to protect them from rioters during the last days of the plague. When the rank and file came to realize they wouldn't make the cut, and only the fantastically privileged had a chance at resurrection, there was no shortage of outraged men and women ready to level the playing field. Many labs didn't make it—stormed, wrecked and put to the torch, Frankenstein's castle at the hands of angry villagers. However, most of the secret labs had survived—Cambridge first and foremost, but also a smaller one in a Nashville suburb, wherein we found something more than we were promised.

Beyond the media mogul's entombed friends and family, here slept soldiers—a private army, outfitted with an impressive array of military hardware. "Security," our man explained, but under questioning it became clear that this strike force was designed not just to protect his life but also to wrest control of the future. If we thawed them out, in all likelihood we'd be making our next extractions under the barrel of a gun.

So we kept them frozen. Much to the mogul's dismay.

He left us wondering: *How many other private armies are buried out there? How many rich and powerful men have hopes of ruling the world—or at the very least, exerting undue influence upon it?*

A would-be tyrant might have a hard time on his own, but not when armed with the knowledge of how to thaw out a loyal combat-ready following. That's why we'd chosen to keep the secret of life and guard it with everything we had. We'd even made a point of not yet reviving any of the doctors and scientists who we thought might be able to reverse-engineer the technique Vashti had pioneered. And that's why we were off schedule. The thinking was:

1. Put everyone on equal footing for now.

2. Once we've thawed all we can, give out the secret. If someone wants to make trouble at that point, it's no longer our problem.

3. Between now and then, get society jump-started as best we can, reestablishing the rule of law, emphasizing cooperation, and discouraging exploitation. Build good habits for humanity, and start civilization off on the right track.

Lucky number three was the Victory Doctrine, meticulously drawn up by the VIC in Victory: Vashti, Isaac and Champagne. However, there was the Doctrine as written and the Doctrine as performed. The more utopian among us—Isaac and Champagne, particularly—liked to interpret it as "fix all of society's ills." Meaning: end racism, sexism, poverty, homophobia, homelessness, hunger and lack of self-esteem. Safeguard the environment, spread vegetarianism and stop the proliferation of WMDs. Swap reptilian thinking for education, enlightenment, culture and the Golden Rule. Dole out hugs. Whereas I interpreted it as something closer to "just stop acting like jackasses for a little while." Both interpretations were far too ambitious.

"You might be overcautious, but I don't blame you for worrying," the President said. "In any power vacuum, warlordism is a grave concern."

"True, but it goes beyond that," said Vashti, and she told him about Richard Ning.

Ning was the force behind New Cambridge's counterculture—in direct opposition to the Doctrine, he'd argued that no great civilization had ever been built without the will of someone at the top driving the sweat of many others at the bottom. He'd authored and articulated a new brand of Manifest Destiny, a school of thought we'd sarcastically dubbed the Manifesto.

Rebuilding the world and in actual fact building a better world are wonderful goals and we're obviously all for them. The only question is how. How do you accomplish it? What we have going here—this brave new collectivist empire we've been welcomed into—thanks, but no thanks, because it's rather a lot of pain with precious little gain. Classless, egalitarian societies are brilliant in theory, but in practice they sacrifice efficiency and practicality. We have an enormous job ahead of us, and if we have any hope of achieving it, there must be a ruling class and there must be a class that is ruled. Therefore, we propose establishing ourselves de jure *as the governing authority, and designating the residents of neigh-*

boring cryonic facilities as our workers. We should revive them, as is only honorable, but as payment for the gift of life, they should work for us until their debt is relieved.

And so on. Very popular with the Social Darwinists in our city, and also with those who just didn't want to do any work. A minority among the thawed, but I'd seen the philosophy spreading at an alarming rate.

There was a split among the followers, half preferring to recruit workers from China as a means of resolving that cold war, the other half not particularly caring where the workers came from so long as they came. Ning himself was cleverly noncommittal about it. I'd pointed out once that many of his followers seemed obsessed with beating China, some verging on a xenophobic hatred. As a Chinese American, did he have no problem with this? How different were these men from the railroad owners who'd exploited his ancestors? Ning simply told me that business was business.

"As you may or may not know," the President said, "there's a secure facility waiting for us in Bluemont, Virginia." We knew. The mysterious Mount Weather Emergency Operations Center, an underground city designed to withstand a nuclear blast. I'd made my way inside once, took my son there to show him the sights. It contained members of the President's cabinet and upwards of a thousand troops. "That base has personnel vital to the survival of this nation, plus all the manpower we need to get started again. More than enough to enforce the law and put down any threat."

"I'm afraid that's not a viable option right now, sir," Vashti sighed.

"Why not?"

"Because, with all due respect, we can't rule *you* out as a threat."

He blinked. "Excuse me?"

"There are people waiting to be revived on every continent. We're working for all of them. We're not working for American hegemony."

He made his pitch. No country on the planet had ever been more committed to global harmony than the United States of America. Look at the tradition of democracy and the number of times the U.S. had led the vanguard of disaster relief. Why should this time be any different? After the worst calamity in human history, he had no interest in putting the rest of the world under an American boot. It simply made more practical sense to reestablish America as a power first, so she could lend a hand to all in need.

Vashti countered that while he might well have good intentions now, his track record showed a bully on the global stage, a man who put big business first, America's wealthiest citizens second, and everyone else in the world a very distant third.

Everything changed when Black Ep hit, he argued, and to be fair, during his last year in office, he gave his foreign policy a radical turn toward accommodation and diplomacy, even with heated rival China. But with Black Ep rapidly becoming a thing of the past, Vashti saw no reason for his change of heart to last.

"You have to think of America first," she said. "There's nothing wrong with that—it's a big part of your job description. But we have to think of what's best for everyone. So we're not going to bring out anyone from Mount Weather just yet."

He turned to me to see if I would contradict her, but I gave him the dead eyes, quietly watching.

"You're not making this easy," he complained. "How am I supposed to run the country without the human resources I need?"

You're getting ahead of yourself, sir, I meant to say, but it came out as, "You're jumping the gun."

"We don't need you to run America," Vashti added, "because

right now there is no America. The country's on hold. All we're asking is for you to add legitimacy to what we're doing, and assure everyone that the traditional power structures will get up and running again. Which they will, Mr. President, I promise."

"So I'm a figurehead?"

"For now."

He stroked his chin, introspective, weighing the situation. I saw a slyness in his face. I wondered if he'd caught a whiff of the truth. We weren't particularly at ease with him thawed out, because his potential to make trouble for us far exceeded his benefit. Vashti would much rather have saved him for later, thawing him only when we were at the end of completing our goal. But there really was no choice—she could see how the populace had begun to chafe under our governance. Bringing the POTUS back into society would buy us some much-needed time. And he was shrewd enough to see that.

"I have a few conditions, but I suppose I can go along with this—for now," he said, which was good, because Vash was ready to put the screws to him. *Needless to say, I'd love to bring the First Lady out,* she would have said, *but she's not in very good shape, so successfully reviving her will take all of my concentration. Now if you could go out and reassure the people like we asked you to, I'm sure that would eliminate most of my distractions.* But no need. We'd keep it friendly and watch him closely.

"That went well," Vashti said when we stepped out into the hall. "Or as well as can be expected. How do you think it went?"

I gave her a look.

"Don't be such a cynic, Hal. Don't you think that went well?"

"Swimmingly," I replied.

· · ·

He went out and pressed the flesh. Reassured his fellow Americans. Reassured everyone else. Sang our praises. Gave a fine speech, and a historic one at that.

And?

And it made Pandora happy. She so wanted this to work.

That night, in the peaceful shadows of our home, she leaned back against me and I hugged her close, my arms secured about her waist—and after I kissed her neck and she reached up to run her fingers through my tangled hair—as my hands rode up to cup her breasts—she tipped her head back—and caressed my face—and found the bruise.

She turned about, eyes widening and then narrowing. "Does it look as bad as it feels?" she asked.

"It's a black eye."

"I should blacken the other one," she said, pulling away to fetch a cold pack from her medicine kit. "Anything else you're hiding?"

"You're welcome to search me," I smiled.

"Vai te fotografar," she said, a Brazilian euphemism for "fuck off," though literally it means "go get your photograph taken."

"Get your camera," I replied, as I always did.

"What happened?"

"Just a fight. But I won. You should feel the other guy."

"Maybe I will."

"That'd show me, wouldn't it?"

"So you're beating people up now?"

"Yeah, pretty much whenever I feel like it."

"Seriously, Hal."

"Seriously, it was all perfectly friendly," I said. And it had been. An hour after the President's speech, I'd bumped into the newly thawed heir to the De Beers diamond fortune. Two months earlier

I'd given the man a walking tour, and I'd barely spoken with him since. But here he'd heard how I'd handled Vegas and he wanted to see how good a scrapper I was. No malice in it, just curiosity.

"I used to box back in college," he'd warned me, but I'd sized him up as another big man who liked to hit and hated to move. And therefore a chance to send a message to those who most needed to hear it.

So in front of a small but passionate crowd, we'd discovered that his jab was quick enough to tag me once but not twice, and that boxers don't fare well when you take them off their feet. Though my genetics are a cut above, I'm not superhumanly strong or anything—all in all, I'm a pretty regular guy—but it's fair to say that what I lack in muscle, I make up for in reflexes, technique, and a willingness to hurt people. When I have to. And between IVR training sessions and occasional sparring with Pandora, I'd learned enough Brazilian jiujitsu to overcome most applications of strength and aggression with a good joint lock or choke. All leverage. De Beers had popped me a good one, but seconds later a *kimura* had won the day. Message sent.

"I don't want you doing that anymore," Pandora said.

"You sound like Isaac."

"No," she said, taking my hand and placing it on her stomach, and instantly I realized it wasn't New Cambridge she was thinking about.

We were expecting. Again.

We'd been down this road three times now, and each time it had ended in miscarriage. Genetically optimized to survive Black Ep, her immune system had terminated each of the pregnancies. It couldn't tell a fetus from a disease. The last one we'd lost in the third trimester—the grief and sheer unfairness of it had sent Pan into a spiraling depression from which work had been her only salvation. I hadn't fared much better. Each lost child burned me with memories of my son, Deuce, and with the ashes of what might have been.

"How do you feel?" she asked before I could ask her the same.

"Nervous."

"Vashti wants me in for regular blood panels, the same old drill. She's got a new immunosuppressant she's looking to try."

"So you'll be prey to every passing microbe again."

"The fun continues."

"Are you sure you want to do this?"

"I'm too stubborn to give up," she sighed. More stubborn than Champagne, who'd stopped trying years ago. Those miscarriages had come with an unexpected price: the dissolution of Cham's relationship with Isaac. Too much wear and tear on the emotions. Pandora and I had vowed not to go down that same path.

"We can always try it another way," I'd said to her many times before, but neither cloning nor adoption were options she felt ready to embrace.

"Maybe we need help," I ventured.

"Don't say what you don't mean."

"I'm not."

"Well, that's a change of heart," she said.

"Who knows our physiology better?"

"Hal, you know we can't bring out Gedaechtnis. Not yet."

My generation had a cadre of scientists to thank for our existence. The workforce of Gedaechtnis had culled our genomes together and whipped them into a shining example of hyper-immunity. We'd never met our makers. Like every other human being, they'd succumbed to the plague when we were infants—however, most of them had been preserved, and were currently hibernating in a smaller cryonic storage facility (a.k.a. "Popsicle stand," as the kids like to call it) over in Germany. Before we migrated to Cambridge, our plan involved thawing out Gedaecht-nis and letting them conduct the Recovery. Let them have the aggravation. Unfortunately, like pungent cat litter, the plan had to be changed.

We'd been curious about the company that made us, and though they'd seemed fairly innocuous at first, the more we dug up on them, the uneasier we became. None of us had expected a multinational biotech conglomerate to be spotless, but neither had we planned on finding rogue pathogen designers in their employ. These Gedaechtnis justified in their official documents as so-called "white-hat designers," former bioterrorists who, having served their time, had been successfully converted and repurposed. And yet we'd found a glut of circumstantial evidence suggesting that links to germ warfare ran alarmingly deep. There had been a confusing tangle of unproven allegations and even a suggestion that the company had been involved in the spread of Black Ep itself. Even though we considered that last possibility unlikely, overall it was troubling news, and we'd had no choice but to question whether turning control over to them was such a good idea.

Isaac had argued it was worth it. We were, he felt, beholden to Gedaechtnis. Whatever misgivings we might have, they were surely more qualified to conduct the Recovery than we. In compromise, we'd thawed out a single employee, one who we thought could shed some light on the company, but who would be unlikely to do any damage to the cause.

The Chief Financial Officer (a.k.a. CFO Bob, as I'd come to call him) lacked a medical background, but he knew where the money went. And sure enough, it had gone to worrisome places. Gedaechtnis had been a player in the "medical arms race" between the United States and China, habitually selling each superpower bioweaponry and vaccines. They'd fearmongered and profiteered. Once Black Ep had started claiming lives, they'd restructured their workforce, signing the personnel needed to create yours truly and nine other posthumans. Clearly, not everyone in the company was corrupt—some were out-and-out heroes—but telling which was which was a Herculean task even for Bob, and the more he told us, the more we decided to leave our creators on ice until the Recovery had taken hold.

So Pandora was right—it was rash to bring out the Gedaechtnis scientists—but when it came to her health, I was willing to break my own rules.

She wouldn't hear of it.

"We can do it on our own," she said. "One way or the other, we can."

We sat together and I found myself thinking about CFO Bob's family. With Pandora's help, Vashti had successfully pulled out the man's wife and young children, whom Gedaechtnis had all cryopreserved as part of Bob's employee-benefits package. They'd made the trip with us to New Cambridge and found new life here. And they seemed so well adjusted. A happy, healthy, nondysfunctional family—I'd never seen one before. Or rather I had, but those were virtual families in a fake world—an illusion of computer programming—while this one was actually real.

Someone beat up Vegas. Not just arm-twisting, someone had stomped his groin, cracked his jaw and knocked out two of his teeth. Did a pretty thorough job on him. Not that I approved.

"So who did it?"

"Good question," my hounds told me through the link.

"He claims he fell down," said Slow.

"But the injuries don't look like any fall to me," said Bridge.

"Is he scared to talk?"

"That's my guess," Slow agreed.

"Okay, maybe someone else witnessed it. Maybe they were even broadcasting. So ask around," I told them. "In the meantime, I'll go pay him a visit in the hospital—there's a chance he's more scared of me than whoever did this to him."

It was worth a shot, but it didn't pan out. What happened to Vegas stayed with Vegas—he wouldn't say a word.

We had our share of crazies. Mostly phobes and obsessive-compulsives, but we'd found all kinds. Coming back from the dead can push a person in odd directions.

We had a Superman. A depressed real estate tycoon who'd convinced himself he was the man of steel. You'd ask him how he was doing and with sunken eyes he'd look up and tell you, "Got no powers anymore. Feel like I'm living under a kryptonite sky."

An ambassador feared there were wires growing under her skin.

We had two apathetics, each totally detached, locked in a catatonic stupor where imagination was preferable to reality.

I'd counted a dozen who were sure they were victims of a mindfuck of immense proportion. Tremulously they'd asked if New Cambridge wasn't artificial in some way, a dream, mirage or IVR simulation.

And we had a good number of amnesiacs, some suffering from the physical damage dealt by Black Ep, others psychologically scarred and desperate to forget the past. Because I'd lost most of my childhood memories to amnesia (the physical kind, though courtesy of electric shock, not plague), I'd been tapped as a mentor. It was supposed to be therapeutic for them and for me, but most of the time I just wanted to live in the present and forget I'd forgotten anything. At a certain point, you have to move on.

Still, I'd agreed to it.

The man who'd recruited me was the king of the grief counselors, our own celebrity psychiatrist, Dr. Danny Chaikin. He'd
amassed quite an empire during the plague years, helping his fellow
man deal with a brutal reality. *Facing Up with Dr. Danny* had earned
his bread and butter, but in my opinion it couldn't hold a candle to
his first show, the much livelier *A Whole Lotta Chaikin Going On.*

I'd mixed feelings about him. Sanctimonious? Yes. Treacly?
Sometimes. But not completely useless. And not without a sense of
humor. You could tell him Vegas got his ass kicked and he'd dead-
pan, "What are the odds?"

"I have an amnesia patient I'd like you to talk to," he told me.
"Extensive memory loss and I'm not seeing much evidence of
brain damage, so it looks to me like a case of post-traumatic stress
disorder. Will you see him?"

"First, I have some names for you."

"How did I know you were going to say that?" he drawled.

"Must be your insightful nature."

"Must be. Let's take a look."

I handed him a list. He scanned it and frowned.

"You know I'm not real comfortable with this."

"You helped me before," I said. "Why not again?"

"People trust me. I'm a steward of that trust."

"Have I ever asked you to break confidentiality?"

"We're in a gray area."

I shook my head. "Nothing gray about threat assessment. This
is a safety issue."

"Yeah, I hear you, Hal, but we both know that's not the whole
picture."

I didn't want to be psychoanalyzed again, so I pressed on
before he could tell me what was wrong with me or how I should
get help. "First name on the list," I said. "Dangerous or not dangerous? And why?"

Threat assessment was ninety percent of my job. I gave walking tours to get into people's heads and know their hearts, to figure out how well they'd integrate and estimate what kind of risk they'd be. What I couldn't find out on my own I got from spies and confidants. It was the name of the game.

"You don't feel real good about yourself," my would-be therapist told me when we'd gotten to the end of the list.

"I'm not your patient, Dr. Danny," I reminded him, halfway out his office door. "Now if you turn up who did a number on Vegas, you just let me know."

The amnesiac turned out to be the hardest of all Pandora's successful extractions, the man whose life she'd refused to give up on those many nights before. Physically, he'd made a full recovery, but mentally and emotionally he clearly still had a long way to go. I checked him out of the hospital and took him to lunch, bringing my friend Kody along for the ride.

"You don't remember anything?" Kody asked him. "Not anything at all?"

He clenched his jaw. "No, I remember some things, but nothing important. Everything important," he tried to explain, ultimately trailing off and making a defeated gesture with his hands.

"But you know left from right, night from day, up from down," Kody offered.

"Sure, I can name all fifty states, quote you song lyrics, tell you trivia. I just don't know who I am. What life I lived. I look at the scars on my body and don't know where they came from. When I try to remember . . ." he said, but then stopped, again unable to articulate the problem.

I said, "Imagine going to a library and instead of books all you have are covers."

"Yes," he murmured. "That's what it's like."

He'd been told his real name but it hadn't meant much to him.

Kody had taken to calling him "Mr. Lucky" based on who he was and how he got here.

"I understand I'm a lottery winner," he said.

"A famous one," Kody agreed. "You may not remember, but I do. Your wife was the Big Pick, there was a huge to-do, massive media coverage when she transferred the prize to you—you both became symbols of hope to all the people who couldn't afford cold storage for themselves."

Cryonics should have been widely affordable, but in the midst of the plague, the supply couldn't begin to meet the demand. In America, two contests for cryopreservation had been carried out. One was based on merit (or, arguably, sympathy)—a multibillion-aire conducting his search for "the best of the best" by inviting the most talented and hardworking Americans to send in footage and make the case for why they should earn a spot. The other was the Big Pick, a lottery draw based purely on luck. Though steeped in kindness, each contest served an ulterior motive—to pacify the have-nots just a little longer, to encourage patience instead of riots and thereby forestall the total destruction of society. And for a while, it had worked. So Mr. Lucky may have been a symbol of hope, but that hope had been used as a collar.

"What happened to my wife?"

"I don't know," Kody confessed. "All this is right around the time I got sick."

"Do you remember her?" I asked.

Slowly my fellow amnesiac shook his head no.

"Do you want to?"

"Of course I do," he snapped. "What kind of question is that?"

"It's possible that you don't," I said. "It might be too painful. You don't want to face what happened, so your mind's protecting you."

"I want to remember," he insisted.

"Then you're lucky," I told him, "for two reasons. Because there's no physical brain damage, you should be able to remember her in time. And if the records are out there, we may be able to find out exactly what's happened to her."

He nodded, offering a brief, encouraged expression, which quickly turned to puzzlement.

"Is that the President of the United States waiting tables?" he asked.

"Yes, it is," Kody said.

Kody told him how Vashti and I had offered the President his pick of jobs—or no job at all—and how after seeing the way New Cambridge was run, the leader of the free world had insisted that he be treated no differently than any other member of our community. And thus, here he was working at Harvest part-time, flanked rather noticeably by the two Secret Service agents we'd thawed out as the first of his conditions. His entry into the service industry was ostensibly an attempt to show himself to be down to earth, no better than anyone else, though I'd noticed the stunt had begun to irritate a certain segment of our populace. They considered it disrespectful and blamed us for coercing him into doing it, despite his (and our) protests to the contrary.

"Good fortune and *mai pen rai*," Kody bid Mr. Lucky at the end of our meal, adding, "That goes double for you, Thursday." He'd bid me *mai pen rai* many times before—it was a Thai expression that didn't translate perfectly into English, but meant something along the lines of, "Hang loose and live for the moment, because nothing really matters."

I took Mr. L to where Brattle Street met the security fence, where those in need of healing often congregated to visit New Cambridge's interminably unfinished memorial museum. Dedicated to those who had lost their lives to Black Ep, the centerpiece commanded attention: a gleaming six-foot-high teardrop-shaped holographic display, which cycled through the faces and life stories of thousands of plague victims. The teardrop was a relic from before the Recovery; we'd been charged with adding faces and names, but with billions dead, it seemed an endless project, like moving a desert with tweezers.

The walls surrounding the teardrop display included access to the media base, where one could link in and sift through all the major broadcasts during the last few years of the plague. We found detailed coverage of the Big Pick—reporters flooding into Mr. Lucky's hospital room, Mrs. Lucky giving a tearful interview—but no immediate sense of what had happened to her after that. It took some digging. At last we found a follow-up story—touched by her selflessness, the world's biggest software tycoon had quietly arranged cryonic storage for her in an unnamed facility.

Before we unearthed the broadcasts, all he'd been able to remember of her was his lying in a hospital bed, with the touch of her hand holding his while he focused on a pain chart at the far end of the room. But watching her here, his face contorted in recognition and grief, and then the tears began to fall. In a matter of minutes, a huge chunk of his memory came roaring back. Over the next few months, he'd recover the rest of it. I couldn't help but wonder what that might be like.

"We can help you find her," I told him.

"God bless you," he said.

Unlikely, I thought. *We're not on speaking terms.*

Dear Hal,
Do the thawed have a god? Is G.O.D. alive in the N.C.? Hit me back, baby.

THE BIG GUY

Yes, whither the religion in the Recovery? Pretty evenly split between believers and unbelievers, I'd say. Atheists tended to point to the sheer unmitigated horror of the plague and argue that no reasonable deity would ever let it happen to his creations. Theists simply pointed to their holy texts.

If you're (1) religious and (2) your faith just happens to involve anything resembling a Day of Judgment, it's a challenge and a half not to think of Black Ep as playing a crucial role in it. Because the obliteration of very nearly everyone—honestly, if that's not an event of biblical proportion, what is?

Christian eschatology traditionally has the Rapture—righteous whisked up to Heaven—followed by Tribulation. Let's say that Black Ep was in fact the Tribulation (as certain New Cambridge Christians claim)—next on the list comes the thousand-year reign of Jesus Christ. While I'd yet to meet anyone in our city who went by that name, the prophesied Millennial Golden Age involved rebuilding society into a utopian paradise and resurrecting the dead, which I had to admit—blasphemously enough—wasn't far off from what we were doing.

In Jewish eschatology, we might have reached the Olam Haba, the World to Come, where after the rights and wrongs of their lives are weighed, every man and woman is purified and knows God directly. Or had we reached Yaum Al-Qiyâmah, Islam's Day of Resurrection, on which the dead rise from their graves to be judged? Sometimes I wondered if that was why we kept thawing people from cryonic sleep: so they could face judgment. And would we be called as character witnesses?

Even the non-Abrahamic religions had found traction in recent events. Hindus could hail the Recovery as the death knell of the Kali Yuga, the Age of Darkness. Now the laws of karma could at long last be restored, with good deeds actually rewarded and wicked deeds punished, instead of the other way around. And cryonic Buddhists greeted the new day with an eye out for Maitreya, the bodhisattva destined to reach total enlightenment and go on to inspire a sustainable civilization of justice, fairness and loving-kindness.

A civilization we aspired to be.

Now I don't begrudge anyone's faith. Believe what you want. Don't believe what you don't want. It's cool. Just leave me out of it.

When I say that, I don't just mean, "Don't push your religion on me." I mean leave me out of it. Completely.

I mean whoever you think is up above, I don't fucking work for him.

Yes, I played a small part in keeping humankind alive. Yes, I'm not purely human from tip to toe. It doesn't make me an angel, saint, holy spirit, genie, prophet or point of light. Don't make me part of your belief system.

We'd say that, and only rarely would they listen. Like children who couldn't help themselves. To make their creeds fit with the time, too many of New Cambridge's devout had insisted on can-onizing all the PH and the Gedaechtnis scientists who brought us into being. It pissed me off. There's nothing holy about me. Not a thing. So thanks, but no thanks—if ever I want followers singing my praises, I'll go back into IVR and raise Lovecraftian monsters again.

Most of my kind felt the same, though Isaac would shrug it off and say, "Let them believe what they want to believe," and Vashti would flash her razor-thin smile before adding, "Honestly, I don't mind being worshiped, but I'd like it to be for the right reasons."

"Kill the Dog," Champagne said, brushing back the strands of golden-blond hair the wind had whipped into her face. A cold snap had brought a fresh dusting of snow to the ground, and the drop in temperature had done little for people's moods.

"Kill it?"

"Put it down," she said through pursed lips.

I gave Brigit a gesture to go ahead without me. We'd come to the dairy (run by the Smartin company—they'd invested heavily in our creation) to inspect the implementation of new tamper-proof seals for our milk, cream, ice cream and yogurt containers. But Brigit's mother had tracked me down with a request. A funny thing about Champagne's requests: they all sounded exactly like demands.

I said, "What did the Dog do this time?"

"Hal, they're trying to bring us down."

They say culture is a living thing—Champagne had taken the reins from the word go, not only driving New Cambridge toward an appreciation of fine art and music, but also spearheading all the minutiae societies depend upon—Apple Festival this, Book Fair that. As Minister of Something to Do, she filled the days, and she did it almost single-handedly. Her primary distribution system and social opiate: Channel One. We'd restored our network to the old standards, letting anyone who wanted to broadcast through the links—while most were lone wolves putting out off-again on-again journals, poetry, social commentary and the like, some collaborated to create twenty-four-hour-a-day programming. And Channel One had the richest programming of all, established as the official state channel, Champagne's voice and the voice of the Assembly. It existed to inform, educate, entertain and inspire. It was also ripe for parody—which was where the Dog walked in.

Unlike Seconds from Disaster, Freezerburn, and the other major humor channels, the Dog's programming consisted of entirely new comedy material with not a single pre-Recovery show plugged into the feed. Only the music was recycled—a medley of rebellious, angst-ridden rock anthems, which needled the adults and helped make the Dog number one with the city's young'uns.

The founder and resident pied piper had been a ruthlessly successful hotel magnate. We'd tapped him to help rebuild the Harvard Square Hotel, but he'd had his fill of the business and wanted only to recapture his youth. Black Ep had changed him, snapped him, arguably for the better, but here he existed as a thorn in the Assembly's side. So much so that I'd nicknamed him the same.

"You really think ol' Thorn has it in for us?"

"Have you seen what he's doing over there?" she asked.

"Jokes?"

"I'm fine with jokes, but there's a certain point where you cross the line."

"You don't like being made fun of, so—"

"No, do you?"

I shrugged. "If you want to censor him, you don't need me. Just pull Dog off the air."

"That wouldn't look good, would it?" she asked, snippy as ever.

"Then why hide behind the pretense of free speech? Confront him honestly. Tell him everything has a limit."

"How about you do it? He's your kind of people, not mine."

"How about no? Everyone needs a release valve, Cham. And we can't all be fascinated by papier-mâché and pottery wheels."

Honestly, there was a lot worse than the Dog. Take the Echo. The Echo was a news channel, not a humor channel, but without a doubt more subversive, because Richard Ning's cronies had infected it. It had become his mouthpiece. The Echo wanted to wipe out the Doctrine; the Dog just wanted to tweak noses and make people laugh.

"Your release valve is spreading poison."

"Such as?"

She glanced around to double-check that no one was watching us—doing so with a measure of distaste, I noticed. We didn't have to look over our shoulders nearly as much back when we totaled in the dozens, and I felt a small fizz of satisfaction that the vast number of people in the world had begun to wear on her the way they had on me.

"He's making jokes about the food," she whispered.

I blinked. "Too bland?"

"He's insinuating that we're spiking it," she hissed, crossing her arms about her chest. "With drugs. To control the populace."

"Well, we're not," I said. "Or are we?"

"No, but we obviously don't want that getting around."

"Because it hits a little too close to home?"

She cut me dead with a look.

"That's it, isn't it? You and Vashti overmedicating your girls?"

Years ago, they secretly drugged their daughters with a mélange of chemicals, designed to keep them agreeable and focused on their work. When the secret got out, all hell broke loose. The healing process was slow and painful, with Champagne and Vashti struggling to regain the girls' trust. But they'd done so—for the most part—and had wrangled promises from each of us not to speak of it to the thawed. It would erode humanity's confidence in us, they argued, and would make everyone's job that much more difficult.

"Want some help off that high horse?" she spat. "We overmedicated our kids. You undermedicated yours. At least we were paying attention."

I gave her a grimace of touché.

"Sorry," she said, looking down. "I'm sorry, Hal, I am. That was . . . Well, let's just say none of us is going to make parent of the year."

"If I press him, there's a chance it'll make it worse instead of better."

"So be nice."

A visit to Thorn—always an adventure. Before you could even get to him, you had to snake through a gauntlet of kids running up to you, asking you stupid questions with their live links. If you said something mockable, you could expect to see it again and again in a loop. Thorn would sit back, directing the chaos, monitoring each feed, cutting between them for his channel. When you finally reached him, he'd talk, but he'd broadcast every word. He had almost no "off camera" life—it was all sent out to the world.

The live episode was a mess, but he recut it and rebroadcast it later in a way that tickled me, filming my approach with old horror flick music, cutting to kids screaming, scattering, running for their lives.

My name is Halloween, after all.

He goofed on the actual conversation by pretending that at any moment I was going to murder him—or at the minimum beat the shit out of him. I went with the flow—conversational *wu wei*—and let him do most of the talking. Bringing up the whole drugs-in-the-food-and-water conspiracy theory would have been the worst thing I could have done, so I didn't. By the end of it, I'd made things slightly better.

Then I went to go find Katrina, the youngest of my nieces. Of all possible assignments, she'd drawn arguably the best or the worst: activity planner for the city's children. I found her in the library with a few dozen younger kids, all sitting on the floor in a semicircle, story time in full effect. Upon an antique cherrywood chair sat the Storyteller, an older woman with short auburn hair streaked with silver. Book in her lap, always, and usually one of her own. She was a much-beloved best-selling children's author who, with a secret white-hot passion, hated kids. Despised them. You could hear it in her tone or see it in her eyes when the polite mask would slip—for long, excruciating seconds she'd stare at the chubby-cheeked five-year-old who'd just asked her what the dragon's middle name happened to be, and it was the look of a life-imprisoned inmate contemplating her warden. Longing for the sweet release of death. But she'd agreed to help entertain the children, and she took her responsibilities seriously. She spent as much free time as possible in Oasis, drinking heavily and trying to get picked up. "I can write adult novels, too," she could often be heard to say.

By contrast, Katrina possessed genuine affection for kids. She was still a teenager herself. And I knew that she and Thorn were friendly—she'd won the privilege of being one of the very few people he'd turn the camera off for—so I played a hunch that she'd been intimating her mothers' secrets to him.

"Guilty," she said, when I took her aside.

She hadn't planned to let any skeletons out but "it just sort of happened," and then she'd played it off as a joke. Which was how Thorn took it. Fortunately. Looking back, she was glad it had come out. It felt good to say it. What her mothers had done was wrong and they'd gotten a relatively free pass on it over the years. All her sisters harbored resentments, but Katrina's kept bubbling to the surface. Maybe from constantly having to settle disputes between her young charges, she'd become intensely focused on what was and wasn't fair. And this wasn't.

"You're right," I told her. "But there's something that trumps it."

Not sabotaging our present efforts, I argued, was more important than venting about the unfairness of the past.

"You're saying safety trumps truth?"

"That's right," I said. And I wondered who the holy fuck I had become. And then I thought of Pandora, and her hope for the future. And my promises to her. I'd sworn to try to make this work no matter what. That trumped everything.

Katrina frowned in confusion, turned it over in her mind a bit, and then agreed. She'd watch what she said from now on.

That was well and good, but the next night someone did to Thorn what they'd done to Vegas. Beat him, stomped him, left him just this side of petrified. Before cutting out, the footage showed a darkened bedroom after hours and poorly lit intruders breaking in—two or three, it was impossible to say for sure—and with mounting realization that our problems were just beginning, my security team and I watched a black-gloved hand close around Thorn's mouth and another yank the link.

Two working theories about Vegas and Thorn.

Numero uno: Someone was trying to make us look bad. Me, specifically. Like I'd orchestrated the assaults, which wasn't true. Or to prove I couldn't protect the populace. Which was partly true—my team consisted of Slow Bridge and scattered spies, with an outer ring of neighborhood watch groups. We couldn't be every-where at once. Either motivation suited Ning's purposes, and from reexamining the feed, I could just make out the shape of one of the intruders—a heavily built man who might have been the Cigar Club's doorman, Fitch.

Numero dos: Mr. President wanted more power. Or at least, his SSPPD did. (That's Secret Service Presidential Protection Detail.) With New Cambridge painted as a dangerous place, the POTUS's special agents could make a case for bringing more of them out of cryonic stasis (thus far, we'd freed only two) and/or supplying them with firearms (inside the city, we'd refused to let any of our citizens carry guns). The moment the news about Thorn got out, they insisted we do more to help them protect the President—it made me wonder if they hadn't zapped Vegas and Thorn themselves.

Upon seeing her friend put in traction, Katrina hunted me down to offer a third hypothesis.

Numero tres: Vashti and Champagne had it done. With beatings and home invasions spreading fear, they could convince New Cambridge of the need for greater surveillance. Let's put cameras everywhere, not just in the links. Let's give our citizens subdermal transmitters that never dissolve, so we can track them forever and ever. Up to this point, the city's civil libertarians had stood in unwavering opposition—privacy was too important, a human right, and no government could be trusted with that much power. But now, maybe they'd bend a little.

"Or maybe it's not about surveillance," she glowered. "Maybe it's manpower."

Numero tres and a half: I did it to justify a larger security force.

Off the mark, I told her. Way off with me. Less so with her mothers, but off just the same. Still, she had company—my conjectures would prove as wrong as hers.

I fed Thorn's footage to the other man in Pandora's life, the one nearly always in her ear: Malachi, her Seeing Eye AI. They worked so well together, most of our populace had no idea Pan was blind. Rather, they saw her as frequently distracted, chatting away with someone they couldn't see—but whether she was linking someone or just talking to herself, they couldn't say for sure.

"It isn't much footage to go on, but did you notice the glove?" Malachi asked, linking me an optimized image. My eyes scanned it for an unusual brand or style—pretty generic, as far as I could tell—but with the light enhancement, I could see a telltale bulge beneath the leather.

"He's wearing a ring,"

"Most people take their rings off before putting on gloves."

"Most do," I agreed.

"So who never takes off his ring? A happily married man?"

"That's a big ring, Mal, a big stone."

"Maybe you haven't noticed, but these aren't poor people we're taking care of," he said, but I barely heard him because that was when it clicked.

I caught up with my ring-bearing suspect in between deliveries. He'd volunteered to bring food and medicine to housebound individuals—not just the elderly, but also those who'd been disabled by Black Ep and whose injuries were beyond our power to repair. He was, needless to say, a good apple. And so I showed up alone, leaving Slow Bridge on double-shift patrol.

"Halloween," said he.

"God's RB," said I.

God's Running Back was Hawaiian, an older man, broad shouldered and sturdy. In his prime he'd been a powerhouse—one of the best rushers in the history of football. (That's American football, not the soccer Pandora used to coach.) Though age had slowed him a bit, he could still boast the physique of an athlete, a trophy to go along with his Super Bowl ring, single-season touchdown record and trip to the Hall of Fame. Always one to credit the Lord for his success, he'd gotten himself ordained and parceled his money into a booming ministry. By the time Black Ep hit, he'd cemented his place as the king of celebrity evangelists.

"Good to see you," he said. "Are you hungry? Buttered noodles are the specialty of the day, and Mrs. Yamamura didn't want hers."

"Not right now, thanks."

"We can break bread another time, then," he smiled, loading a tower of trays back into his van. "What's on your mind?"

"Let's walk and talk," I said.

We took a stroll to the fence. He told me he'd been hearing howling at night—a pack of wolves or wild dogs (hardly a difference between the two these days) nosing the perimeter. I promised

I'd look into it. Then I intimated what he'd done and he nodded, relieved, unwilling to deny it.

"I'm glad you found me," he said.

"Yeah, me too. It's nice when these things work out for everybody."

"No argument here."

"So why'd you try to make chopped meat out of Vegas and Thorn? I have to say, it doesn't seem very Christian of you."

"You may be right about that," he acknowledged. "I've been praying about it. He's yet to give me an answer."

"You've yet to give *me* an answer," I said. "Tell me why."

With an earnest expression, he told me he was looking at the reason why.

I was his inspiration.

"Gabriel," he began, palms outstretched, but I cut him off right there.

"I don't go by that name anymore," I said. "And even if I did, it's just a name. I'm no angel, believe me."

He chuckled. "Even Jesus had his moment of doubt in the desert. But I'm happy to call you Halloween if you like. Some of us haven't forgotten its real name: All Saints' Eve. A night not of darkness but light."

"You're killing me," I said.

"Halloween, I'm contending for the faith. All right? I'm contending for the faith by opposing evil men."

"Vegas and Thorn? Obnoxious, maybe, but evil men?"

"Have you read the book of Jude?" he asked. "Woe unto them who despise dominion and speak evil of dignities."

"And you gave 'em woe, huh?"

"I delivered a message."

"Let me get this straight. You think you're helping me?"

"Yes."

Misguided son of a bitch, I fumed. "You really think this makes my job easier instead of harder?"

"I think it shouldn't be your job at all. In fact, I *know* it shouldn't."

The serenity in his eyes, the certainty in his baritone voice . . . something gave me pause. Probably a combination of the two.

"Sinful men," he continued. "Plenty of them. I see them prowling around like those wolves out there. And I see you fighting the good fight against them. And sometimes a fight takes more than words. I see that. But you shouldn't have to do it. God has made unto you wisdom. God has made unto you righteousness. God has sent you to us, and there's no reason for you to sully yourself with this. You can stay as pure as his thoughts, and that's how you will stay if I see to the problem instead."

The religious convictions baffled me, but we agreed on one thing: the Doctrine couldn't sustain itself without help. Someone had to play the heavy. And as far as he was concerned, better him than me.

He was desperate to protect me—or whatever he thought was me—and he wasn't alone. Just as New Cambridge had cabals aligned against the PH, here was one aligned in our favor. Supposedly. But with friends like these. . . ?

I arrested him and he was perfectly agreeable, except when it came to telling me who else was involved. Or how many. That he wouldn't do. He implied there were others in the movement, men and women of faith, though not all belonged to the Christian faith.

So the city had been seeded with an unguessable number of loose-cannon vigilantes. It was the last thing we needed.

"No, we're exactly what you need," God's RB insisted. "We do what has to be done, and because we're not associated with you, what do you have?"

"Plausible deniability," said I.

"And clean hands," said he, and smiled.

Quite a scandal when the story broke. For a hero to so many to fall—some felt it threw gasoline on a smoldering fire, but others saw it as a breath of fresh air. Some praised us for taking a dangerous man off the street; others blamed us for creating the conditions that allowed it to happen in the first place. It sent ripples through the Christian community. While most didn't care much for Vegas or Thorn, they loudly condemned the assaults. "We're Christian," they said. "We don't wish that on anyone." But I sensed a definite sympathy for God's RB bubbling underneath.

Of course, the Assembly made an example of him. Came down strong to reassure the community that the law was the law; no one was above it; no one had to live in fear. And of course, that didn't sit well with everyone. Angry notes were scribbled. "Only God can judge a human soul. What authority dare you claim over the righteous?" When the anonymous threats started rolling in, I wondered if the loose cannons had reconsidered deifying us and had instead thought to put us in their sights.

One of them sent an excerpt from the Old Testament, the Book of Zephaniah. Instead of sending it to the Assembly, he sent it directly to me.

Ah, soiled, defiled, oppressing city!
It has listened to no voice; it has accepted no correction.
It has not trusted in the Lord; it has not drawn near to its God.
The officials within it are roaring lions; its judges are evening wolves
    that leave nothing until the morning.
Its prophets are reckless, faithless persons; its priests have profaned
    what is sacred, they have done violence to the law.

On stupid impulse, I crumpled it up. But I couldn't throw it away. I smoothed it out, folded it and kept it in my pocket. I didn't wholly agree with it, but God, there were times I hated the city, too.

Excerpt, New Cambridge Assembly Transcript, Session 606

THE CHAIRMAN. The meeting will please come to order. This morning the Assembly will take up the issue of expanding the city's constabulary. I would like to start by recognizing our Chief of Law Enforcement, Mr. Hall, for any opening remarks he'd like to make.

MR. HALL. No remarks.

THE CHAIRMAN. Then next up is Assemblyman Ning, who has a prepared statement, I understand.

MR. NING. Thank you, Mr. Chairman. Security is the backbone of any democracy, and our community is no exception. The citizens of New Cambridge cannot be expected to live their lives in a constant state of fear. Given the recent string of violence, it is imperative that we add more capable, able-bodied men and women to the ranks of those who have dedicated themselves to upholding the law. This is not the first time this call has been sounded, but one can only hope that this time it will be heeded. If Mr. Hall is unwilling to increase his personal security force, I propose we establish a supplementary agency that can round out his efforts to effectively police the streets. I call not for another half-measure, not for yet one more neighborhood watch, but rather a highly trained, well-armed—

MS. POMEROY. Is this an end run?

MR. NING. Excuse me?

MS. POMEROY. Are we back to firearms again?

MR. NING. I was under the impression that I had the floor.

THE CHAIRMAN. You do, Mr. Ning, but Ms. Pomeroy has a point. Whether or not private citizens should be allowed to carry firearms within the city is a separate issue, and one of your favorites. I trust this proposal—

MR. NING. No, I've conceded that vote. This has nothing to do with private citizens owning guns, as members of any officially sanctioned police body would by definition no longer be private citizens. Let's not become ensnarled in this. Alarming though it may be, trying to enforce the law with insufficient firepower is a less dangerous experiment than trying to enforce it with insufficient manpower, particularly when coupled with insufficient confidence from the people of this city. May I put a question to Mr. Hall?

THE CHAIRMAN. Go ahead.

MR. NING. When New Cambridge was first established, you assembled a force of three, yourself included. Tell me, how many are in that force today?

MR. HALL. Three.

MR. NING. Three? Protecting a thousand plus. And how would you explain this egregious lack of recruiting?

MR. HALL. There's no reason to recruit when I can do more with less.

MR. GETTY. If I may interject? Mr. Ning, until recently the crime rate has been minuscule. There's been no reason to expand the force.

MR. NING. That may be, sir, but now we have good reason, and this Assembly needs to know if he intends to do something about it.

MR. HALL. I'll consider recruiting.

MR. NING. With all due respect, your consideration is not enough. New Cambridge deserves better security, and if you won't make the hires—

MR. HALL. You're saying I should surround myself with people I don't trust or you'll petition the Assembly to train and arm them instead.

MR. NING. If you have a problem with trust, you really ought to seek psychological counseling. Dr. Chaikin?

DR. CHAIKIN. Hey, my door's always open.

MR. HALL. Enough. You're not interested in security. It's power. You've opposed the Doctrine the whole time you've been here. You want a coup, and this is an attempt at positioning.

MR. NING. Really, that's outrageous. Patently ridiculous. Just because I disagree with certain points of policy, that doesn't make me an insurgent trying to bring our society down. Do you deem every critic of your job performance as untrustworthy and dangerous? Dr. Chaikin, is this not an exhibition of paranoid thinking?

DR. CHAIKIN. Well—

THE CHAIRMAN. Let's come to order—

MR. HALL. Let's not.

THE CHAIRMAN. Hal?

MR. HALL. I've got work to do, Isaac. Let me know what you decide.

It used to be easier.

When we had only a few thawed to worry about, or a few dozen, they pretty much did what we told them. Once we hit fifty, the questions starting coming. "Why do we have to live in community housing when there are better accommodations all over town?" So we let them spread out. When they got into the hundreds they wanted mansions. So we tried to accommodate them there. Then they asked, "Why are you rationing the things I want?" Now they wanted to come and go as they pleased, taking advantage of the benefits of the city without contributing their share of the work. "Why should I do this dirty job when we can just thaw other people to do it?"

I often felt like I was herding cats. If they'd no interest in playing by the rules, I wished they'd just leave. Go to Zurich. Or the

French Riviera. Or Timbuktu. Some of them wanted to leave as well, but they were bound to the city, unable to stay away for long. Leave all their friends behind? Leave a sense of normalcy? Leave their creature comforts? They'd been bound by golden handcuffs and no one could find the key.

The Dog went back on the air, but after the attack, Thorn was so jittery he forgot how to be funny.

Francisco Fierro had a full-blown nervous breakdown—or just a tantrum, depending on whose diagnosis you accepted—trashing Harvest's kitchen after hurling a saucepan of beurre blanc at an impertinent sous chef's head.

Superman's powers came back, or so he thought. He tried to fly off the Harvard Square Hotel.

Just another week in Victory City.

One bright spot: we found Mrs. Lucky. ("I thought *I* was Mrs. Lucky," Pandora had taken to teasing me.) Mr. Lucky's lottery-winning wife had apparently gotten her freeze on in Amarillo, which fittingly enough happened to be the coldest part of Texas. The Amarillo cryofacility kept a head count just shy of two hundred—it originally housed twice that number, but some time in the last few decades a meteorite had punched a large hole through the southern part of the building and "melted half the Popsicles." In spite of the explosion, Mrs. Lucky's cryostat had—according to our records—survived the blast, safely tucked away in the northern wing.

Citizens of New Cambridge could go wherever they wanted, but without help from the Assembly they typically found the wilderness to be wilder and woolier than they would have hoped. Most of them weren't accustomed to roughing it and held only a passing interest in trying. To enlist help, a person could go to his fellow private citizens (the Yacht Club, for instance—some of the more nautically inclined thawed had formed a water taxi service, specializing in retreats to Martha's Vineyard and Nantucket), or he could petition the Assembly. Bureaucracy kept petitioning far from a swift process, but upon approval, Isaac would fly a team to the selected destination to scavenge all they could for the community. "Shopping," they called it, the term "looting" having been deemed vulgar and impolite.

Slow as the bureaucracy was, we had a rule about reuniting families as quickly as possible whenever possible, so an Amarillo shopping trip immediately shot up on the schedule—Mrs. Lucky being the first item on the list. Carefully, Isaac would transport her back to New Cambridge, and just as carefully Vashti and Pandora would try to thaw her out.

Another bright spot: the kick.

Cloning is all about following a formula. It's like a marathon of cake baking, except you don't lick the batter and you use an artificial birthing chamber instead of an oven. It's controllable, whereas natural pregnancy takes place inside another living being—so it's less controllable, with more room for error. But less controllable has an upside: it makes the experience magical. To put your hand on the woman you love and feel your baby quicken—that's magic.

Especially to someone like me, who'd grown up amidst so much artifice. In a strange way, I'd spent my entire life looking for something magical and real—some spark of light to entrance my inner moth—and with Pandora I'd found it at last.

Her hope, her need, her dedication—it drove me. It deferred my slip back into the shadows. I didn't like the thawed, didn't care about the thawed, but for her I would. For her, I'd do everything in my power. My three-part plan:

1. Help build the world she wanted.

2. Give her a child.

3. See to their safety.

And then I could die.

Or at very least, sleep. Sleep might be better. I'd been drawn to self-destruction for such a long time, I'd little skill separating the sleep of the just from the sleep of the dead. I'd cross that bridge when I got there. I'd cross it on my own terms.

In the meantime, I had a war to win, an ongoing counterinsurgency against all our splinter groups. With the Cigar Club (exploit the frozen) and the Strangelove patriots (ensure American hegemony) overlapping on one side and all the loose cannons (frighten anyone from crossing the PH) stirring things up on the other, I'd come to think of everyone having their fingers somewhere they shouldn't.

They didn't. Most didn't. Most were actually pretty okay. I found that out later, when it was too late to do me any good. But in the thick of it, my well-honed cynicism and mistrust had me overestimating our enemies' numbers, though not their threat. Looking back, it was a justifiable mistake. There's no way to count all the crocodiles until you drain the swamp.

"Because now, more than ever, we're all in this together."
—PRESIDENT JOHN HENRY COLEMAN'S PUBLICITY SLOGAN, 1 AR

The President got kicked in the groin.

Metaphorically, I mean.

He'd established himself as a positive force in the community—outwardly, at least—by repeatedly calling for unity. *"Ich bin ein New*

Cambridgian," and the whole shebang. In a short time, he'd gotten on familiar terms with every one of our citizens, and not once had he called any Tim "Ted" or any Bill "Bob." Excellent recall for an older man, especially one glazed out of his mind when we first thawed him out.

"He's campaigning," Pandora observed. And, unofficially, he was. He'd set his sights on leading a united world government after we'd finished our work. I'd noticed him paying special attention to the non-Americans in town—the Europeans and Asians, most of all. To sway potential constituents to his side, he'd taken to serving as an ombudsman, listening to what they wanted, nodding from time to time and making all the noises that signify empathy. Then he'd voice their interests in the Assembly. (We'd made him an honorary member.)

Because he'd been behaving himself, Vashti had thawed both the First Lady and the press secretary rumored to be his mistress. They made an interesting trio. And though the opportunity for a good, solid groin kick popped up on more than one occasion, the one I'm talking about was delivered not by the women in his life, but by the Green Mountain Boys.

Named after the wild cards of the American 1770s—Vermont-based guerillas who'd fought both the British *and* the Province of New York—our Green Mountain Boys had left New Cambridge to found their own state, a libertarian paradise where freedom and guns were as plentiful as the government was slight. The GMB were a loose confederation of hunting enthusiasts, free spirits and pioneers, several dozen scattered around the Connecticut River in southern Vermont, roughly a hundred miles to our west. They had the distinction of being our first (and only) successful colony, a realistic alternative for thawed who didn't want to deal with the Assembly. Their numbers rose and fell with regularity—those who pissed and moaned about life in New Cambridge would often join up to find that life with the Boys involved more work than they'd expected. Heaps more work. They'd typically tough it out and stay, or return a little wiser and more accommodating. Win-win, as far as I was concerned. Which was why I'd had a hand in the group's creation.

The exodus to Vermont began with the thawing of Charles "the Ax" Axakowsky, whom Vashti hadn't wanted to bring out at all. Too unpredictable, too gung-ho about the issues, he'd only foment and agitate our community. Not so, I'd argued. He'd go off and blaze his own path. With the media base, I'd researched his many careers—decorated war hero, motivational speaker, best-selling author, state representative, pundit—and I'd pegged him as the sort who'd light a candle instead of cursing the darkness. No reason to bring our society down when he could start one more to his liking. And so he had.

"Too much government," he'd complained of New Cambridge, peering at Vashti, Isaac and me from behind the auto-focusing emerald green mirror sunglasses he'd made synonymous with his person. "And what's with the gun control? 'A free people should have sufficient arms and ammunition to maintain a status of independence from any who might attempt to abuse them, *which would include their own government.*' That's what George Washington had to say on the subject, and you'd do well to listen to it."

Though a thorough critic of the society we'd propped up, he appreciated the work we were doing and seemed to like us personally, me most of all, as I'd fought for his escape from the freezer. Beyond that, he'd picked up on the fact that the city I protected wasn't my particular slice of heaven. "What are you still doing here?" he'd ask me whenever he came to town, on perennial visits to recruit new Green Mountain Boys and return those who couldn't cut the mustard. "You'd be much happier with us."

Maybe.

They'd roll up in a convoy of black SUVs, twenty-five of them, a suitably tradable deer harvested and tied to each hood, each antenna flying a green, white and blue flag. And we'd meet them at the gates, Slow Bridge and I, running the Boys through the scanners and confiscating all their guns and contraband. But this time, the Ax had something special in his inventory. "A gift for the President," he said, with the puckish grin of a delinquent child displaying his newest, ill-gotten toy.

"Is that authentic?"

"The one and only," he replied.

Everyone had a gift for the President. Every social club and society wanted to name him Person of the Year, having selected Vashti for the year before. Champagne coordinated all the congratulatory presentations, an endless parade of syrupy speeches, which I would only half listen to, scanning the crowd (as usual) for signs of trouble.

By most accounts, the President and the Ax were—politically speaking—on the same page (or at least reading the same chapter). The former had even given the latter a medal back in the happier times before the plague. Here in the city, they met privately and rehearsed the presentation before it happened. Everyone seemed comfortable with it—and unfortunately for the President, the Ax just sandbagged him.

"You're not carrying any matches on you, are you, Mr. President?" the Ax joked, and everyone laughed. "I wouldn't want you to burn it now."

He held the venerable, many-times-refurbished parchment aloft, scavenged from an undisclosed location on a recent trip to Washington.

"That belongs to every American," the President acknowledged. "I'd sooner burn everything I own."

More laughter and scattered applause. That's where it should have ended. Instead, with a smirking "It's funny you say that," the Ax deviated from the script, launching into a scathing critique of the man's time in office, lambasting him as nothing less than a traitor to every American who believed in that document.

For years, libertarians had to endure being pigeonholed as simply "Republicans who liked to smoke pot." Here, the Ax sliced the last strand holding him to either major political party. When I look back on the incident, I see him playing keep-away, raising the Bill of Rights high with his right hand, and using his left to keep a shorter man at arm's length, pie-facing the President, stopping him from making a grab at it.

That isn't what happened, though. What happened was the President stood there with a sour expression while his supporters booed and Champagne cut the Ax's microphone. By the time I'd secured the Bill of Rights, Green Mountain Boys and Strangelove patriots had started shoving each other, bumping hard at the base of the stage, to make what I could only term as a decent mosh pit. Punches were thrown but few landed; Isaac got on the mike to plead for sanity; Slow Bridge helped me break up the spectacle of so many captains of industry, senators and ambassadors making fools of themselves, yelling and flailing and falling ass over teakettle.

It reminded me of watching chimps fight—not the ones in the jungle, who'd learned how to tear each other's throats out, but rather chimps raised in Hollywood with cigars and funny hats and years of doing what humans wanted, now trying to reclaim their wild heritage and failing miserably.

Sad to say, the Green Mountain Boys were as close as we got to the kind of rough-and-tumble postapocalyptic bandit gangs you used to see in the flicks. Yes, they were survivalists, but only in the way a men's encounter group can be considered such. They'd find their inner warriors in the woods with the enthusiastic self-deception of lifelong non-athletes cracking weak softballs at fantasy baseball camp—"How gifted I am!"—and then they'd retire to their luxury riverside condos to wash their venison down with Chablis. Surprisingly, not a single mohawk among the thawed. And the only spiked wristbands, studded collars or black leather chaps I'd seen anyone wear had emerged from our city's resident clothing designer throwing a tongue-in-cheek "postapocalyptic fashion show" with a double helping of kitsch.

Still, with this attempt to publicly embarrass the President, the Ax might as well have been wearing antisocial regalia—overnight, the Green Mountain Boys had become a bad element, personae non gratae. They'd proven themselves dangerous, erratic at the very least. So said the community.

"How many guns do those lunatics have out in Vermont?" they asked me. "How do you intend to deal with the situation?"

I don't, I thought, for there was no situation to deal with. Ax and his Boys weren't about to storm the city, guns blazing—it wasn't in them. I was sure of it. But by following his heart and insulting the President, the silly ass had cursed New Cambridge with yet another poisonous distraction, exploitable by every bad apple who wanted to ratchet up the fear and bring the system down.

Hold on. That's the mantra now.

We're down to the homestretch. Nine out of ten thawables already thawed. Maybe another month. Maybe two. Then it's a new city.

Just keep the empire from sliding into barbarism for a little longer.

Not much more. Just hold on to the reins.

Hold.

If happiness is a warm gun, hundreds wanted to share the joy.

In the wake of the Green Mountain Boys debacle, a groundswell of Second Amendment activism surged to the fore. Protests aplenty. A vote to repeal the firearms prohibition rushed through the Assembly, failing to pass by a whisper of a margin. Some claimed the vote was fixed.

"Calm things down," Vashti directed. "Placate and mollify."

Or, at least, sidetrack.

Enter the mechanical men.

On a trip to MIT, Isaac's team recovered a few dozen brickbots. Four-foot-high robotic butlers, lightweight Lego-like plastic brick shells encasing a hodgepodge of electronics, silicon and steel. They were the most advanced of their kind, which is to say they were junk. Not that they weren't capable of a good many things, and not that they weren't entertaining—they were. They could even boast rudiments of artificial intelligence, like the driver technology in many cars. But countless bugs had made brickbots more trouble than they were worth. Time and again they went kaput, shutting down with such frequency they'd come to be known as "breakbots." And after decades of disrepair, these sad salvage jobs were sure to bite the dust with even greater regularity. Still, they could serve a useful purpose.

They could have the semblance of an underclass.

If there existed a basic human need to subjugate and exploit, as the Richard Nings of the world exemplified, robots could serve as a substitute for the poor. For decades, they'd been heralded as the saviors of leisure. If only everything could be automated, some cried, human beings might never have to toil again—why, a person could incessantly relax; he could be artistic, witty and erudite; he could philosophize; he could play games. He could sit around, thumb up his ass, and enjoy the life of the mind. Though not without its wars, its famine and its poverty, civilization was surely heading in that direction when Black Ep popped up to ruin things—and, in retrospect, if only that goal could have been reached, our city would be plagued with fewer problems today. It's hard to argue for the exploitation of other humans when everyone has his own multipurpose automaton.

"Give the breakbots to the Cigar Club," Pandora suggested, on the grounds that they would make them feel important and distract them from dreams of conquest. But they didn't go to Ning and his cronies—everyone wanted to be the first on his block with a junky new toy, and Isaac couldn't justify "rewarding" the bad apples with special treatment—it would only encourage more of the populace to make trouble for us.

We had the same predicament with IVR. The hard reality we'd inherited had disconcerted many of the thawed, and some longed to escape into a gentler, happier simulation of life. Why not plug into a virtual universe, one that could fool you into thinking its computer-generated wizardry was real—trust me, I know—to while away a few hours? Or days? While its designers had envisioned it as an instrument of education and entertainment, in Victory City it had most value as a painkiller. To prevent overindulgence, we'd regulated IVR time—gave everyone an allowance, and those who didn't want theirs often traded it away for something more tangible. (Besides, there were unrationed entertainment alternatives—thousands of hours of live and recorded programming via the links.)

Ironically, the citizens who received the most time in IVR were our criminals: Parker and God's RB. Locked in artificial dreams for long stretches of time, they didn't have to be guarded as closely. The Assembly considered it a more humane prison than any alternative the city had to offer—on the other hand, didn't the promise of long stretches of fantasy encourage discontent citizens to become criminals?

Ultimately, the breakbots got distributed via a lottery system.

One had glitched beyond repair, so I dragged it out to the shooting range. The range served a dual purpose; it kept the shooters sharp (officially, me and my security team, but I insisted all the PH practice from time to time), and it let the bad apples know who not to mess with.

I'm a good shot. IVR shooting games for the first part of my life, regular target practice since. It relaxes me. I like competing against myself, and the two times I've had to take aim against others, it didn't fail me.

Executioner and *avenger* get tossed around from time to time, yet *killer* is the word I can't get away from. It keeps me up nights. So I hit the shooting range with a passion to show off—and thereby frighten away potential threats. Please don't be on the wrong side of my gun. For my sake, if not yours.

Six shots to paint a smiley face on the breakbot's chest: two for the eyes, four for the mouth. Plastic shrapnel with each impact.

It was a face in honor of my old friend—the brash, fickle, mentally ill Fantasia, "that poor girl," as my fellow PH used to call her. She had a thing for smileys, the vapidly amused expression plastered on all the soldiers in her virtual army. That was a long time ago, back in the war games we used to play. Since parting ways at eighteen, I'd seen her exactly once.

A year to the day before I sent a breakbot to Valhalla, a white-haired Fantasia appeared at the city gates. She looked like she'd seen a ghost, which is what she said of me while I stared in mute astonishment. She'd isolated herself for years, and so had I—neither of us would ever be mistaken for people persons. I'd heard she'd contacted Vashti once before, around the time I'd buried my son, but since then we'd seen neither hide nor hair of her.

More surprisingly, she sounded normal. Almost. Saner than I'd ever heard her. Some of the delusions remained, but the rocking and lip smacking had stopped, and her speech had organized. In the old days, we had to wade through malaprops and word salad. When she'd wanted to say, "too many cooks in the kitchen," it would come out as, "too many cookies in the cookie jar," and there was no correcting her.

I asked her how she'd become so lucid, and she told me she'd slipped on a mountain trail and bumped her head. Upon waking, for the first moment in her life, absolute clarity had ensued.

"Really? A whack on the head? I'd heard that could—"

"No, idiot, I'm on the right medication now."

After decades of looting pharmacies, she'd hit the right pill combination. Vision quest complete. Beyond that, she wouldn't say what she'd been doing all this time, except that it involved "fixing things" somewhere in the Pacific Northwest.

I brought her into New Cambridge and reintroduced her to all her old friends. An emotional homecoming—there might have been hugs, but she still didn't like to be touched. She stayed for a week, got to know all her nieces, complained of wanderlust, promised she wouldn't be a stranger and vanished once again. But before she left, she took me aside and said she had two words for me.

"Won't work."

"What won't?"

"This," she said, waving at the city.

"Why not?"

"You know why," she said.

She haunted my thoughts while I peppered the breakbot, the smile I gave it more lopsided than I'd planned. Brigit joined me for target practice, and when Sloane took her place the aim was way off and I knew something had gone wrong. After the third wide shot I took the pistol from her and saw it wasn't hers.

"Where's your Glock?"

She cleared her throat and said she'd gone to the armory for a lighter piece. I repeated the question. In a voice I had to strain to hear, she said she didn't have it handy.

"Handy?"

She'd "temporarily misplaced" it.

"You lost your gun?"

Biting her lip and looking away, she told me she'd been looking for it. She hadn't told me because she didn't want me to worry.

"Sloane," I said, "where did you see it last?"

She told me of her carelessness, a fuckup par excellence.

"I know," she said, fighting tears. But she didn't. She thought this was about my being disappointed with her. I had no time for that. If we were lucky, I would. I put a bullet between the breakbot's eyes and turned about.

"Where are you going?" she called.

"To clean up your mess."

Decades back, self-cleaning clothes were hailed as the invention that would force a death rattle from laundries everywhere: "Nanoparticles react with natural light to break down dirt!" But not everyone felt comfortable wearing so many chemicals (much less bacteria—"self-cleaning bacterial underwear" had been a marketer's nightmare), so the Crimson Cleaners on Massachusetts Avenue existed as a diversified business: one section dedicated to traditional liquid carbon dioxide cleaning, the other to reimpregnating fabrics with nanoparticles.

I found Mars by the second section. He'd drawn work detail here, and though a chocolate factory it wasn't, he seemed to be getting on okay. We kept our voices low, just loud enough to hear each other over the din of the machines.

"Down the laundry chute?" he asked.

"Our best guess."

"A pistol?"

"Thrown out with her clothes."

He nodded. "I haven't seen anything, but I can ask around."

"Subtly, if you don't mind."

"Of course."

"You feel comfortable doing this?"

"No problems pitching in, Hal, and if it passed through here, I bet I can find out what happened to it." He smiled. "I've got a face people trust."

"I can see that."

"And if I catch word of it, I imagine there's a reward?"

"Naturally."

"Can I name my own price?"

"Within reason."

His smile broadened—the easy grin of an opportunist.

Vaginal bleeding is not what you want in a pregnancy.

"Your baby's all right, and Pandora's all right," Vashti reassured me. "It's placenta previa—that's where the cervix is blocked, but partial, not complete. Treatable, eminently treatable. Aside from that complication, we're looking good. Better than good, actually—best yet. Her immune system's accepting the pregnancy. If we can stay the course for another eight to ten weeks, I'd like to take a shot at a C-section. I don't want to give you false hope, but I really think this might just work."

I nodded so she knew I understood what she was telling me. Without the nod, there'd have been no sign. The good news could only get so far before it hit a protective wall of deadness. We had tried too many times and lost too many children.

"Sleep," I told Pandora an hour before. Beseeched her, practically.

"Look who's talking," she said.

"You're the one who's in the family way. You need rest."

She laughed. Brushed hair from her face. "I'll rest when I'm dead."

"You keep up this pace and that might be sooner than you'd like."

She waved that off, telling me she needed to start her rounds. Then the cramps and the bleeding and the mad rush to obstetrics.

"She won't like it, but I'm stopping her from working—suspending her indefinitely," Vashti promised. "Like you suspended Sloane."

"That had to be done."

"You did warn me about my wayward girls."

I shrugged. "It was a calculated risk."

When we'd first set up shop in New Cambridge, I recruited Brigit and Sloane not for their limitless potential as security personnel, but rather to reform them (at best) and/or keep an eye on them (at least). Though they'd spent their youth largely as bullies and troublemakers, Vashti had hoped I'd be able to turn them around. In some ways I had, instilling a sense of duty and honor—they took their jobs seriously, and I took pride in the fact that they were completely incorruptible. Unfortunately, Sloane was proving to be cursed, a magnet for spectacular mistakes.

How much would this one cost?

"The older girls always were more trouble," said Vashti. "I imagine Cham and I got better at parenting as we went along. What's the old saying? Children are like pancakes—you have to throw the first ones out."

First *one,* actually. Whatever. I don't think she ever made pancakes in her life.

I followed her down to the hospital basement, where artificial birthing chambers clicked and hummed to bring a new generation of posthumans into being. Ten heartbeats from ten amniotic sacs, each not many months from birth. Boys, these. Her first turn at bat, she'd only gengineered girls, but this time—chromosomally speaking—the Ys had it.

Call it an attempt at further integration. Her adult PH daughters would bond (she hoped) with garden-variety humans, and these families would adopt a new generation of infant PH boys. Integration to make our kind less "other." As much as she enjoyed being exceptional, Vashti struggled for the future where we could not be painted as threatening and strange.

I watched her cross to a desk and—in a smooth, graceful motion—pull a hidden water pistol that had been strapped to its underside. Extending her arms, she whipped about to aim it at the door we came in. Strong stance, good grip, left index finger on the trigger, right thumb toggling the tiny microwave attachment—a blast of superheated liquid a squeeze away from eradicating the imaginary threat.

"Decent," I said, "but twist farther so you're a smaller target."

"I'm already a small target," she muttered, Napoleon complex bare. She made the adjustment. "And aside from that?"

"Aside from that, you're good."

"So I haven't forgotten everything you taught me," she crowed, relaxing her stance and lowering her weapon. "I can defend myself in a pinch."

"Hopefully, I'll recover Sloane's gun and that pinch won't come."

"An open ticket to Fantasyland," said Mars. "No time limits. Whenever I want."

"You want to run away?"

"The option," he nodded. "That's what I want."

"And fuck all of us in the real world?"

"God no, I have friends here. I like what we're building here. But I want the option. Do you understand?"

You want to be a little kid again, carefree, entertained, shamelessly indulged, with no need to contribute to society until you decide you're a grown-up again. Check.

"I hear you, Mars."

He'd named his price: the bottomless illusions of IVR. He kept going on about the things he couldn't have otherwise. Kobe beefsteak. Fresh Beluga caviar. Orbital skydiving. Sex with every James Bond girl. Riding killer whales around the Hawaiian Islands.

"So do we have a deal?"

"If you can help us."

He could. I made a note to introduce him to my niece, Olivia, who maintained the IVR—a job Pandora used to do back when New Cambridge was just a fever dream. Then I linked Kody, the best jigsaw piece to connect me to the man who had the gun.

A backroom at Oasis served as neutral ground, banging dance music partly muffled by the soundproof door, the rumbling bass line still loud enough to make cocktail glasses vibrate.

"I don't know who told you what," said the doorman of Ning's Cigar Club, "but I don't have what you're looking for. Even if I did, why should I help you?"

"Don't help me," I said. "Don't help anyone. Keep trying to put a boot on the future."

"How can I? Yours is already there."

"Let's not make this about ideology," Kody suggested, arms outstretched to keep us apart. "We're here to talk business. Fitch, listen to Thursday. Thursday, give Fitch a good reason to do what you want."

I won't have to shoot him down like a mad dog, how's that for a reason? I did not like Fitch. A lifetime ago he'd been a public relations wunderkind, running a firm that boasted among its clients nearly every dictatorship on the planet. Scandal-plagued, he'd retreated from the public eye for a while, only to return here in the Recovery as Richard Ning's friend and consigliore. A tough customer, notoriously so, and I knew he'd be trouble from the day we brought him out.

"Helping earns you my goodwill."

"And what's that worth, kiddo? Are you so terribly important?" he sneered, lighting a black and oily cigar. "Funny, when I went to sleep, I didn't think I'd wake up to take orders from some sawed-off, sarcastic little goth mutt."

"That *is* funny," I agreed.

"You should never have unthawed us, pal."

No argument here.

"How long do you think you can keep this farce of a government running? You grow the city with the speed of a glacier, you sacrifice all common sense for politically correct egalitarian propaganda and you cap it off by standing in the way of freedom. Textbook stupidity. If this were a business, you'd all be fired."

Predictable complaints, only half of them true. I didn't bother arguing with him. Instead I said, "Then fire me. Hell, let's discuss severance packages."

"The moment you spill your trade secret. Right when you teach us how to wipe out Black Ep and bust your monopoly on thawing."

I shrugged. The timing on that was Vashti's to make.

"*They're* management and *we're* workers," Fitch ranted at Kody. "Does that sound fair? We could all be management—Amarillo's just a short plane ride away and full of worker bees."

As Kody tried to steer the conversation back to common

ground, I heard myself paraphrasing the antistratification portion of the Doctrine, part of the repeated call to oppose the "us vs. them" hardwiring in the primate brain: "Does there have to be management and workers? Why make that division at all?"

"Because we're not all assholes," Fitch spat. From the school of thought that life is a zero-sum game in which there are winners and losers—and the losers are assholes. With everyone equal, no one's a winner and hence everyone's an asshole. You could use the same logic to say that with everyone equal, no one's a loser and therefore no one's an asshole—an "is the glass half-empty or half-full" matter of perspective.

"Ideology," Kody reminded us, but the big man railed on, shaking his cigar at me: "Do you even believe your own bullshit? Aren't you the big nonconformist here? I'm sure there's a special place in hell where they throw hypocrites on the fire."

Actually, no burning, but a whole lot of tromping around in lead-lined cloaks, according to Dante, I didn't say, because I was too busy saying, "You know, it's not every day my morality gets questioned by a child molester."

"Ho, Thursday, way over the line," said Kody.

"Those were baseless allegations by scumbags with an agenda to bring me down," Fitch raged. "And they were fifty years ago."

"If you two are just going to trade insults—" Kody began.

"No, fuck this," Fitch said, already up to leave.

Something banged against the door. Everyone reacted but no one reached, which meant if Fitch had the gun, he probably didn't have it on him. We gave ground as the knob turned and the door swung wide. A gin-soaked couple lurched in, trying to keep their balance in mid-kiss and already fumbling with each other's clothes—tired of dancing, the lovebirds were searching for a romantic hideaway.

"Oh!" said the Storyteller, upon seeing us there.

"Uh-oh, it's the fun police," Dr. Danny Chaikin joked, clutching her tighter as she giggled. "We're sorry, we didn't realize anyone was in here."

"That's okay, I was just leaving," said Fitch, but Kody stepped up to cut off his path and shut the door on the lovers.

His back to the door, Kody raised an index finger and said, "Experience is the comb Nature gives to Man after he goes bald. Understand? You walk off, or you drive him off, you're both going to gain a pantload of experience. You're going to regret not making the deal you could have made."

"Pantload of experience?" I said.

"Look, you two are never going to give each other a kidney, but you don't have to be friends to do business. Thursday, make Fitch a serious offer."

I took a lungful of air and offered the deal I'd given Mars.

"You want to put me in a box? Now I thought you might be keen to put me in *a* box, but I didn't think *that* box. I prefer reality to that virtual bullshit, so if that's your big offer, you know what you can do with it."

"Fine, name your price."

"You can't afford me."

"Try me."

He asked me for things I couldn't give, concessions that would have compromised our security far more than any firearm.

"Then what do we have left to talk about?" he said. "There's nothing you can give me."

Maybe so, I thought. *Maybe this comes down to me searching the Cigar Club and Fitch's apartment, trying not to get shot.* Nevertheless, I turned it over in my mind and said, "Am I negotiating with you or your group?"

"What are you talking about?"

"What do you want—personally? Not what you think is best politically. What would make you happy?"

"What would make me happy?" he scoffed. And in a sardonic tone, he threw out what he considered a ridiculous request. But one I could accommodate.

"You can't be serious," Champagne scowled. "Hal, that'd be insane."

"We *do* have it," I said.

"It's not a bargaining chip; it's priceless."

"Priceless," I acknowledged. "But how valuable is Sloane's missing gun? You want me to recover it but you don't want me to crack any heads—well, here's a way to get it *sem tumulto,* as Pandora would say."

She gnawed her lip and shook her head. "Fitch? Of all people?"

"Pearls before swine, Cham, I know."

We walked in silence to the Fogg, crossing its Italian Renaissance-style courtyard, navigating past the security I'd installed and dropping down to a subterranean vault. Aboveground, Harvard's oldest art museum housed treasures, but they were positively meager compared to what lay beneath. In the bowels of the Fogg, a temperature-controlled, light-sensitive, dust-free chamber housed an irreplaceable collection of paintings, sculpture and drawings: da Vinci, Michelangelo, Picasso, Goya, Bacon, Blake, Bosch, Rembrandt, Kahlo, Magritte, Monet, Mondrian and on and on.

Over the past twenty-five years, we posthumans had looted. Habitually. The best finds were the time capsules. Most had been built with time-release locks, protecting cultural/historical artifacts from thieves and vandals during the plague, but set to—over the duration it took us to wake up and find them—pop open like flowers in bloom. Some of the designers had prepared for the possibility their capsules wouldn't be found by humans or posthumans; instead, these were a gift for far distant future anthropologists to discover—extraterrestrial explorers, presumably—because pains had been taken to explain the intricacies of human existence to those who might have no grasp of them. And one had actually been booby-trapped—a "fuck you" to any who dared live after the capsule makers had succumbed—but Isaac and I had worn our biohazard suits, the liberal misting of nerve gas not affecting us at all.

"It's kind of funny," I told Champagne.

"What is?"

"Fitch and the rest of Ning's cronies like to call us fascists, and stepping into this room, it's hard not to think about what Göering hid around Berchtesgaden, or the bunkers beneath Kaiserburg castle—all the art the Nazis stole."

She didn't find it funny.

"We're protecting, not stealing. And don't tell me that's what the Nazis said. Once society's stable again—and I mean truly stable, Hal, not this 'drunk elephant on a high wire' act—we'll give them back to the people. Except, apparently, the *Mona Lisa*."

"The 'fucking *Mona Lisa*,' to use his exact words," I said.

"Is he such a big art fan?"

"It's an ego thing."

"What, to be the man who owns the most famous painting in the world?"

"Sure, everyone measures himself against everyone else—maybe this is a way for him to feel less ordinary, more valued, special—special enough for him to cough up the gun. Or maybe it's just something he said, never expecting we actually had it."

She stared at the hoard of precious objects, feet unwilling to move. "Can't we just reason with him?"

"Either we trade him for the gun or I go in and take it. Words won't cut it."

"What if we don't go along? How dangerous is a single gun?"

"You tell me, Cham. You're the one who said we had to remove all civilian-owned firearms from mainstream society. Keep the deadly weapons out of the city and we won't need a repressive security force, remember? That's how everyone was supposed to get along."

She narrowed her gaze at me. "I don't remember you loudly disagreeing."

"Not my job. You, Vashti, Isaac—you make the rules, I enforce them—that's the beginning and the end of it," I said. "So what do you want to do about Fitch?"

"Do you think he can tell the real thing from a fake?"

"If it's a good forgery, then no, I don't think he's the sort who could tell the difference. But I can't guarantee you, and I can't rule out the possibility that one of his friends might sniff it out."

She sighed. "All right, let me think what I want to do," she said.

Outside, Kody let out an appreciative whistle. "Sweeter than candy, Thursday," he said, running a hand through his thinning hair. "Is it real?"

We stared at the painting. It smiled.

"Yes," I lied. I didn't know.

"It seems a shame to give it to such a rotting fish."

"Bad apple," I said.

"Same difference," he shrugged. "One bad apple spoils the bunch; one rotten fish makes the whole basket stink."

"Do you think he'll take it?"

"No doubt."

"How do you know?"

"Ah, I know his type. He'll make the deal reluctantly and suggest he's only making it because of me," Kody said. "You watch.

He wants you to trust me completely, and then use me against you. Typical Tzuperman."

"A typical Superman? How?"

"Tzuperman—a Sun Tzuperman. A big admirer of Sun Tzu's *Art of War*," he explained. "Make as many business deals as I have and you can't help running into them. Spies are vital to Sun Tzu—he calls it 'divine manipulation of the threads.' So in Fitch's book, information is the best weapon of all, something he can use to disrupt your plans and prey upon your fears."

"So he's talking to you?"

"He's recruiting me, he thinks."

"Should I worry?"

"What," he laughed, "you think I'm a rotten fish? *Mai pen rai,* Thursday, relax. I've got him completely snowed."

When he found out we had the *Mona Lisa* available, Fitch held out for two additional masterwork paintings, but did in fact relinquish Sloane's gun. Reluctantly, as Kody said. After the swap, the man tried to ingratiate himself with me, hailing the exchange as a positive step in our dealings. Maybe our two points of view weren't so far apart, he said. And while saying so, he went to work on Kody.

Three days later, I stopped trusting Kody. Not Fitch's fault, though. It had nothing to do with him.

"He's your friend, so I came to you first," said Tomi. The quietest of my nieces, Tomi worked cryonics with Vashti and Pandora. With long black hair, fine features and the soul of a warrior-poet, the appellation suited her well—she'd been named after Tomoe Gozen, the most celebrated female samurai.

"You say he said it as a joke?"

"No, he played it off as a joke afterward. He looked serious at the time."

"I don't see why he'd ask you."

"He knew where I worked; I had excellent access."

"No, I mean his motive," I said. "Why would Kody want you to kill someone?"

"*Kill* isn't a word he used."

"Then are you sure it's what he meant?"

She gave me a single, decisive nod. Sure as shooting.

Into Grendel's Den I ventured, interrupting the 9-ball game Kody was winning, and thus reluctant to leave. I spoiled his shot, grabbing him by the forearm and pulling him up from the pool table. He stepped back and rubbed his arm ruefully.

"Sorry," I apologized. My anger had snuck up on me and tightened my grip.

It seemed I was always inflicting limb damage in the Den. *Channeling Beowulf,* I supposed—the Old English hero had defeated his Grendel by tearing the monster's arm right out of its socket.

"What's so important?" he asked, and so I told him. "Oh, that." He flashed a grin worthy of his native Thailand, the Land of Smiles. Not quite reassuring me. Behind the cheerful, dismissive guise I saw the strain of guilt, the kind a man carries for years hoping and not hoping for a chance to unload.

"Sort this out for me, Kody," I said. "Come on, put me at ease."

We walked and talked. The more we talked, the more the smile faltered, and the more hangdog his expression became.

Now on schedule to be thawed: the more difficult cryonic extractions, the plague sufferers who'd been so damaged by Black Ep they were unlikely to come back to life. We'd already thawed all the easy breezies. Among the remaining stragglers was a captain of industry named Van Caneghem—no relation to the escape artist. Tomi had estimated his chance of recovery at twenty percent; Kody had asked her what it would take to drop that down to zero.

"Who is he to you?" I asked.

Kody shrugged. "No one really."

"Then why?"

"He knows me."

I studied him. He sighed.

"Let me tell you how I got frozen."

In the wrong place at the wrong time, Kody breathed his last. Got himself killed. The limo ran afoul of a riot and lost, have-nots shattering the windows and ripping the hapless captain of industry out, stomping him to death on the pavement. Ugly, not peaceful, not "dying with the eyes closed" as the Thai say.

R.I.P. the real Kody—not the one who'd befriended me.

My Kody? In the driver's seat, bloodied from broken glass, fortunate to survive the violence, speeding off into the night.

"I was his chauffeur," he explained. "My boss didn't like to drive and didn't trust a computer to do it. And I was also his bodyguard—body double, technically—he'd hired me because we looked enough alike to fool people who didn't know him personally. Not that it helped him in the end, sitting in the backseat while I was up front with a chauffeur's cap. Thursday, I was never so happy to wear that cap. They were hitting me, pulling at me. Trying to do to me what they'd done to him. 'I'm just a driver,' I yelled. 'I'm a workingman, leave me alone!' They listened. I made them listen. I got away and didn't know what to do. I remember wanting to call my family—but what family? I didn't have anyone. I started talking to myself. Said I'd rather live as someone I'm not than die as who I am. So I came here pretending to be him."

"And no one caught you."

"No one," he said. "I had his ID. I had his passwords. I'd learned all his mannerisms. No one knew him here—he was a very private person—I kept thinking someone would expose me but I had his voice in my ear, his ghost's voice telling me how white people thought all Thai looked alike. He'd said it before, and this time I guess he was right."

Kody had every intention of continuing the impersonation indefinitely. But Van Caneghem had made several deals with the genuine Kody—he knew who the man was and who he wasn't—and if successfully revived, could expose the charade.

"And so you wanted Tomi to pull his plug?"

"Just joking," he said. "I knew he was coming up on the list and I wanted to know what his chances were. To see if I had to come clean or not."

I wanted to believe him, but couldn't give him the benefit of the doubt.

"Honestly, Thursday, I haven't been truthful about this, but that's it. I'm not out to murder anyone. Seriously. Hiding who I am doesn't mean so much to me that I'd want to take anyone's life."

"But it does mean a lot to you," I said.

"Sure it does."

"Or you would have come clean from the day we thawed you."

He said nothing.

"Did you think we'd prosecute you?"

"At first."

"And when you saw we had bigger problems to worry about?"

"It's complicated."

"Maybe I'll understand. Stranger things have happened, right?"

He shook his head and I thought he might stay silent, but in a rush of breath he said, "I'm trying to do some good here. I'm working with you because I know what's right and what's wrong. And I know what you're doing is right. So I'm trying to make a difference—but I'm doing it as Suchart Shinawatra," he explained, invoking his boss's real name, the latter half of which translated as "does good routinely."

"Do you understand? I'm only here because of him. I want him to get credit for whatever good I do. So, yes, it's important to me, but if I have to be myself again, I will. No foul play required."

I didn't care about the lie itself. Pretend you're whomever you want. Pretend you're the king of Siam. But had Kody been willing to kill to protect his secret? I couldn't prove it. I couldn't rule it out.

Betray or disappoint. That's what the people closest to me tended to do.

So I stopped trusting him. I kept him as an informant, but stopped telling him anything that could pose a threat or come back to haunt me.

In a shark tank of prosperous, privileged, self-centered big fish, I thought I'd found a half-shark—or mershark—someone who could speak their language and mine. And no. No, he was just faking it. That's what bothered me most.

Maybe I should have suspected him. Since starting this, I'd had an inkling that the facilities had made mistakes, and not everyone who'd been cryopreserved was who they were advertised to be.

Take Amarillo.

Isaac returned from that expedition without his objective. He'd led Mr. Lucky to Mrs. Lucky's cryostat—and the sleeping beauty there was a stranger. Mislabeled. They scoured the building, but the real Mrs. Lucky was nowhere to be found. A heartbreaking mistake, if in fact it was a mistake. It wasn't hard to imagine crooked proprietors running out of space and double-booking their cryostats, tossing clients out for family and friends. Dumping the old for the new.

Better to try and save the people you love than strangers. And if by some miracle, on some hypothetical day, Black Ep could be beat, stand trial then.

On the other hand, with no sign the plague could be stopped, what did it matter?

Everyone was done for, anyway.

Who'd ever know?

I'm outside the gate, serving venison. Feeding the wolves. There's a good-sized pack now, brown and gray with keen yellow eyes. Apex predators at the top of their food chain, nothing eats them but curiosity, watching me with measured caution as I offer to supplement their diets with strips of deer, and digging in only when I retreat and the alpha gives the signal. I'm halfway to domesticating them. I don't want them domesticated; I just want to keep them around. I want them howling at night so everyone in the city can hear. Let the thawed know something's out there. Let them unite against a common fear.

The light is strange. Judging by radiance alone, it could be an overcast day. It could be twilight. Or it could be a moonlit night. I've forgotten what time it is and I don't think to look up. I'm utterly in the moment—the universe is just wolves and meat, with me as the middleman—and then there's the hat.

I see it out of the corner of my eye. A navy blue snow hat, crumpled, discarded like rubbish. My heart starts beating. If that's what I think it is. Oh, if it is.

Before the wolves can get to it, I'm there. I clutch it. My hand shakes. When I reverse the hat and hold it up, there's the telltale 2 in white at the top. This is the 2 hat, special to me because it was my son's. Deuce and I shared the same DNA, so he wore it as if it were necessary to tell us apart. But over time, the hat became less of a joke, evolving into a staple of his identity. One of his favorite things.

It's supposed to be safe at home. Locked up. Someone broke into my personal things, took my son's hat and threw it away where I was sure to find it.

To fuck with me.

I'm sick with fury. I feel like I've swallowed razor wire. I tuck the hat into my inside pocket and I get up. I hate the city. I turn around with every intent of—

No, it's already happening. Huge plumes of smoke are rising up, and even this far away, I can feel the heat. Flames consume, windows break. The city is burning.

Good. That's how this should feel. But I can't take pleasure in it. Can't let it happen. I'm already in full sprint, off to save lives and catch the arsonist.

Inside the gate, I spy something familiar. Amidst all the screaming and running, a flash of orange hair. My son, Deuce, hatless, walks through the chaos like it's nothing, stainless steel lighter in hand. I call his name and he doesn't hear me. Or doesn't want to. He flicks the lighter's case open and thumbs the wheel, looking for something new to burn.

I chase but don't catch. Keep losing him in the smoke. When I do see him, I race to close the distance, but his arms and legs warp and stretch in ways that defy all logic. I am chasing a ghost.

"Where's the fire?" calls a voice to my left. I recognize the voice. Only now do I realize that I'm dreaming.

From the eighteen years of behavior and mannerism my generation logged in IVR, artificially intelligent programs were built—so anytime I felt nostalgic and morbid, I could plug in and hang out with fairly sophisticated phantoms of my dead peers. Except for one. Upon making the decision to betray and murder us, my oldest friend scorched the earth behind him, wiping himself from the logs. So no personality composite can be made—and the only time I get to talk to him is in dreams.

Where the Statue of Three Lies should be, Mercutio dangles upside down from a gallows tree. The rope's about his right ankle and his left leg is bent to form an inverted four. It's the pose of the Hanged Man, a tarot card of introspection and sacrifice. With each hand he gives me the finger.

"Fuck you, too," I reply. That earns a smile.

"Hey, where you running off so quick? Where's the fire?"

"All around us," I yell. "Can't you feel it?"

"No, but don't go by me. I don't feel much these days."

"You want me to say I'm sorry?"

"Hell no," he laughed. "What happened happened. Shot is shot."

"And not is not."

"That's right, we're both just victims of circumstance."

"No, you did what you had to do. So did I. We took actions; actions have consequences. So none of this 'victims of circumstance'—you don't get off the hook so easy. Neither do I. Now I don't have time for—"

A flash of color through the smoke—streaking two directions at once—I'm tracking forked lightning, and his name is Deuce.

"Why are you burning the city?" Mercutio's asking me.

"I'm not. That's my kid."

"No, your kid's still nestled in Pandy's girl parts. Bang-up job, by the way—good luck with that."

"Thanks."

"I still say you're the one making the city extra crispy," he says, stretching down to scratch something in the dirt. "You hate Harvard or something? Go Yale?"

I glance down and see he's written BOOLA BOOLA.

When I look up, he's gone. Escaped. I'm staring at an empty tree.

"Dreaming," I remind myself.

I can't decipher the full extent of my brain's backwash, but I know I'm dealing with fear and guilt. Haunted by people I couldn't save—that's the guilt. Unable to save the city. Having it burn on my watch. That's the fear.

I drop my head back down and what Mercutio's written now reads BREATHE. I can barely see it through all the smoke. Breathe, why not, I'm oxygen-addicted—don't mind if I do. In this case, it's bad advice. I'm conscious of the acrid stink of chemicals—whatever's burning here is unsafe to inhale, but it's filling my lungs and—

The bottom's dropping out.

I'm coughing up poison. I've been contaminated. It's not smoke—not a chemical cloud. It's a biological cloud, a swirling miasma of microorganisms besieging me, seeping into my skin, and I'm breathing in more and more of them. And it's getting easier. Like they're terraforming the architecture of my internal organs. With the kind of certainty that comes only in dreams, I know something within me is changing.

Now I can hear voices bubbling and overlapping, shooting up like grass bursting through concrete. Every speck in my blood wants to tell me what it thinks.

But whatever language they're speaking, I don't understand.

I drop to my knees. I'm not well. The babble of voices keeps getting louder, and I'm in touch with a wellspring of emotion: fear and fascination, but mostly a jaw-clenching, teeth-grinding, un-reasoning anger. Theirs or mine? Mine, I realize—the anger's mine.

"Get out!" I yell.

I could yell myself hoarse.

Enough of this, I decide, working to assert my mind over the litany. Out with the last gasp: I exhale as much of the toxic vapor as I can, forcing a cone of it back into the atmosphere, where it scars the air itself. I'm seeing my breath on a cold day, hanging there before me, but it snakes into a pattern before it dissipates.

The pattern spells FREE.

At last I can see the city again—or what's left of it—the ashes of New Cambridge whipping around like inky snow. This is the nuclear blast site, the dead city, the smoldering afterbirth of combustion and ill will.

Off in the distance I catch sight of the fire starter. He strides toward me, closing to a gunslinger's range, pausing when I call him Deuce, then drawing near enough for us to box. He's not Deuce. Mercutio's right about that.

I'm opposite a corpse-faced version of myself, black lipstick, black fingernails, black eyeliner, the self-indulgent depths-of-despair, nothing-to-live-for, think-twice-before-you-dare-talk-to-me wardrobe of my youth. There's a silver medallion around his neck in the likeness of a tarot card; I don't have to look to know it's Death.

With a satisfied smirk he lights a clove cigarette, and in the lighter's glow I can see he is crawling with microbes. As am I. He takes a drag and my eyes are open to the hidden life that covers everything. His eyes mirror mine, identical but for distortions of each iris reflecting twin ankhs alight.

"Have we met?" I ask, and when he exhales the puff of sickly-sweet smoke, it hits like a shotgun shell, and I am flung back like a moth introduced to a hurricane. The wind screeches past me as I twist, but it's an electronic-sounding screech, one that sounds increasingly like my alarm clock. And the clove smoke expels me from the universe; I'm waking now; I can feel the dream slipping away, stretching off into the distance, leaving only blackness behind.

I'd sworn off dreaming years ago. Gave it up for Lent. My unconscious mind hadn't listened, disobediently serving up phantasmagoria like that far too often.

Traitor.

Dreams are supposed to be a way for the brain to work through unresolved issues, but the prospect of tugging at the loose threads of my life struck my conscious mind as painful and pointless—why struggle with knots you can't possibly untie? Better to leave them be. Or reach for scissors and be done with everything.

The dream melted and flitted away—parts of it would come back to me at odd times, but upon waking, I only remembered two things.

I remembered the word *free.*

That word alone. Which summoned up a conversation I'd had with Kody a month prior. I'd asked him about the Thai word for freedom—not *thai* as I'd originally thought, but *itsara.* A linguistic kissing cousin, perhaps, of a word Isaac once taught me, *istiqara,* a request for spiritual guidance in the form of a dream.

"Yeah, *itsara.* Means 'liberty,' 'freedom,'" he'd said, as we watched the heads of two Fortune 500 companies shout at each other over ownership of a breakbot. "That's what it means in Thai, but the word originally comes from another language, Pali. Meant something completely different there."

"What's that?" I'd asked, as the younger and louder of the two CEOs forced the other to retreat.

"It meant 'the power to control other people.'"

"That's not so different," I'd cynically said.

The other thing I remembered:

I remembered the city burning down.

And the very next day it did.

Not by fire. By treachery, it burned.

I'd discovered one of the President's Secret Service men teaching two of Harvest's busboys how to fashion homemade explosives from common cleansing products. Ammonia and nitric acid make ammonium nitrate. Nitric acid and sulfuric acid make nitroglycerine. Plant nails in the bombs to up the lethality. Dip the nails in rat poison to up it some more.

I have a nihilist's temperament. I know from bombs. This wasn't unexpected.

Surveillance led me to one of the old fraternity houses. They'd set up a lab in the basement behind a door that blended into the wall—I found it mostly by nose, following the concentration of cloying floral-scented deodorizer and the ghost of chemical smell buried underneath.

I called my hounds in; we came down hard. Three arrests, and no one resisted. But it took time. It put me across town.

Miles away, at the community park, the boys and girls of New Cambridge chased a softball game with an ice cream social. Typical Saturday afternoon, clear skies, sunny weather, perfectly innocuous until the sickness. Stomachs turned; faces went green; half-digested ice cream and stomach acid shot up to paint the grass.

A parade of nauseous children funneled into the hospital, carried there by worried parents and obliging Good Samaritans. The health emergency pushed Vashti's staff to the limits, and in the rush to treat everyone, amidst all the shrieking, crying and vomiting, security procedures went unfollowed.

A disaster because the Good Samaritans weren't. By the time Malachi linked me, they'd overpowered the staff and barricaded the entrance. It was a well-orchestrated attack. They immediately took Vashti and Tomi as hostages, catching each by surprise before either could find a weapon. To her credit, Tomi performed not one but two makeshift rhinoplasties before being subdued, the first assailant's nose fracturing to a looping uppercut, the second to a high back elbow. But Vash went quietly, calm and cool, trying to reason with the unreasonable.

Pandora—

"Safe at home," Malachi assured me. Which helped. I was already taking it personally. Too much of that can cloud your thinking and get in the way of your *zanshin*. You want to stay aware. Combat ready. But really there was nothing personal about the siege. In the mind of the man who architected it, at least, business was business.

Everyone had told me I'd overestimated the threat he comprised. They'd said he was just espousing the minority view, the old guard's elitist concerns, and his Manifesto was a useful dissent, one that could help the community burn off steam. They'd said when it came to actually taking the system down, Richard Ning was all show, no go. And they'd said I carried a grudge against him, an unreasonable grudge, fixated upon him, because one of his companies made my son's favorite lighter.

So? Deuce didn't meet his end in fire. He just liked to burn things, that's all. He couldn't help how he was wired. Being the father of a pyromaniac didn't embarrass me, though many felt that it should. Screw them. My paternal failings had nothing to do with fire. I just didn't give him what he needed.

That wasn't anyone's fault but mine. The lighter coincidence meant nothing. My misgivings about Ning came purely from the coldness that always lurked behind his smile.

"We'll see what happens," I told Ning's defenders, time and time again.

He never entered the hospital himself, but this was his baby, a Cigar Club venture all the way. Right-hand man Fitch ran the operations from the inside, the *Mona Lisa* buying me Sloane's gun only and his loyalty not at all.

It doesn't take a lot of people to effect change. It just takes a willingness to do whatever it takes.

Step one: Poison children.

To repeat, they poisoned children. Wait, it gets better: Some of the hostage takers were parents. In a perverse twist on the already perverse Münchausen by proxy, they'd made their own kids sick just to get into the hospital to gain the upper hand.

Step two: Secure the hospital.

Step three: Don't let anyone treat the kids until Vashti gives up the secret of life.

I'm sure Ning phrased it in more heroic terms. The Resistance making painful sacrifices to outwit Nazis. Prometheus stealing fire from the gods.

Trouble was, they'd picked the wrong nut to crack. Vashti could be stubborn as Catholic guilt—if need be, she'd call their bluff and let the kids wither and rot. She could be cold. Which meant they might blink first, necessitating a step four.

Step four: Panic, do something criminally stupid and let someone die.

That's what I worried about most.

All attempts to link Fitch failed; he only wanted to negotiate with Vashti. On my order, the hounds brought Ning into custody, while I hit the arsenal.

"Ready to go in?" I asked Malachi once I'd loaded up for war.

"Whatever you need," he replied.

He'd already tapped into the infrastructure. He could provide invaluable tactical support, turning cameras, locks, alarms, lights, links and ventilation on and off as needed. And if worse came to worse, he could do something more.

"Ready for applesauce?"

"You don't really want to do that," he said of that particular contingency plan.

"No," I agreed.

"I'll be ready," he promised.

Past Isaac and Champagne and the rest of the gathering crowd,

I moved invisibly toward my goal. Stealth in, negotiations or firepower out—their choice—I'd made a point to bring whatever I needed to get the job done. Except . . .

Except it was over before I got there. Vashti caved in almost immediately. Not what I'd anticipated.

"I just kept thinking of Penny," she told me after the fact. Her late daughter, Penny, my son's partner in crime, haunted Vashti much the way Deuce haunted me. "I kept thinking of Penny and I didn't want to lose another daughter," she said, looking down at her hands.

Among those felled by the tainted ice cream: the activity planner for the city's children, Katrina—Vashti and Champagne's youngest child.

"They wouldn't let me examine her," she said. "I didn't know how sick she was."

Not very, as it turned out. The hostage takers had slipped the kids a powerful emetic to force vomiting. The effects were nasty and startling, good enough to produce a serious scare of food poisoning, but in no way life threatening.

But Vashti hadn't known that. And now she was alone, sitting on the waiting-room floor, refusing both to leave the hospital and to talk to anyone but me. "I've saved so many, Hal, but in my head it was just Penny, Isaac's kids, your kid, all the senseless tragedies. To see and hear that suffering and not be able to do something about it," she said, trailing off to bite her lip hard enough to draw blood. "They wouldn't even give them water to fight dehydration, not unless I told them what they wanted. They made those kids suffer on my watch."

She made a derisive, self-deprecating sound, something between a snort and a sigh. "I thought I was stronger," she said.

"Nobody blames you," I told her.

"Then that makes me nobody."

"Vashti," I said, "you can't live life in a state of complete immunity. What happens affects you—one way or another. And what happened to Penny didn't leave you untouched. That's probably a good thing."

"But to not have control over it? I mean, hell, I cured Black Ep—I should be able to do anything. Yet I couldn't go numb when I needed it. Not like you can."

I didn't correct her.

"Is it chaos out there?" she asked.

"Lots of angry people. The kids are scared but okay; the President's out pleading for calm; the Assembly is meeting right now to figure out what to do."

"But the secret's out."

"Yes."

"Well, that's going to change things."

"I imagine so."

"We tried running it our way. Maybe they'll do a better job."

The desperately hopeful expression—the atypical vulnerability—stopped my *don't bet on it* in its tracks.

"You never know," I said.

"That's right, you never know."

We sat together until I could coax her back to the outside world. We walked through Victory City at dusk with the moon already high in the sky, and we could feel everything she'd built quietly collapsing. The peace she'd worked for was over. We knew. We walked and we knew.

In the days that followed, we enjoyed the moral high ground. What happened at the hospital was plainly unconscionable. No one dared defend it. Buoyed by an outpouring of popular support, we caught most of the culprits. But some disappeared. And none of it stuck to the architect of the crime.

Knowing that someone had to pay for this, Ning made certain that person wasn't him. He sold out Fitch. He told us exactly where we could find him. I gathered a team of twenty—loyal citizens, Slow Bridge, a couple of Green Mountain Boys—my *posse,* some called it—and tracked Fitch to a heretofore-unknown Popsicle stand just a stone's throw from the Metro Toronto Convention Center.

We pierced the security of the lab to find it choked by corporate branding, a kaleidoscope of red and white. Here we discovered a private security force—small army, really—waiting to be thawed out. As expected. And attempting the thawing: Fitch and two co-conspirators, the top execs of a major soft-drink corporation.

We stopped them at gunpoint. Then put them under the lights. Caught, and recognizing how they were caught, they proved only too eager to turn against the man who tipped us off. Which fit neatly into my plans.

Unfortunately, by the time we returned to New Cambridge, I'd been outmaneuvered. Ning had spent the moment well, sharpening the findings made in the aftermath of the hospital siege into dangerous political weapons. He'd taken his message to the streets and roused the city's rabble, upper-class rabble though they were. With a slick combination of fearmongering and legitimate complaint, he'd put a stutter of doubt in the Assembly's leadership. And, worse, he'd annihilated Vashti's credibility.

Why, after the most horrifying health crisis in human history, had she deprioritized the thawing of doctors? Look how many highly skilled medical talents she'd left on ice, downplaying their value to the city. All for fear of her secret getting out. All because she'd wanted to protect her monopoly. Wasn't that selfish?

The lesson to be drawn from children getting sick, he'd argued, was not just that some citizens were ruthless. Virulent microorganisms lay in wait, immediate and close. What if the plague made a return? How safe were we? Medical genius though she was, by neglecting to thaw enough doctors, Vashti had put everyone at risk. And the Assembly had let her. It was irresponsible to the point of criminality.

Plague culture did us in; the terror of Black Ep trumped all. After bumping shoulders with extinction, how could it be any other way? Richard Ning tapped into the city's nightmares and worked those emotions into white-hot indignation. Whispers of an ouster cranked up to a shout; Vashti stepped down; the Assembly imploded. I'll give the man his props—it didn't take him long to unravel everything we'd built.

PART TWO

applesauce

·

(to rein in hell)

fantasia

Long day. Very. Everyone screaming. Being pests. Pushing my buttons.

Mommy's tired.

Chose this. My choice, no one else's. Knew the work it would take, must tough it out, lie in bed I chose to make.

Vacation when this is done. Where? Somewhere warm?

Tried green this morning. Green top, black jeans. Liked it. Brought out the color of my eyes. Couldn't do it. Held on for fourteen minutes, then changed into red cammies. Feel safer in red. Residual sludge of my mental illness.

Was obsessed with violet, now red. Color substitution hardly a cure.

Find new medication for OCD? Probably not worth risking negative interaction with antipsychotics. Mild OCD small price to pay for clear mind and delusional thinking ~~almost~~ gone.

Whole zoo calls me Red now. George's idea to first use the sign for "red" instead of "caretaker," and now that's spread to everyone. George, trendsetting abstract thinker. Smart girl. No dummy. Do they associate all reds with me now? If red means me and this is a red toy, is it a me toy? How to parse that question so they understand?

George as trendsetter encouraging for experiment. Fears of subject group exhibiting passivity slightly allayed. Intellectual passivity dragon maybe slain, physical passivity dragon maybe still breathing fire. Foul up years of research.

Have I wasted the past eight years?

Subject group too passive = failure. Subject group too hierarchical = failure. Signs of both today helped throw me in tailspin. Signs, but not clear signs. Control group played keep-away with George's favorite cup and she didn't chase. Rising above it or intimidated? Ringo beat up Paul pretty good in a wrestling match. Dominance or rough play? Much harder to read signs now that puberty's come calling.

Control group's easy. Behavior dynamics could be read in the dark, or in Braille through freaking oven mitts. Mick's king of the mountain. He's proven it over the past year. Balls have dropped. When he takes your treat or toy, the teeth are out, and if you challenge you're getting hit or bit. Keith's the beta behind Mick. He robs the females, they scream, Mick chases after to remedy the theft. Enforcing the pecking order.

I'm sick of stitching up wounds, but my job's observing behavior, not encouraging or discouraging it. Sorry, kid, Mommy's here to fix you up, not tell you how to live.

Not just sick and tired. Nervous lately. Growing tickle that one of the two primal forces is coming for me. Kept checking the surveillance cameras ~~for an agent of N or D.~~

Won't believe it. Won't relapse. Just acknowledging it so I can quiet the thoughts and move on.

Want to be warm, safe, healthy, wholesome, sane. Can't be. Not completely. Never be perfect. But sometimes weakness can be an even greater power than strength.

It takes a special kind of crazy to think you can change the world.

isaac

Regimes never last. Never. Let's not lose sight of the fact that no empire is infinite. Power can be held but never kept. Looking back, I believe we made the best of our short reign. We saved lives. We inspired. There is no reason to be discouraged.

Had we elected not to govern and merely presented ourselves as practitioners of medicine, the situation would be different. Better or worse, who can say? I refuse to claim victory for a path not taken.

Lazarus, old friend, how I wish you could have been there. You had a way of keeping everything in balance. How many contributions would you have made, had you not been murdered those many years ago? More than ever, we are poorer for your absence.

A pang of apprehension tells me it's a mistake to remember you in times of trouble. It seems I only turn your way when the situation looks grim. But I find your influence calming, even though you can never answer me.

Have I told you about the AI simulacrum Malachi fashioned of you? It does you no justice. It boasts your personality but not your wisdom. Digital or no, I will not speak to a foolish ghost.

No, it's much better like this. Like brothers, you and I.

Let me say this much about New Cambridge, counterintuitive though it may seem: Sometimes, it's best to give up power. You knew that, didn't you? There are those who have accused me of being broken by the mistakes I've made in my life, crippled to the point where I would rather cede power than wield it. Nonsense. From the very beginning, I have wanted to cede power.

For who among us is wiser than the Gedaechtnis corporation? Why should the men and women who outmaneuvered Black Ep be left sleeping while we take control? They designed us. They are the architects of our continued existence, surely more fit to make monumental decisions than we.

When our friends deemed Gedaechtnis too great a risk, I sought the United Nations instead. Alas, that cryonic facility had been compromised, a casualty of the riots, so I suggested we cede to the United States, but once again I was outvoted, our friends unwilling to trust President Coleman with the reins.

Vividly, I remember warning Vashti about the rise and fall of Akhenaten. Akhenaten, pharaoh of Egypt, in all probability the father of King Tut. Akhenaten, who rebelled against his family and against all common mores by outlawing the worship of traditional gods in favor of praying to the sun, by constructing a new capital and by making his name and the capital's name synonymous.

We're not forbidding anyone's religion, she said.

We are imposing the Doctrine.

Presenting, not imposing. You're afraid of a backlash, Isaac, but these people can't go back to their old lives. Look at the state of the world. They need something new.

Admittedly, but you expect too much of them. You're intent on making Cambridge the new cradle of civilization, instead of letting it be what it is: a temporary shelter. And you call it Victory City, after Jaipur, India, where you spent your youth, and after your very surname, Jai, meaning victory.

It's just a nickname. And I did stop Black Ep. Permit me *some* indulgence, won't you?

Vashti, I said, when have I denied you anything?

With retrospect, we can add those to the list of words that

sting my conscience. Champagne and I stole two hours together today. Two blessed, breathless hours, churning feelings long sleeping but never dead. Vashti must know. We haven't told her yet, but she must.

As I say, regimes never last. America is our concern no longer. Europe is next. The British royals, the German magnates, and the Vatican all crave freedom. That is why we have returned to "the world city with a heart," Munich, where my children are entombed. Then China, and the task will be at end.

We're within walking distance, Lazarus. We're already thawing out Gedaechtnis. To think how many years I have waited for this opportunity, and how tantalizingly close it has crept. How often does a chance like this come? To look behind the curtain? To meet your makers? And make sense of the world?

sloane

That's Sloane with an *e,* not just an *n,* and not fucking Slow. Christ, how I hate that. I'm not slow. Unlucky as a whore at a eunuch convention, but not slow. My name is Sloane with a capital *S.* I'm the last PH in Vic City. Last, like I could set up a big-ass sign that flashes *Posthuman Pop: 1* here, and everyone could gawp all slack-jawed to wonder who that one could be. Well, you're looking right the fuck at her, geniuses—it's me, baby, it's me. I'm the one still here in the trenches. All the others hightailed it back to Europe. Who can blame them? I wouldn't be here if I didn't have to be.

And I do have to be. Absolutely have to. No one understands that. They all think I'm crazy for sticking around. Especially my mothers. Even my twin. Never mind that I can do some good here, they want me over there. That's where my instincts tell me I should be, too. Sorry. Not this time.

My existence is shit. I am a colossal fuckup. Period. No, make that an exclamation point. Everything I try fails, everything I touch collapses, everything I want gets away from me. That's not woe is me. That's not poor Sloane has it so hard, little baby wants some sympathy. Fuck sympathy. This is the way it is for me. My whole life I've been cursed. Someone cursed me with—take your pick— the worst luck ever, or a combination of terrible choices, appalling instincts and deep-seated character flaws. Maybe they all go hand in hand. I don't know. But as you might imagine, I'm sick of it. So sick I'm willing to do something drastic.

There I was when it all went down. Out of position. Showing up to the rescue too late to do anyone any good. Mother and sisters taken hostage. Information extracted. I'm thinking how typical this is. How representative of my shitty life. And I'm talking to myself the way I do when things go wrong. Not just about the siege. About every mistake I've made. If you take a job in law enforce- ment, can you do much worse than lose your gun? Can you really? I'm a fucking punch line and I know it. And it occurs to me that my worst enemy is in my gut. All my impulses and feelings. Every instinct. That's what I have to get rid of. That's what I'm doing.

Whatever my intuition tells me to do, I'm taking my best shot at the opposite. It's an experiment. It's how I'm going to break the curse.

And it's the number-one reason why Sloane-o is flying solo. After the sheep lost faith in our shepherding, with the majority grumbling and making the city a hostile work environment, I gave my ear to the vocal minority who wanted us to stay. Wait, that's not entirely right—I didn't listen to the well-meaning shmoes, or the ones who were frightened to see us go. I listened to Richard Ning, who invited my sisters and me to be a part of the city's future. His city's future. I didn't trust him, so I said yes.

It's a business deal. He gets a splash of legitimacy, a wedge against my family, eye candy and a potential hostage. I get a chance to beat this curse and earn some redemption, plus a much-needed vacation from my family, a break from being a twin (hey, Bridge, don't let the door hit your ass on the way out) and the whole double-agent Mata Hari thing. If my new benefactor needs to be taken down, maybe I'll be the one to do it. I believe in takedowns. I subscribe to the philosophy that some people are better off drowned at birth. My dearly departed sister, Penny, was a prime example. Ning might be another. I'll have to get to know him better to make sure.

Strangers are starting to creep into town. They're not on any of our lists—I checked. Dollars to doughnuts someone had them defrosted from another freezer, one of those hidden vaults everyone's so worried about. I've seen about a dozen now. By age and physique and most of all attitude I'm guessing they're soldiers. Ning's new security team. Normally, I'd try to hang with them, so I'm keeping my distance, mixing with fashion-conscious trophy wives and spoiled debutantes instead. For now. They want to take me to Aspen and I'll let them. I love to ski. Meanwhile, the President's skipped town. Back to Washington, or Virginia, or wherever Presidents go.

I'm biding my time.

You watch. I'm going to do something valuable here.

halloween

Phase B—B as in banished, bounced, booted from Boston back to Bavaria—overtook Phase A so quickly, you'd have thought it was A all along. "This has always been the strategy," Vashti reminded anyone who would listen. "We're simply accelerating the timetable to meet the situation at hand."

I said, "Don't rationalize this to me. You know how I feel."

She couldn't help it. She'd been put on edge and had a need to justify every path taken. And to be fair, those choices were under attack. Many of our supporters felt we should have stayed. Or at least left more of our number behind in a symbolic or supervisory capacity. By pulling out of the government so completely, we risked leaving a power vacuum in our wake—which in turn risked violent instability. But trying to hold on to a bucking bronco wouldn't have been safe, and our continued presence might have only inflamed the outrage, what with our enemies becoming increasingly successful at painting us as villains. Perception is reality; well meaning or no, we were unreceptive to the needs of the community. Particularly the medical needs. So said Ning, and so said the voice of the people, which meant it must be true. That's how popular opinion helped drive Vashti, Isaac and Champagne's groupthink toward a policy of retreat. Better to go and help the rest of the world and return later, perhaps, once things settle down. Let the thawed govern the thawed; there were human members of the Assembly who still supported the Doctrine, and who could pick up right where we left off.

I said, "That's not how it's going to shake out." Coming events would prove me right.

Further Monday-morning quarterbacking among the faithful: Had putting all our eggs in one basket really been the best choice? In retrospect, might it have been wiser to split into groups—one in the United States, one in Europe, one in China? We could have had three weaker cultures, but that had struck the group as inefficient and dangerous. Better to leverage all our assets in the U.S., in the hopes of creating a single, strong society, one that could be started off on the right track—hence the Doctrine.

I said, "Looking back won't solve anything."

For as long as I'd known them, Vashti, Isaac and Champagne had belonged to a conspiracy of optimism. *Everything will work out. Expect the best, not the worst. With persistence and passion, any goal can be reached.* In times of trouble, they'd relied on one another to reinforce the shared conviction that the universe and those who inhabit it are essentially benign. That someday humanity will achieve a destiny that eradicates all war, poverty and crime. That order can always be imposed over chaos. Over the years, I'd noticed something preying on that seemingly unshakable enthusiasm— beaten down by one betrayal after another, my friends were gradually starting to understand. *Quae nocent, docent.* Things that injure, teach. Like enormous animals with sluggish nervous systems, the pain took longer to reach their brains, but here it was, reaching them at last. Watching them on the flight back to Munich, I could see they were becoming more cynical. More disillusioned. More like me. I didn't like it. I didn't wish that on them. I didn't wish it on myself.

Of the three, Isaac worried me most, the fearful, desperate glint in his eyes betraying an otherwise placid mask as he spoke about perspective, the importance of taking a longer view. "This is a flash," he told me. "Just a flash of white light, bright enough to blind us, and too quick to offer us anything more than a glimpse. It's impossible to accurately gauge what's happening now without the prism of history. Good decisions, poor decisions, give us some years to look back and we'll know." And then, as he would increasingly do, he steered conversation back to Gedaechtnis, how they might be the best evaluators of what we'd done, a hero worship I could barely stomach. So the company gave us life, granted, and they'd pulled a choke chain on human extinction. They'd also lied to us, made us guinea pigs and set us on unfortunate paths. To a good end, I suppose, so pay no attention to the means.

"Do you doubt they can justify the choices they made?" asked Isaac. As if they were infallible. With a perfect plan. As if they were a substitute for God.

Under no circumstances would the holy trinity of Gedaechtnis answer any of our questions. The three project heads—Ellison, Hyoguchi, Koppel—were simply beyond saving, having worked obsessively on our creation even as Black Ep did its heaviest damage. That kind of determination carried a price—Koppel had already been laid to rest at a local cemetery, and though Ellison and Hyoguchi had chosen cryonic preservation, the disease had ravaged them terribly, and they were too far gone for us to do much good.

"We can't try it," Vashti decided. Too much risk of ruining what was left of them with a failed resuscitation attempt. So they'd sit on ice indefinitely, like Isaac's children, waiting for the hypothetical technological advance that might restore them, someday, to the land of the living.

Even though God was dead, the angels were still kicking. (Isaac's metaphor. To me, it felt more like breaking the titans out of Tartarus.) One by one, we brought out an assortment of Gedaechtnis geneticists, epidemiologists, IVR programmers, sociologists, administrators and engineers, each overjoyed to see us—or anyone, truly—but especially us, their creations, the living proof that their experiment succeeded, and all their hard work was not in vain.

Welcome back. Yes, you're safe now. Disease free.

That's right, it worked.

Right, you saved the human race. Well done. Gold star for you.

How long has it been? How long do you think? No, longer than that.

But we look so young, yes. Must be the good genes you gave us. Good immune systems. Good metabolisms. Vampiric good looks.

Would you consider us your greatest creation? Or Black Ep?

You say you didn't midwife Black Ep? It isn't one of your bioweapons? It didn't spring from one of your labs?

Vigorous denial on unleashing the plague. Yes, they'd engineered biological WMDs for their clients, but never anything that couldn't be contained. For them, the real money had been in biosecurity, because no politician ever wanted to admit to his constituents that he'd put too low a price on their health. By introducing the occasional new germ warfare agent, they'd played on fears and increased profits, but—so they claimed—they'd always approached their work from a position of safety first, and had been far too careful to ever create as robust and ferocious a microbe as Black Ep. There was no profit in Armageddon. Other companies had been less careful and less scrupulous, and some had carried political agendas beyond the desire to make a buck, the Gedaechtnis employees were quick to argue—maybe I should investigate one of them.

When the bodies had started piling up, "Who's to blame?" had been the number-two question on everyone's lips, second only to "How do we stop it?" Millions had sought the answer in vain. Was it a naturally existing organism? Was it manmade? Did it come from outer space? God? The Devil? If anyone had known the truth, he'd stayed silent about it—and while I'd always had a hunch it was man-made, how could I prove it? Short of a smoking gun or a confession, I'd no hope of doing so, and without solid evidence of a natural origin, I'd no hope of proving the opposite.

Any other questions?

Here's one: Why'd you lie to us? Why didn't you tell us what we were up against from the beginning? When you spent all this time and effort building a virtual world to give us our "normal upbringing," didn't you realize how much more painful learning the truth would be? Did you give any thought to the kind of damage it does to suddenly find out you're alone?

They'd debated it, they assured me. If they'd told us what we were and what was ripping its way through the human race—if they'd taught us that back when we were kids, the pressure would have wreaked havoc on our childhood development. What if we had cracked from it? The whole project would have been compromised. So which was the lesser evil? Which choice was more responsible?

"Honesty," I said. "Always better."

Ah, the look on Isaac's face when he asked these thawed about their plan. "Which plan is that?" they frowned. If they'd plotted a course for us, they'd plotted one for society. Hadn't they? The answer always came sheepishly: "Hell, kid, we just did the best we could to get this far. And you guys really came through. Hopefully, we didn't screw you up too bad along the way, huh?"

Society had been a complete afterthought. They'd left post–Black Ep thinking to the governments and think tanks, distant hypotheticals for strategists with little faith in Gedaechtnis's ability to pull off such a grand experiment.

One odd thing. When they were throwing us questions, using all the old names—calling me Gabriel, Champagne Charlotte, Pandora Naomi, and so on—and we had to explain how half our number were either missing (Fantasia) or dead (Mercutio, Tyler,

Lazarus and Simone), one of the geneticists quietly asked, "What about the others?"

"What others?"

"The Hong Kong program," she said. "The other children."

isaac

Tinted glasses have never suited me, be they rose-colored or dark as the very center of an eye. Unreasonable optimism serves no one, nor does a jaundiced view of humankind. I have always believed we must see things as they are and then act from that awareness. Nonetheless, my vision has been shaded for years. I can admit it only now that I can see it, and I can see it only now that the lenses have been shattered.

It's as if I've been wearing Beholder Spex. Do you remember that fad, Lazarus? Lenses that distort light into a famous painter's style, and make the world a work of art. Fantasia favored them. One flip of a switch and objective reality slips behind a filter.

The old heart-to-hearts have been coming back to me today. Everything you said about a collective calling. How within each psyche lives the potential for abject purity of motive—the pursuit of the most good for the most people. And how some of us, some tiny fraction, will become the embodiment of this pristine thought, word and deed—and they would be the best of us, the transcendent pinnacle of human achievement. How deeply I believed this was Gedaechtnis, the architects of your destiny, mine and so many others.

Everything for a reason. Arab-African bloodline for genetic and cultural diversity. Male to even out the ratio of boys to girls. Raised Muslim to represent the populous Islamic faith. Raised Sufi to mitigate the perceived rigidity of Islam. Raised in IVR New York to furnish an appreciation of Western values, yet familiarize a wide range of cultures. Mother a UN Humanitarian Affairs Officer to teach negotiation, cooperation and compassion. Father a cultural anthropologist and a curator at the Met to teach the importance of studying ancient civilizations. Pushed to study those civilizations to be a link in the chain of living history. Pushed to study medicine to fight Black Ep. Sent to Idlewild to bond with my counterparts. Every major event in my childhood made for a specific reason. And so I asked why. Why the accident.

Verisimilitude, came the hesitant reply.

Explain.

We wanted healthy, well-balanced children, so it made sense for most of you to hail from stable, two-parent homes. However, had all ten of you grown up in such a fashion, that approach would have been not only unrepresentative of society but also disrespectful to the large number of single parents who have raised successful children. Thus, after careful deliberation, the decision was made for two of the marriages to end in amicable divorces and one to end in a head-on crash.

Drunk driver killed my mother.

Yes, we considered a disease. We even considered Black Ep. But we feared it might create undue pressure for someone we needed to combat microorganisms. To increase your personal stake like that could have been motivating, but might have been overwhelming. We couldn't chance it. A traffic accident seemed more humane: tragic but sudden, scripted without gratuitous suffering.

Without *what?*

Suffering. Her suffering. You never saw any. Just your father breaking the bad news. Closed-casket funeral. All by design. That's not to say you didn't suffer. I'm sure you did. But we all lose parents, and it's always sad. In a sense, you were all bound to lose your parents the moment you discovered the extent of the IVR simulation. We hoped you'd be able to help the others, having lived through the experiences you had.

And why my mother?

Haven't I just explained that?

No, you haven't. Of the ten subjects, why was I chosen?

Oh, that. That was an impossible decision. None of us wanted to cause any of you pain, so we let an RNG make the call.

A random number generator. A roll of the dice. It shatters everything, Lazarus. I am unable to view it rationally. Except to say, of course it was random—how can bereaving a twelve-year-old child of his mother be anything but arbitrary?

Inconsolable, unaccompanied on the flight back to New York, how I wept. But I laughed and danced at her funeral as my father commanded. We lived the words of the Sufi poet Jalal Al-Din. "When the human spirit, after years of imprisonment in the cage and dungeon of the body, is at length set free, and wings its flight to the Source whence it came, is not this an occasion for rejoicings, and thanks, and dancing?"

Absolutely, it is—if one believes such a Source exists. I do not. I am a fallen Sufi, an apostate Muslim, and well on the path to becoming an ex-humanist as well. Belief in God spun me in circles for the first eighteen years of my life, but faith in Gedaechtnis has spun me in circles ever since. Now the vertigo has caught up with me at last. No wonder I had to excuse myself from the quiet heart of Nymphenburg to find a place in which to be sick. I lost the contents of my stomach at the thought of all my folly, and at my creators' surrender to pure chance, and at what I almost did to my children in their name.

They're just men. Men and women with a certain talent, wisdom, passion and purpose, all born from desperate circumstance. Ethically and spiritually, they are the embodiment of nothing more enlightened than a survival instinct.

Never have I felt more in touch with the random cruelties of the universe.

Life isn't fair, they told me. We tried to prepare you. Your parents, your teachers, they all warned you. We made a special point of it.

So this is disbelief. To be isolated from that connection I once valued more than anything. To be disconnected from any presence greater than one's self feels spiritually crippling, mystifying and fearsome. The devil's name has roots in the word for despair, but without the devil, the despair remains, and without God or heroes, it only deepens. Belatedly, I have empathy with Halloween and Fantasia. I can understand the loneliness and desolation, the desire to push everyone else away. But I will not. There's too much work yet to be done, and if I have no betters, the task is mine.

The new call is Hong Kong, Lazarus. We are not alone. Or were not. There once were others like us there and I must know what happened to them. Evidently, the Chinese launched a parallel program, hoping to gengineer immuno-optimized descendants. In defiance of company policy and government embargoes, a fraction of the Gedaechtnis team clandestinely shared technology with Chinese geneticists to help them along. It was the right thing to do, though out of favor at the time.

The Trade War might have been the only geopolitical conflict not to be put aside in the dark days of the plague. Too much damage had been done to China and the West, and though politicians said much to the contrary, neither side was willing to put the bad blood behind them, Apocalypse or no Apocalypse. As you have so often told me, far beyond power, the most corruptive element to the human spirit is offended pride.

I promise to keep that in mind as I seek my paradise anew—a search that leads to neither God nor Gedaechtnis, but to my heart and conscience. The first step is Hong Kong, though whether I go as a diplomat or an archaeologist, I have no idea.

fantasia

Fireball low on the horizon. What some call a blood sunrise. Wrongly. Blood is much darker, redder. Womb color. No womb on the horizon. Have yet to see a bloodball sun or the bloodmoon of Rev. 6:12. No rush. Inspired, this dawn, blue light submissively scattered to let great streaks of red stain the sky.

So. Born Gina Rojas. Means Red Queen. *Through the Looking Glass* homage, someone at the company had love for Lewis Carroll. Always liked the name Rojas. Wore red all the time. Stopped when I realized I wasn't like the other kids. Thought differently. Not just quirk, something mad wrong with my mind. Burgeoning delusions, paranoia, thought disorder. Sick. Bad sick. Couldn't be Red. Had to be Purple. Purple was sick. Learned that studying American history. Roaring Twenties. Purple Gang crime syndicate got its name because they were rotten. Mobsters deemed "purple, like the color of bad meat." Me, too. Bad meat left out in the sun. Putrefying. Knew it. So. Embraced my illness. Became Violet Queen.

Friends started calling me Fantasia. Can't remember why. Let them call me anything. Called myself Mystery. Whispered it in the night so no one could hear. Convinced I was the Whore of Babylon. "And the woman was arrayed in purple and scarlet color." Rev. 17:4. Terrified I was she. Horrified I would traffic the Antichrist. Unleash the Beast. Annihilate the Universe. Laugh was on me, of course. By the time I was two, Black Ep already had made its slaughter.

Crazy vs. sane, a primer. Sane person wants a cookie. Knows she shouldn't eat it but wants it anyway. She eats it or doesn't. That's it. Crazy person has same conflict but can't keep it inside her. Has to bring in outside forces. The Devil wants her to eat the cookie. Jesus doesn't want her to have it. Or maybe the government wants her to go on birth control. Or terrorists. Or aliens. Someone impossibly grandiose. Someone who makes her feel important. Less lonely. How I wanted to feel.

Over the years, what did I do? Herded every single thing into my delusions, every power I'd ever heard of, moral, immoral, mortal, immortal, hell-bent or heaven-sent. Put them all to work. As pawns. Of the two primal forces: N & D. Two secret societies at war since the beginning of time. Each deadly enemy with inescapable reach. Not to be trusted, not to be crossed. All major historical events caused by their invisible parries and thrusts.

Really just an inner conflict externalized. N: Nutritious. What's good for me. Versus D: Delicious. What I want.

Nothing more than that. Nothing at all.

There. Owned it. Spoke it aloud. Wrote it all down.

Taking medicine now. Won't relapse. Can't. Work far too important. Chimps need me. Plus, prognosis excellent. Mental illness all but contained. Neurotic, first to admit, but no more psychotic episodes. In this moment, as clear as I've ever been. So.

Why do I feel like I'm being watched?

halloween

The soul secure in her existence smiles at the drawn dagger and defies its point. The stars shall fade away, the sun himself grow dim with age and nature sink in years, but thou shall flourish in immortal youth, unhurt amid the war of elements, the wreck of matter and the crush of worlds.

That's an excerpt from *Cato*, George Washington's favorite play. It's about standing up to tyrants. And about not taking power when that power will corrupt you. You can see how Washington, who shot down the proposal that he be made King of America with the line "You could not have found a person to whom your schemes are more disagreeable," might have appreciated a story like that.

I haven't read the whole play; Gedaechtnis never put it on any of my reading lists, and since coming of age I've yet to take the time. I discovered it through an unlikely intersection—my lifelong interest in cryptography mixed with a fondness for the macabre stories of Edgar Allan Poe. (Second only to H. P. Lovecraft in my formative youth.)

Poe enjoyed crafting ciphers; employing a pseudonym, he encrypted the *Cato* passage above; it took over 150 years for anyone to crack it. As homage to the man, I'd made a habit of using that same passage as dummy text to test my protocols.

Smile at the drawn dagger and defy its point. Words to live by, no?

Though based in New Cambridge no longer, I retained a few eyes and ears about town—Slow, Kody, Mars, a few others—who would send private (and often coded) messages to apprise me of the evolving situation. I put complete faith in none of these, fearing manipulation from Ning. To minimize the potential for misdirection, I refused to take anyone's word without corroboration—fortunately, the initial reports diverged only slightly, and so from a choir of spies, details began to emerge.

No end to the fear, I learned, Ning playing hard to the phobes. Steadily jacking up that worst-case scenario of a new strain of plague finishing what was started. How safe is safe? Only a doctor-centric society, an iatrarchy, could hope to keep everyone from death's door. Hence the "reorganization," Ning pushing to prioritize health care above all else—which I imagine wouldn't have been particularly offensive if he hadn't been doing it so dishonestly.

With no solid evidence of a health crisis, this was simply an opportunity to seize control. Even prior to the poisoning incident, Ning had been putting doctors in his pocket one by one. To me, it seemed nothing more than a pretext to institute the same morally questionable policies he'd wanted all along. Fear makes a fertile soil.

So the few New Cambridgians we'd failed to thaw were woken up and introduced to the underside of a new class system—*hello and welcome back; sign here, please; though committed to your civil liberties, we remain in a state of emergency; for successful cryonic retrieval one must remunerate the city, and according to this policy, you have been temporarily conscripted to a period of service.*

Unfair? Possibly. Yet, it could be argued, a vital and a well-meaning policy, if the indentured servitude went to the purpose of preserving all our lives.

Not quite as persuasive as the Doctrine, but then Ning had leverage. What we'd done once with the President, he'd instituted as a matter of course. Thawing a husband and holding off on the wife. Or not bringing out the kids. Leverage to ensure compliance. All policies enforced with new muscle—a cadre of soldiers trickling into town, their numbers growing with each passing day. None of my operatives could pinpoint the origin, but "unknown cryonic facility" and "private corporate army" seemed the consensus.

To all appearances, the Assembly kept jurisdiction over the city, but behind the scenes Ning and his cronies had been wrangling not just influence but dominion. A smoother transition that way—no reason to tear down old institutions when they can simply be perverted to new ends.

And disturbingly, Ning had gotten himself engaged. Disturbing, because by all accounts the prospective missus was a widely respected, lovely and beautiful woman who was sure to soften his image. She'd allow him greater flexibility—callous acts could be explained away with warm-sounding aphorisms and homespun reassurances.

Threat exaggerated to justify subjugation, check. Bullshit washed down with political lubricant, check. I had a sense where the man was going. Some truth in that old saw about positively identifying waterfowl from their visual, auditory and behavioral characteristics. If it looks like a duck . . .

My first thought: *Who cares? Let him do his worst. It's not like I owe these people anything.* Followed by: *I can take the son of a bitch out now, before he can consolidate his power. If I want him dead, he's dead. It won't be difficult. Far from it, it'll be the easiest thing in the world.*

And I couldn't. Not because I didn't believe in killing. Not because I felt it was none of my business. Not because I owed him a chance to reform.

I'd done it twice before, each time with the discharge of a gun. The decision to squeeze the trigger comes at the speed of thought, but then you have to live with everything that follows. You feel the weight of death. No matter how justified you were, you feel it. You feel it the rest of your life.

Shame on me for doubling that number; two more lives to hang on my conscience, both suicides. Four people. Hardly enough loss of life to justify my Grim Reaper rep, but more than enough to convince me I didn't want any more blood on my hands. Not if I could help it. Not with my baby almost born.

And speaking of blood on one's hands . . .

"You've got to hear this." A gallows-humor twinkle in Vashti's kajal-accented eyes. "One of our creators wants to make a confession."

"What, to a priest?"

"No, to us. He wants to confess a crime. Homicide," she added when I didn't answer right away.

We fell into step together. Toward the lake, colonized by the swans that fascinated my son, Deuce. Dozens of them now, their long necks bent to make question marks in the water. And slumped on a bench: one of the Gedaechtnis employees, a picture of misery, eyes downcast, chin to his chest, neck bent like the swans.

"Glenn Watkins." About whom I felt next to nothing. "This a recent crime? Since he was thawed?"

"No."

"Are we now prosecuting crimes from before the Recovery?"

"Not as a rule, no."

"So what gives?"

"He says he killed our friends, Hal."

I almost laughed, but something in the way she carried herself—hands balled into fists, tension creasing the bridge of her proud, straight nose—reassured me that this was not some elaborate joke. "You have got to hear this," she repeated.

Had I misunderstood what she'd meant by *our friends*? "Which friends?"

"Lazarus, Simone, Tyler and Mercutio."

"So he's crazy, then. He wasn't there. He'd been locked away in cryonic storage for years and years before any of that went down."

"I don't think he's crazy," Vashti said.

sloane

My new best friend is Claire. How I fucking loathe her.

She's a bubble-headed bleach blonde from Beverly Hills. Nature's cruelest mistake: a goddamn waste-of-space trust-fund-baby fashion-zombie wannabe pop star. She can't sing. Or dance. Or do anything but make people look at her. Claire isn't her real name; it's her stage name. Claire Isabel. Like clear as a bell. She isn't clear yet, though; she says she still has thetan energies trapped within her. Yeah, she says she's only Grade III, but that gives her freedom from the upsets of the past and ability to face the future. Neat. Would I like to learn more about Scientology? Not on her life, hell, not even on any of her past lives. Only I said yes. Yes to that cult, yes to laughing at her jokes, yes to hanging out with all her stupid friends in Aspen. I have to break the curse, so I have to say yes.

Brigit and I had a thing where we'd pretend to be nice to our sisters only to cut them down later. This is like that but without the cutting down. Feels like bad sex with no payoff. Worth putting up with Claire, though, because she's about to be Ning's stepdaughter. Which makes me a friend of the family, which gives me primo access. That's worth the damage I'm doing to my face with this forced fucking smile.

Because I'm her friend and maybe her bodyguard/mascot, Claire gave me these fat rainbow pills to flip on the slopes, an ecstasy-and-synthetic-serotonin cocktail called Wretched XS. Expensive shit, the caviar of polydrugs. Well, happy's somewhere I love to be, so I took a bunch and spat them out in the snow when no one was looking. No room at the inn, happy. I don't do the things I want. Break the patterns, break the curse.

Crying shame, because blitzed I might even enjoy Claire's company.

Want to hear a joke? Here goes. Big tycoon wanted to divorce his wife, but he also wanted to stay friends, so he told his lawyer to meet with her lawyer and agree to anything she wanted. Anything? Yes, anything. So the two lawyers meet, and apparently she doesn't want much from the tycoon because they both had money before getting into the marriage. All she wants is child support for their two kids. Sounds reasonable. How much?

Three hundred thousand dollars per day.

His lawyer hems and haws but has to agree to it. The client said anything. But for curiosity's sake he has to ask how she came up with that figure.

"Simple," her lawyer says, "the children like to go skiing."

"So?"

"So they're shy. They don't like a lot of people watching them when they ski."

"But three hundred grand?"

"That's what it takes to shut down the slopes. They rent every room in every hotel on the mountain and no one bothers them."

Shut up. I didn't say it was a funny joke. True story, though, and they were twentieth-century dollars, so it's even more ridiculous when adjusted for inflation. That's commensurate with the kind of lifestyle Claire and her friends used to enjoy, so today's big bad world doesn't suit them so well. Aspen without creature comforts is hardly Aspen. And unlike the kids in the joke, these witless wonders aren't even outdoorsy. So with no restaurants, clubs or arts festivals in which to be seen, what was the point? Just to ski? Please.

If they'd realized this before piling into the plane, we could have saved some valuable time, but everyone was flying high and deaf to reason. I'd have had a much better time shredding virtual snow, which for me is saying something. Outside owns Inside any day of the week.

Here in the city, the weather's bad and the links are fritzing. Everyone's pissing and moaning, the smart ones about the new watch lists but everyone else just because they're inconvenienced by sputtering connections.

Watch lists tell us who's in the news, so if I've got Claire on mine and she's featured on someone's channel, an alert lets me know. Watch lists are also a measure of popularity, so the more watched you are, the better. Slick way to get citizens to enjoy being watched. "How do I get more people to like me? How do I move up in the rankings?" Total crap, and it's catching on because Ning's making it work. Most of these jokers are desperate for distinction now that their money can't buy or sell anyone.

If someone's using a link anywhere in the city, I can find out where he is and what he's linking—another person, an information site, entertainment, you name it. Blows my mind how many citizens are willing to give up their privacy. Total transparency may be the selling point, but the goal is control.

Anyway, since the watch lists have been installed, the links have gotten fritzy. They've put the engineer on it, what's his name, the one they call Mr. Lucky. He doesn't look happy to be working for Ning, but then I don't think I've seen him smile since the day Pandora pulled him from the freezer. He looks how I feel.

Tomorrow, I'm having breakfast with Claire, her mother and Ning, whom I've started calling "Emperor Ning" or "Ning the Nerciless," though no one gets that joke but me. Halloween might, but he's not here, and it does no good to spend any time on that. I was thinking about him too much when he was here, bad idea with his being my boss and already spoken for. I could handle one or the other but not both.

Dumb fucking daydreams. Like he'd take a second look at me.

Instead, I'm getting attention from the Popsicle army. Ning's jackbooted private security organization. It's not unwanted attention, because they're badasses and I have no problem with badasses. Especially the lieutenant who's been flirting with me. Lodune. Pronounced "low done" with a useless *e* at the end of his name, just like mine. It infuriates me I think he's hot. The main attraction is his combat experience. He's killed in battle and he's completely cool with it. Not bragging, not tormented, just cool. You can see it in his eyes. We could have a fling, and it could mean something to both of us, and then if he had to shoot me for going after Ning, he'd be cool with that, too. Every instinct tells me that hooking up with him would be a mistake.

Which sucks, because it means I have to do it.

halloween

"The guilt's killing me," said the geneticist, two fingers to his carotid artery. "Palpitations, I swear. Feel like I'm having a panic attack." Sweat-soaked and miserable, he met my eyes, Vashti's and the unseeing eyes of Pandora (who, with Malachi's assistance, had come to join us), searching us for sympathy, before dropping his head again and taking a sidelong glance at the lake.

Without shifting his gaze from the swans, he took a bottomless breath and said, "I just want you to understand. It wasn't from bad motives. I didn't do it intentionally. It backfired. I tried to do something positive."

The story of that alleged positive came haltingly, nugget by nugget, like black pearl tea sucked through a narrow straw. Ultimately, the choice he'd made had come down to ideology. The last century had been hamstrung by what he called a "catastrophic failure of leadership" with no one for the world to rally behind. Democratic globalization had been a grand goal, but what had it achieved? Endless litigation? Governments sitting around with their thumbs up their asses, mooing about feelings? Governments controlled by corporations? Who would make the hard choices?

"I didn't want that to happen to you," he explained. "You were our last hope. You had to make choices, and the thought of you paralyzed with the same indecision terrified me. Don't you understand? We made you strong, but for this to work, one of you had to be *stronger*."

Back when my friends and I were embryos, this sad and inconspicuous Gedaechtnis employee had gone rogue, clandestinely tweaking one of our genomes in an attempt at producing a natural leader. Someone with the drive and aggression to lead the others in a quest to defeat the plague, so Man could walk the Earth again. "I thought this would give you a better chance," he said, hugging his arms to his chest.

"You lit the fuse." Pandora's face darkened as the implications played themselves out in her mind.

"Adam," he nodded, using the old name for Mercutio. The

briefest of glances at her swollen belly and again he looked away. "When you told me he'd gone mad, the sabotage he did, the murd—" He shook his head, unable to free the word *murders* from his lips. "I couldn't believe it. And yet I knew I was responsible. My fault. But you have to realize it wasn't my intention. I wanted the best of you, not the worst."

Heredity and environment. We'd spent years dissecting the environmental factors for why Merc did what he did. Now we had the other side. Put them together and . . .

No, I didn't want to put them together. What good would it do me to know what had made him a ticking time bomb? What good after he'd already exploded? Long ago, I'd rejected the concept of healing because if I couldn't be healed, I couldn't be further hurt. So there was no solace for me to take in this confession, and no outrage. The loss I felt couldn't be touched.

Sharply, Vashti interrogated our man about how he'd pulled it off, both from a technical standpoint, and how he'd evaded detection. The former he was more comfortable explaining, but his tone grew more hesitant about the latter, the shame stifling him, disgrace in perverting the efforts of his coworkers, and accomplishing his goal only after his boss had committed suicide.

"Dr. Koppel," he sighed, remembering. "We called her Blue because of her eyes, but it was also her moods. She ran the show, but after she died, there was a period when the lab was in total chaos. No one knew who was in charge anymore. I saw my opportunity and took it."

Furiously, he swept a tear from his cheek. "She believed in me and I betrayed her. By fucking up her work, thinking I knew better. I almost destroyed everything. If it wasn't for you, Gabriel," he said, head still turned, "I don't think any of us would have made it to today. And I can only imagine how terrible it was to have to kill your friend."

"Best friend," I said.

"Why Mercutio?" Pandora wanted to know. "What made you choose him?"

He made a helpless gesture with his hands.

"Because he was the firstborn?"

"Yes."

He'd answered too quickly. "I don't think so," Pandora said.

"But he was."

"But that's not the reason," I said. "How are those palpitations?"

He'd come to us wanting to confess his sins. Real sins. Good intentions gone astray wouldn't have made him this distraught. Not this man.

Sure, he'd wanted one of us to lead the others. Not for the reasons he'd claimed.

Jaw quivering, he kept opening his mouth to speak and thinking better of it. Gaping like a fish. *Should I or shouldn't I?* I could tell he didn't need much pushing. A pointed question here, a gentle reassurance there, and I'd squeezed out a drop of truth. Then a few more. Then . . .

The screed that followed bemoaned the decline and fall of the white man, a slow but sure reduction of power over several centuries. The worrisome feeling one has of slipping down the food chain, with those unlike you increasingly vilifying you as a racist, sexist, imperialist, no matter what your personal beliefs might be. Wincing as multiculturalism overtakes your society, celebrating every heritage but your own. Stinging from memories of what once was, especially in the face of China casting a wider-than-ever shadow of influence, and both America and Europe weakened by the Clash of Civilizations, unsure what to do.

"Here I was helping to engineer children," he said. "Children who would be the future of the world, if any kind of future could be had. We split you between boys and girls and tried to represent every color under the sun, partly for immunological diversity, no question, but partly for political sensitivities. And I . . . I don't hate anyone. But I couldn't embrace the universality of what we were going for. It felt so damn politically correct. I knew you needed a leader, so I picked the one who looked most like me."

That meant a white male of European descent. Which left out everyone but Mercutio and me, the melanin challenged. And with Gedaechtnis peppering my otherwise lily-white heredity with dots of Korean and Cherokee genetic material, Merc got the nod.

"Do you think I'm an AWM?" Dr. Watkins asked, sharing my partiality for acronyms. "An angry white male? And if I am, does that make me racist? I don't mind a level playing field as long as I still get to play. But if you bench me and keep kicking dirt in my face, how is that fair?"

Regardless of what he was or wasn't, he'd acted selfishly. He knew that. He hadn't been thinking of what was best for the project. He'd made his decision based on what he wanted, and because of that, four people had died.

Possibly. But for the genetic manipulation, would Merc have gone mad? Or what if Gedaechtnis had never lied to us? What if Malachi had never crept into our heads? Would he have been all right then? What if I had been a better friend to him, what then?

Funny how we all wanted to take the blame for a killer's actions. I found myself smirking about it, but no one would have laughed harder than Mercutio himself.

"What can be done about this?" asked Watkins. Would we put him on trial? Sanction him? Ostracize him? Forgive him?

"It's your guilt," I said. "You deal with it."

"There must be some way I can make up for it," he stammered, but really, what was there for him to do?

isaac

Years ago, the digital trickery I mistook for my father brought me to the digital trickery I mistook for Hong Kong. Six days, seven nights, a bonding exercise to fill the spring break after my mother had been written out. What did we talk about when I returned? Did I tell you about the dizzying skyscrapers? Back then I had not even an inkling that I'd grow up to mourn the architect I was born to be.

Among my souvenirs, you must remember the dragon carving I gave to your Simone. It was inscribed with the Chinese word for life force, *qi,* the same as her last name. Life from the city of life, she said, and when you asked me how much it cost, I assured you that wasn't important. Actually, it cost me nothing.

When I close my eyes, I can see the harbor at night, perfect dark blue water hosting junks, trawlers, water taxis and freighters, dotted with lights that sparkle like phosphorescent fish. My father has led me to the Jumbo Floating Restaurant, where I have been served a dubious delicacy, sea cucumber stew. The novelty of eating something that scrapes across the ocean floor doesn't appeal to me in the slightest, but I did ask for it, having insisted quite foolishly on ordering in Mandarin. The waiter compliments me on my adventurous palate, and I'm too embarrassed to admit my mistake, but too squeamish to eat. I can only stare longingly across the table at a plate of steaming dim sum. My father, programmed to be receptive to my needs, smiles knowingly and pushes his plate toward me. Before I know it, he has taken my bowl and extended it out the window, offering it to a poor fishing family on a tiny skiff. An exchange is made, and I have an empty bowl and a carved dragon souvenir to show for it. All without what the Chinese call *tiu lien*. Losing face.

With my eyes open, I see nothing I would recognize. This place has been swallowed like so many others, Lazarus, unmade by the forces of time. This is what happens when a civilization has no one left to support it. It succumbs to nature, in this case, to a string of unmerciful hurricanes. Geostationary weather satellite logs confirmed my firsthand assessment: storm-tossed over many years.

Calm now, but the wind made itself known as we disembarked, a mournful sound, a distant echo of what came before. The phrase that crept to mind, *all else is wind,* once was said of the prophet Muhammad's words. But Champagne's words were the ones that pulled me forward, a dulcet call to escort her. Side by side, we blazed a trail through the debris, leading an expedition to the counterparts we never knew.

Underground, our destination, beneath an unremarkable and mosquito-plagued patch of land not far from the wreckage of what one of the Gedaechtnis scientists assured me is the Hong Kong Disneyland Resort. She's one of the few who shared technology with the Chinese. We have six with us, as chatty and eager as sugar-laden children.

The vault took longer than I expected to open, but we managed it. Then down the shaft, harnessed together, autorappelling for want of a working elevator, descending to the sepulcher itself. The heart. Still beating. We have a faint hum of power here, but too faint to keep our ten cousins alive. Container after container, we exhumed them, with the same results as when you yourself were exhumed: too late to do any good.

With two exceptions. One man, one woman. Slow and helpless as turtles who'd been flipped on their backs, but alive nonetheless. We carried them out and kept them from going into shock. We cleaned them off, kept them oxygenated, assured them they'd be all right. We rescued them, Lazarus, saved their lives.

The woman, Li Quan Yin, vacillates between gratitude and outrage. Thank goodness we came, but why did we take so long? The man, Zhang Zhao, carries no resentment toward us, but is a little unhinged, behaving like someone who is living a waking dream.

Their English isn't very good, but it's much better than my Mandarin. Champagne was the one to find the common language: French, which we could all speak quite passably. In the language of diplomacy, Li Quan Yin told us their tale.

They were raised much as we were, in IVR, coming of age in a virtual China. Unlike us, no secrets were kept from them. They were told from the beginning what they were, what Black Ep was doing to humanity, how they would one day cure the disease and start the world anew. They knew we existed, though we never knew of them. They were told that we would all work together or, more specifically, that we would work for them. To that end, they would be released at age fifteen, three years before we were scheduled, but the release mechanism malfunctioned. Was it a design flaw, billions of dollars jammed up from a faulty relay? Was it sabotage? Whatever it was, they were stranded, unable to escape, unable to signal us for help. The artificial intelligences that governed their care and education recognized that the only way of protecting their charges was to ration the existing nutrients. To make the supplies last as long as possible, sacrifices had to be made. Li Quan Yin and Zhang Zhao were told that because they were the most promising, they would live on in the hopes of someday being rescued, but for them to live the others had to die. That was decades ago.

Though it broke her heart, she was able to accept the rationale behind her friends' demise, while he rejected it and rebelled. Retreating to fantasy, he could process the deaths and the abandonment only within the confines of an old Hollywood movie, one of many stored in their media base. Wracked by survivor guilt, it was more comforting for Zhao to believe that nefarious machines hated humans, working to destroy them or enslave them to their will. I suppose this explains his perplexing behavior, treating me like an old friend, calling me "Morpheus," repeatedly asking, "How deep does the rabbit hole go?"

Here we have one person who likes me and seems open to what I say, but only because he's living in a fantasy world. And then there's the other who, while happy to be rescued, sees me as a representation of the West—and, according to her, the West can't be trusted, not after the United States defaulted on its Chinese debts, igniting the Trade War. Champagne and I have been explaining how we don't represent any one exclusively, we are world citizens, and wouldn't be here if we didn't care about everyone. That seems to be making some headway, but there's an existential horror in Li Quan Yin that I can't seem to penetrate. She spent her whole life preparing to cure Black Ep, only to be rescued by Westerners who'd already done it. What point does her life have now?

It can have any point that she wants it to have, I'm going to tell her. Like the old expression, *Eli fat mat*—the past is dead. Now it's up to her. I'm hopeful that I can encourage her to find a new purpose, and in so doing, perhaps I will find mine.

sloane

So Lodune and I are finished getting it *done low,* if you know what I mean, and we're in that rare postcoital conversation moment, where the guy doesn't roll over and fall asleep. I say rare because it's the first time it's happened. And out of the blue I'm wondering what it's like to kill someone, so that's what I ask.

He turns on his side facing me. "You never killed anyone?"

"My sister Penny tried to kill me."

"Sisters. Mine tried to put my eye out with a fork."

"This one?" I try to playfully tap him on the eyelid, only my aim isn't good and it turns into a poke.

He swats my hand away, "Can't remember, whichever one was closest to her fork at the time."

His eyes are the most perfect blue I've ever seen. They're sniper's eyes, enhanced by genetic tinkering. We can thank the military for that, but he won't tell me which military. In any case, he's a better shot than I am, maybe even a better shot than Hal. I've seen him on the range. That's where we are, out underneath the stars, blanket over us and grass stains beneath.

"What it's like to kill someone?" he says. "You just kind of do it. And you don't think about it afterward. Thinking's not so good."

"I wonder if I could do it."

"I'm sure you could, you're a hell of a shot."

"I can hit a target. The difference is the target's not going to scream or start bleeding or something."

"That's why you can't think about it. Why, who you thinking of killing?"

My instincts tell me to lie, so I don't: "Your boss."

He leans back and laughs. "Join the fucking club."

"And then maybe Claire?"

"That gutterslut? I'd think your bullets are worth a little more than that."

We gossip for a while about our respective employers. I feel like we're the maid and butler talking about the Master and Mistress. When really it should be reversed, because Lodune and I are cut from better cloth, genetically speaking. But while I'm really aware of being different, posthuman and all, he's convinced we're all basically the same.

"You've got a great immune system," he says, brushing my hair back from my face, "and maybe some other guy doesn't. But he can juggle and you can't. You're killer in the sack, and maybe some other skirt isn't but she knows how to do calculus in her head. We're all basically human, it's just a question of who can do what when you want that thing done."

Bitch, I think. *I can do calculus in my head. And when have you ever seen me wear a skirt?*

The more we talk, the more I realize he's pressing me for information. Being subtle about it, but basically doing threat assessment on all my relatives and me. Which is the same thing I'm doing to him. I think we both notice it, but we're too polite to say. He wants to know which of my elders are still pissed about the coup. Apparently, the President's alive and well and bringing out an army, and Ning doesn't want to follow the leader. No ceding power. New Cambridge will remain autonomous. No one wants a war, but neither side wants to give in, and each is looking for an advantage.

Playing for hearts and minds is where we are. Grab them by

the balls and their hearts and minds will follow, that's how the saying goes.

I wonder if Lodune's secretly working for the President.

One thing's for certain, the mood in the city's getting worse. The links might be fixed now but I've noticed everyone on edge. They've been catching wind of what's in the air, and most don't seem to like it. The ripe aroma of fear.

Doesn't bother me, though, because from where I'm sitting, it smells like opportunity.

fantasia

Refilled termite mound. No termites. Artificial. Filled it with pie filling. Cherry. The one they like best. Dig it out with little sticks. Gives them a chance to use tools. Like how they'd get termites in the wild.

Surveillance camera got me running. Mick just slapped the holy hell out of Keith. Wanted the orange, fought for it, got it. Victory screech. Gloated by sucking and chewing the pulp with wide bright orange rind smile. Had to soothe Keith. Pretended to cluck disapproval at Mick. Mother's work is never done.

Zoo here. Total zoo. Always something to do. Starting to favor the subject group because they cause me less work. Less fighting, more sharing. Oranges for all. Can't favor them. Have to stay objective.

Believe in better living through chemistry. Found workable combination for myself. Halfway done. Why treat when you can fix? Subjects prove experiment is working. NCBI and GeneWatch both singled out Dr. Erlich as dangerous rogue, whatever that means. Erlich not crazy, the man was on to something big, and I get to finish what he started.

How to take that next step? Need help? Losing objectivity with chimps = losing objective sense of reality? Is my thinking clear?

Doesn't make sense. Taking meds and still feel paranoid. Can't shake sense of being watched.

~~Paranoid delusions. Am not being followed by anything Nutritious or Delicious. No one here but us chimps. Function of loneliness. May be sabotaging self for reasons unknown. No agents after me. Nothing holy or unholy. Just thoughts. Thoughts can be controlled. Must be. Must force self to keep perspective. Up dosage if necessary. Too close to finish line to fall down now. Why would~~

I am being watched.

Someone is watching me.

halloween

I twitched myself awake, accidentally jostling Pandora. The baby kicks her enough; she doesn't need it from me.

"You all right?"

"Dreaming," I said.

"Same one?"

"Variation on a theme."

Ever since that first dream of New Cambridge burning, I'd been catching it again and again in my nightly trips into unconsciousness. I couldn't always keep them from slipping away, but very often I'd wake with a sense of déjà vu. This time I remembered it completely:

This time, the dream is much the same, the city burning, except I can see cancerous shapes writhing and buckling within the toxic cloud. What I see and what I don't quite see makes me wonder if I've found something nastily Lovecraftian, some impossibly evil nightmare monster from the Plateau of Leng. I expect it'll favor me with its unpronounceable name shortly—Ygllammaog, let's say, or Ctelh-mei—offering me a hideous, slime-drenched tentacle to shake.

But soon I'm facing myself again. A look-alike of me, at least.

The clove cigarette that smolders between his fingers is Sendiri-brand Indonesian kretek. My old brand. With a pang of longing, I recognize this black-clad, ankh-eyed goth as a "purer" version of myself, a lovelorn, antiauthoritarian and somewhat sinister twin. An idealized self-image I've since outgrown. I'm facing the teenaged version of myself all grown up, untouched by the world, while I myself *have* been changed by it. Changed perhaps too much. It's unfair. The longing gives way to resentment, though I can't tell whether or not I truly want to be this thing.

"Have we met?" I ask. And before he can launch me into orbit with a gale-force exhalation of Indonesian smoke, I add: "Of course we have. You're the ghost of Halloween past."

"Angler," he tells me. "Bill Angler."

The name throws me; I don't remember any Anglers in the waking world.

"Not me?"

"Not you. In your dream but not of your dream," he says. "You breathed me in a few weeks back."

"That was careless of me."

"You can't prevent every infection."

"So you're a disease."

"Please," he says, making a small show of being offended. "Microorganism."

"A microorganism named Bill Angler?"

"It's your name for me. I'm piggybacking on the language center of your brain. Likewise, the übergoth look I'm sporting—that's all you."

"Do you think I want you commandeering any of my neurons?"

"It's not anything you need."

"That's not your call to make."

"Well," he says, ankh eyes sparkling, "it's the only way we can talk."

"I'm listening, Bill."

He waves his hands like a magician doing a parlor trick, and now I'm looking at a floating ball that hovers in the air between us. It looks like the sprites my friends and I used as calling cards back when we were kids. Unlike my old ball of orange and black, this one is solid black, except for tiny points of brilliant light. Somehow I know that this sprite contains the entire Milky Way.

"This is you," he says, indicating a single star, which has brightened enough to show me a familiar-looking solar system. "And this is us." The black orb spins about to display an unfamiliar corner of the galaxy. I try to recognize what I'm looking at by constellation, but I'm not seeing anything I know.

"Us, as in you and your kind? You're telling me you're an alien microbe? I've caught the Venusian flu?"

"Does this look like Venus?" he asks, indicating the unfamiliar section of space with a black manicured fingernail.

"Look, I don't need an astronomy lecture from Gothy McMakesnosense," I snipe. "What are you trying to say?"

"I've said it. I've come a long way to get here and many of my kind died trying to make this happen. So I'd appreciate if you'd shut up and listen to me."

And he tells me how, ordinarily, he'd be toxic to me. Only my heightened immune system allowed me to survive him. His species worked very hard to find a form in which they could make this communication take place. He is a vanguard for his people, but more are on the way.

"You're the first. You should be honored," he says.

"Maybe if I believed you were real," I reply.

"Believe what you want. The facts will bear out the truth."

And he tells me how his people created Black Ep and unleashed it on our world. It was a test. It's what they do. They believe in survival of the fittest. They bring the best challenge they can dream up to an emerging civilization. If we survive, we're beloved. If we fail, we were never meant to be.

"So you're responsible?"

"Me. My people. The Free."

"Free?"

Angler nods. "That's the best word you have for what we are."

"You're saying you love us. And you killed billions of us."

"Yes, and billions of Free died in the process, too. But for a good cause. Because we love you."

I think about it and say what comes to mind.

"Shove your love up your ass."

"You're angry," Angler says. "We knew you would be. But with time, after the healing process—"

"No anger—I don't think you exist. I don't know why I'm dreaming you, but I'm going to make an effort to turn you into the back-in-school, didn't-study-for-the-big-exam nightmare I know and love."

"Just think about what I said," he replies, taking a drag off the clove before dissipating back into the smoke.

"Pregnant women have bizarre dreams, too," Pandora told me, getting up to pee. "Maybe you're having sympathy dreams."

"Or maybe I'm so self-important I'm fantasizing that aliens would reach out to me before anyone else on the planet." Flippant, but as I said it, I felt a prickle at the back of my neck. What if this wasn't a product of ego and imagination? Had I just met an extra-terrestrial being? What would that mean?

The dream had unsettled me more than I let on.

"What if aliens really appeared to people like that?" Pandora said, as if echoing my thoughts. "Sort of an Old Testament type of first contact," she mused.

Before I could answer her, Malachi paged me through a link. He had Fantasia for me, which carried on the surreal quality of the evening, because she hadn't done that since we were kids. She valued her privacy as much as I had back when I'd pushed away the world. Maybe more so.

"Hal," she said, "you have to come here. You have to help me move."

Typical, I thought, *you don't hear from certain friends until they need to move.*

"Right now?"

"Now. My life depends on it."

isaac

There's a Ferris wheel of emotion in the expressions of those we bring out. After they see another Chinese face in Li Quan Yin, the joy of being rescued might swing to concern when they notice the rest of us. We are foreigners, after all, *lao wai*.

Over three hundred meeting halls, lounges and offices, and one famous auditorium comprise the Great Hall of the People, but during the plague nearly all of these rooms were repurposed for storage. Now they house cryostats, thousands of them, the future of Eastern Civilization. You would marvel at all the possibility contained in these sterile prisons. I have been working to help realize that potential, but along with the resuscitations I've caught myself fooling around with the thought of being an architect again. I've even started doodling my old line drawings. This place inspires me, Lazarus. Though the structural design has changed much over the years, the original ceilings are still intact. The auditorium features recessed lighting in circular and semicircular patterns that make me feel like I'm standing inside an enormous flying saucer or even a time machine. Perhaps that's what appeals to me most: the thought of turning the moments back.

When we've done our work here and in Europe, too, that's what I'll be able to do. It's there when I want it, the chance to play at what I once wanted to be. You always said my designs were more expressionist than functional; once I've put my time in here, I can be as impractical as I like. That could recharge my batteries and give me the space I need to figure out what lasting mark I want to leave on the world.

Champagne tells me that bringing so many people back from cryonic sleep will leave more of a mark than anything, and yet I see that as mere responsibility. It's the only decent course of action, setting things right as best we can. But my mark has yet to be made.

We're a man down in Zhang Zhao. He took his leave when the fantasy faded and reality set in. Raised to serve his people, he has turned selfish, feeling betrayed by his government and by fate itself. My heart goes out to him, more because of his faults than in spite of them. He reminds me most of Halloween. But the lure of community may be stronger with Zhao, and no one suspects he'll stay out for long. We linked him up before he left, contact numbers so he could reach out to us when he was ready.

Malachi has picked up the slack he left behind, helping to orientate the newly thawed. It's a bit impersonal for my taste, letting an AI play such a large role in bringing the nearly dead to a place where they feel safe and purposeful. Even so, I have to admit he is a useful tool.

Did I tell you that a few of my children befriended him? Or perhaps it was the other way around. There was a special bond, he claims. I don't know. They talked about him like he was human. Clearly, he is not. It's one thing to appreciate a wonderful invention and it's another thing to confuse the semblance of life with life itself.

You and I were tricked into thinking our parents and so many others were real, when they were all but constructs of programming. No one can be blamed for being tricked, but to willfully accept a fabrication makes no sense to me.

A distant part of me remembers the call to know my true nature and to thus know God, and never be swayed by self-deception. Now and then I think back to the peace I felt when I had my faith. When it lived in my heart, and not just my words. And not even my words anymore. There was a kind of wisdom, which eludes me now. But I can accept this loss. I can accept it with eyes opened.

We've let Li Quan Yin decide the order of resuscitation. I have yet to determine a pattern, as she seems to be alternating between dignitaries, soldiers and cultural icons, based on criteria I do not understand. The mind-set differs here. For one thing, Champagne has noticed that not everyone is from the upper social strata; contrasted with the United States and Europe, preservation required not treasure but connections and initiative. There are less-privileged individuals and their families who earned their way into cryostats by simply refusing to take no for an answer. Li Quan Yin describes it as *xian lai, xian chi,* which means, "first to come, first to eat."

Speaking of food, a failure of planning has led to a supply shortage. While the Great Hall itself has been fortified against natural disasters, the nearby stockpiles were not. Much has been destroyed. Exacerbating the situation: a portion of what survived has since spoiled, thanks to the traditional Chinese reluctance to employ harsh ultrapreservatives in their processing plants. How many times did Maestro warn us of this back in school? No one plans to fail, they merely fail to plan.

Champagne has tapped Hal to airlift supplies to us once we get an accounting of how many viable survivors we have. Additionally, she wants to reassign some of my nieces from the work they are doing in Europe, in the hopes of making the Chinese extraction run quicker. But with Pandora so close to delivery, Vashti claims she has no one to spare. I wonder if this is true. The undercurrent of jealousy cannot be ignored, and this may be a small, petty way of punishing us. Everyone mourns what they lose.

As do I. I have counted over two hundred children waiting for new breath, and when I stand at each cryostat, looking in, the faces I see are the faces I have lost. This one reminds me of Haji. That one favors Ngozi. That little one looks as spirited and pure as Dalila. I have lost all my children. And the three youngest, there is no known cure for what struck them down. Yet these two hundred can be saved.

Every time we resuscitate, I feel that much closer to redemption. I may never reach it, but this is what I must do. My children deserve nothing less.

halloween

I'd never been invited to Fantasia's stomping grounds before. I knew she was somewhere in the Pacific Northwest, probably near Aberdeen, her hometown in the IVR. For years I'd respected her privacy; it would have been hypocritical of me to invade her space and come barging in. Back when I'd had a mind to push the world away, I wanted exactly the same number of visitors that she wanted: none. For Fan to summon my presence now meant something serious was going down. The only question: Was this something real or within the confines of her pathology?

She'd holed up at Central Washington University, a couple hundred miles east of Aberdeen. Large enclosed compound just on the edge of campus, and smack dab in the center of it: a downed helicopter, plumes of smoke trailing up to the sky.

Dropped into VTOL, landed and locked, then dashed to the crash site to find the pilot slumped over the control panel, dead on impact. Thirty feet away I found a human arm still in its sleeve. The copilot himself was a bit farther off, legs bent in impossible positions, his face a pulpy mess.

"Bad, huh?" said the voice behind me.

"You do this?"

"No, but I'm responsible."

Fan wore khakis and a red T-shirt. Red, a good sign. The lettering on the shirt read *Two out of the three voices in my head are telling me to f**k you up.* A sense of humor about her condition, also a good sign. I noticed she'd traded her crossbow for a tranquilizer gun. Couldn't tell whether that was a good sign or not.

"Do you know these guys?" she asked.

I didn't. She'd searched their pockets and had come up with nothing that could point to their identities. Maybe they were out doing reconnaissance. Maybe they were joyriding. Either way, they crashed hard.

"Mechanical failure," we agreed. Careless. Decades of neglect had made aircraft risky—so if you lacked patience and discipline, you could get screwed. Burst fuel tank or bad circuitry, if you don't put the time in, you take your life in your hands.

I'd said as much to Deuce before taking him up for flying lessons. "What are you worrying for?" he'd complained. "I know all this—I've done the safety training like a million times."

"The simulator isn't enough," I'd said, and we went over it again.

Fan pried me from memory lane: "Whoever they are, you can bet more are coming."

"Expect a search party?"

"Let's get me gone before they come."

"So long as you clue me in. It wasn't mechanical failure that ripped this one's arm from its socket."

"No one likes an uninvited guest," she shrugged. "C'mon, I'll explain."

She led me past platforms, hammocks and tire swings. Then I got a strong whiff of monkey. Chimpanzee, to be exact, as she brought me into a spacious bungalow, which housed eight cages. In those cages, seven chimps slept, sedated from her tranquilizers.

"Since when did you become Jane Goodall?"

She told me how she'd acquired the secret of life from Vashti a few years back. Vash hadn't been planning on telling her, but Fan got her talking, and people tend to underestimate Fan's intelligence just because her mental state is historically confused. She rattled off how she'd cloned chimps from DNA samples, applied what she'd learned from Vashti, "and there you go."

"And that's what did in the copilot?"

"See for yourself."

She showed me footage from the security cameras. Played the helicopter hit and fast-forwarded until the copilot staggered out the side. The sight of a free-roaming chimpanzee startled him, and he shot it dead with a pistol. Screeching, other chimps mobbed him, one bringing him down and holding him long enough for two more to join in the fray. Back in school we learned that chimps are about six times stronger than a human being. The footage proved it. I shot Fan a raised eyebrow.

"It's actually a very encouraging sign," she said. "Sad as this is, I'm heartened by their show of unity."

"Well, as long as you're heartened."

She scooped up a series of journals, pausing to scribble a note in one, drumming her fingers rhythmically as she searched for the right words. I remembered sewing three of those fingers back onto her hand what seemed like a lifetime ago. We'd been through a lot together, Fantasia and me.

"Van's out back, could use your help loading these cages."

"Right."

She grabbed me before I got there. "It's important, Hal. I don't want my research compromised."

"Chimps are research?"

"You think I spent all these years with them because I love animals?"

"Don't know what to think."

She dug her fingers deeper into my forearm. "I'm not crazy."

"Didn't say you were."

Out back I noticed her bumper sticker: *Forever Free*. And halfway through the loading, a call came through, telling me Pandora was in labor, my baby on the way.

sloane

So it's all "The British are coming! The British are coming!" except instead of the British it's the U.S. Special Forces. But all we've got right now is a lot of rumor and false sightings. No hard evidence. Satellite photography would be really useful, but I don't have the access. I've been asking Hal's little buddy to help me out, but Mr. Malachi says he can't use the spy satellites anymore. He's been locked out of the sky.

Meanwhile, the boys are back in town. It's the Green Mountain Boys, flying their stupid flag. They work for Ning now. Showed up in a convoy, as usual, but this time with a bunch of Popsicles. Slaves, once they're thawed. Oops, did I say slaves? I meant to say "valued additions to the workforce." Ax and Ning are pretty chummy. They've brought a lot of firepower into the city. They must think they need it.

Ning's doing everything he can to paint the President as a dangerous man, a loose cannon, prone to combat flashbacks from his time in the military. Probably bullshit, but there's enough erratic behavior in the man's past to make these points seem credible.

On the other side, we've got continued calls from the Prez for Ning to step down. Patriotic Americans don't know what to do. Some are leaving to go join the President's Mount Weather compound. Others are swayed by Ning's argument that Black Ep may have sprung from a government lab. That one plays nicely with the phobes.

I'm sharing a city with panicked sheep. Oh, no, the sky is falling! What do I do? Which oppressive egomaniac should I support?

Victory City has officially become Victimy City.

Did I mention Lodune's gone? Split, sayonara, didn't even say goodbye. I've been told he's out playing the Paul Revere role, reconnaissance, so he can mount a defense if things go from bad to worse. Or maybe that's just a cover.

It's kind of funny how Paul Revere is in the zeitgeist right now. Keeps coming up in conversation and on the link channels. Especially funny, considering how the guy spent the last part of his life opposing Thomas Jefferson and arguing for a system where the rich should get special privileges. I mean, that's just perfect for this place.

In other news, I'm still biding my time, playing nursemaid to Claire, who's got some dental problems. A tooth's rotting and has to come out. Lucky thing. God knows if I were attached to Claire, I'd rot just to escape as fast as possible. She's got Ning's ear, so he's going to start incentivizing dentists, giving people special benefits if they take all the IVR training. We didn't need dentists back in the beginning, but we sure do now. After a couple years of poor dental hygiene among the thawed, the demand is overwhelming the supply. Don't these Neanderthals ever floss?

Fucking Claire. I guess she hasn't reached whatever Scientology class it is where you don't get toothaches anymore. Not that I'd tell her that. She's too valuable. I'm over at their house every single day. The family friend. You couldn't ask for better access. Ning and I just played a game of badminton, for Christ's sake, with Claire clutching her jaw and laughing about the word *shuttlecock*. And I let him win, so he wants to play again.

If I need to take the guy out I'll be at the right place at the right time. I just don't know if I can catch him alone. He's got round-the-clock security.

halloween

We made good time back to Munich, Fan periodically checking the sleeping chimps in the back like a nervous mother. I called her on it and she said she was just protecting her data.

"What's this experiment of yours all about?"

"Altruism," she said.

"Go on."

"Primates look out for each other. They can even be self-sacrificing, though they're naturally inclined to establish dominance hierarchies. I want to isolate what makes them altruistic. Is it kin selection, indirect reciprocity, mutual aid?"

"There's research on this."

"Doing my own experiment."

"Why?"

"Why do you think? We're lucky to have survived Black Ep. To get any further, we're going to need some serious unselfishness. Where does that live, Hal? If we can bring it out in apes, maybe we can bring it out in men."

She told me how she was piggybacking off the research of Dr. Caspar Erlich, whom I knew next to nothing about, and what I did know sounded dodgy. One of many who'd been vilified for irresponsible experimentation. When Black Ep hit the populace, and no one knew where it came from, those types were practically strung up from lampposts. Some literally.

Everyone needed someone to blame. And we needed a way to feel protected from it ever happening again. *What kind of world are we leaving to our children?* And with that thought came thoughts of my child. And Pandora . . .

When Kody called to keep me abreast of how New Cambridge was crashing and burning, I let Fan listen. "Told you it wouldn't work," she said when he was done.

"I'm getting by with a smile on my face," Kody told me in the course of that conversation, "but you should know things are getting out of hand." He painted a grim picture of running low on pre-Recovery supplies, having to switch to a more agrarian existence, and hence needing more live bodies to work the fields. Fear, fascism and fakery from Ning, now buoyed by tactical support from the Green Mountain Boys, while to the west, the old U.S. government struggled to reemerge, trotting out a comparable plan for the future called the Turnaround. Each laid claim to being the "real America," and each refused to rule out the use of force in pursuit of its goals.

I said, "I'm not going to step in. I'm not in charge, and I'm nobody's revolutionary. You'll have to work it out amongst yourselves."

"Thursday, you can't give up on us here."

"What do you expect me to do? I can look out for you, Kody, but beyond that . . . ? You know if it's getting too hot and you need an escape, I'll fly you out. Say the word."

"Not yet."

"You tell me when."

A few of my nieces met us, surly for having drawn the plum assignment of helping Fan clean the Ape House at Tierpark Hellabrun, the time-ravaged Munich zoo. No animals had survived the demise of their keepers, except for the "Villa Dracula" exhibit—the macabre-looking bats seemed to be getting along fine, emerging from their grotto to swoop past us into the gathering night. Guano spatters throughout the park made the going unpleasant. No longer my problem; I simply made the dropoff and vowed to return with additional supplies.

Back at Nymphenburg, Vashti met me at the gate, offering me a weary smile. Bad news: I'd missed the birth. Good news: I was in time for the afterbirth. Actually, I'd missed that, too, but mother and daughter were healthy and safe.

I ran down the halls, nodding at those who offered congratulations.

Pandora lay half-asleep, exhausted yet beautiful. Hope rested on her chest, eyes wide and unfocused. I knelt by the bedside. And stared.

Deuce had been a clone of me, but this little girl was entirely new. And with that newness came sanctity. Never had I felt more responsible for anything in my life. If you don't have children, you won't know what I mean. If you do, I don't have to explain a thing. I can only describe it this way: it feels a bit like dying, but it's the most wonderful feeling in the world.

She hiccupped. Tiny body shook from the motion. Instinctively, I reached out to soothe her, and reflexively, Pandora did the same. Our hands met. Time stopped. Everyone else in the world disappeared. Vanished all together.

When I look back on my life, that fragile moment was greater than all the other moments combined.

I wanted it to last forever.

I never wanted to let it go.

fantasia

New digs not as good as old digs but workable. Everyone there for me when I needed them. Hal especially. Owe him big time.

Both groups skittish, adjusting to new environment. Have to be coaxed. Mick throwing tantrums. Rest grieving, signing George's name. What to tell them? No George. That's not good enough. How to explain it to those who never knew death before? Part of life? Natural? Not to be feared? Do I believe these things? Does it even matter? No, because chimp sign language vocabulary won't allow complexity. Limits what good I can do.

Words always treacherous anyway. Words die before deeds.

Vashti came to visit. Had that sucking-on-a-lemon smile. Said she was concerned about me. Blah blah blah. Brought some shrink with her. Sanity check. Medication check. Relax, I'm fine. No threat to you. No threat to myself. Let me stay on your turf and leave me be. Only if the doctor can evaluate you first. Right. I can't tell what's a dream and what's reality most likely, so my job's to jump through hoops to prove I can. Your standards, your hoops. That's fine. Jumping. How high?

She took me aside, asked what I was trying to prove. Would I break the experiment down for her? Gave her the quick version. The half-truth. Research, that's all I'm after. Nothing practical about the work, Vashti. It's not delicious or nutritious. It's innocuous.

Felt like a beta female mollifying an alpha. Probably how she saw it, too.

Shrink was typical pop psychiatrist. Full of catchphrases. Out to get me. Best strategy was to nod at his wisdom, stroke his ego, get him on my side. Shook his hand at the end. Smiles all around. Vashti seemed pleased.

They have no idea what I did.

sloane

Holy shit. Claire doesn't have a toothache, it's oral cancer. Bleeding gums, jaw swelling up like she got punched. Curable, no doubt, but the cure's brutal. It's the start of a long journey for her. We have doctors, but we don't have engineers to repair the medical equipment that's broken down. My mom has a knack for that kind of work, and Uncle Isaac, and Aunt Pan, but they're thousands of miles away. So we're not really set up for this. Ning's much-touted healthcare system is all about prevention, not treatment, and it's overtaxed as it is.

"Too many chiefs and not enough Indians," the guy keeps bitching—a real failure of planning that not enough technically minded people were frozen, so now he's going to have to incentivize engineers the way he'd planned to do for dentists. Of course his wife wants it done yesterday, shrieking at him behind closed doors about her darling daughter. "We didn't survive the fucking plague so my Claire could die of cancer—a fucking curable disease!" Not shrieking in public, naturally—there she's all smiles and apple pie, hanging on his arm to lend him likability.

The cancer's covered up. Just a toothache as far as most people know. I'm one of the lucky few who've got the truth.

All this time I've been seeing Ning as playing me. Pretending I'm a friend of the family to keep his friends close and enemies closer. But somehow I think I *am* a friend of the family. If there were thought crimes, I'd be public enemy number one, but I've kept my temper in check and acted sweet, and they're taking me at my word.

How pathetic is that?

halloween

"I see something deeper, more infinite, more eternal than the ocean in the expression of the eyes of a little baby when it wakes in the morning and coos or laughs because it sees the sun shining on its cradle," said a fellow redhead, the brilliant but unstable Vincent van Gogh. Presumably he said it well before his breakdown and disfigurement. Either way, there's something to it. A sense that possibility itself is wide open, that a baby is the beginning of all things.

On the other hand, it's poetic bullshit, as DNA has a bit of fun with us. We lend poetry to something that's purely chemical—we feel joy about our kids because if we didn't, no one would have any. The species would die out.

Whatever it is, it ran me over pretty good.

Having a kid means immortality. You don't have to exist anymore. You can go away and the world will still have a part of you. That's how I used to feel. If you know me, you know I'm no stranger to suicidal thinking. But there's something about the gift of life, the responsibility, something about fatherhood . . .

It put me more at peace than I've ever been. Which in turn made me a hell of a lot more tolerant of others. When he wasn't writing George Washington's favorite play, Joseph Addison was penning maxims like, "It is only imperfection that complains of what is imperfect. The more perfect we are, the more gentle and quiet we become towards the defects of others." And even if you think gentle and quiet are overrated, there's something to this quote as well.

I have to rely on other people's words because this is uncharted territory for me. I don't have the vocabulary for it. I spent so much time raging at everyone and everything, infuriated even at existence itself, that I have a hard time putting calm into words. I can say this much: Anger doesn't melt away all at once, but when you feel it leaving you, even just a little bit, it's like you can breathe deeper than you ever thought you could.

For the first time since I could remember, I wanted to be part of the world.

The sense of harmony I felt lasted long enough to filter into my sleep. Back into the dreamscape I ventured, back to the charred remains of the city.

First Deuce came to me, long hair whipped by the wind.

"Hey," he said with a lift of his chin.

"Hey," I said. "I've got something for you."

"Been looking for that." He took the blue knit cap from my outstretched hand, happy to have it back. "Still fits," he said, covering his head with it, the white number 2 at the front now replaced by a red triangle, the alchemical symbol for fire.

"Looking sharp."

"Thanks."

He turned and began to walk away. Whirling about after a few steps to look back, still walking backward, apprehension pulling at his (and what once was my) youthful face.

"You're not angry with me, are you?" he called.

"Just myself."

"Don't be."

"It's my fault."

"Mine, too. And if I'm not mad at you, why should you be?"

A shadow stepped out of the smoke to walk beside him, still bleeding from where I'd shot her. Penny, the catalyst to my son's suicide. She caught my eye. Still a deep, empty sadness that would never be filled.

I called my son's name. To warn him.

He took her hand. Smiled at me. "Dad, you don't have to worry anymore."

They left together, a couple. He wouldn't forsake her, but I didn't have to accept her. It was his life, even if he didn't have it anymore.

Then Mercutio made himself known. From nowhere, he collapsed at my feet, his body broken. Someone had used him like a piñata.

"Who did this?"

"Who do you think, Sherlock?"

With dream logic, I deduced the ones he'd killed had inflicted the damage. My old love Simone, my old friend Tyler, my old enemy Lazarus.

"You want a piece of me, too?" he spat.

"I think you've had enough."

"More than you know." His eyes were glazed and watery, the stare of a beaten man, but deep at their center I saw a defiant glint. That told me he'd do it all again if only he could. But he couldn't. He'd left this world. All that tied him to it now was my memory, my guilt and my blame.

"Don't I owe you something?"

I crouched down to his level, and as he flinched back I extended my arm to offer a parting gift. I can't remember what it was. A dream object. Maybe nothing at all. Whatever it was, I recognized it as the thing he'd wanted most in the world. Uncertainly, he took it from my hand, the way a starving man accepts food from his most hated enemy. I watched him hold it high to the light, let out a breath of pure relief, clutch his fist around it and grin.

"Well, all right," he said.

And I remembered how he'd shown me mercy. I'd shot him and he'd had a perfect chance to kill me, yet never took it. Over the years I'd wondered if it had been an act of cruelty to leave me living, knowing me as he did. But seeing him smile so genuinely here, I became convinced it had been mercy and nothing but. He'd never hated me. We'd remained friends despite his demons. Friends to the end.

"Do you know what this is worth?"

"Enjoy it," I told him.

"Count on it."

Before I knew it, he was gone.

As Angler rode up on a mount with a wet and grimy mane, the smoke became as dust, the sky grew dark with hovering night-gaunts, and the words *dead but dreaming* whispered on the wind. Trailing behind rider and horse were Jasmine and Doom, and earlier, less-realized, more grotesque IVR playmates I'd fashioned out of zeroes and ones. My long-ago creations from back when I'd first embraced the goth-chic of being despondent and misunderstood.

"Just the Free."

At my command, everything dripped into nothingness, save Angler, who landed gracefully on his black steel-toe leather boots. He and I became all that existed, the glowing ankhs in his pupils the only source of light.

"I've decided you don't exist."

"Have you now?"

"I wouldn't be here if it weren't for Black Ep," I reasoned. "I've been blaming that microbe for every terrible thing I've seen in my life, and even for that life itself. So who created Black Ep? Someone working out of malice, or maybe just careless tampering, but human, I should think. A human being. That's why I carry my anger and despair. But now things are changing. I'm tired of hating people. I don't want that anymore."

"You think I'm a scapegoat?"

"Absolutely. You're 'other.' Alien. If I believed you created Black Ep, I imagine I could make peace with everyone else. That's what I want right now, so of course you don't exist. You're too convenient. You let everyone off the hook."

"That's quite a theory. Got any proof?"

"The burden of proof is on you, Angler. You know what they say about extraordinary claims. . . ."

"Extraordinary evidence will follow," he snapped. "I'm just the *first* to arrive. Wait until everyone you know dreams of the Free."

"Until then, I'm passing you off as a figment."

"Do what you want. See if I go away."

I sucker-punched as hard as I could. He reeled back, lip split, blood trickling down his chin.

"If you're real, you can expect more where that came from, and if you're not, what does it matter?" I turned my back and strode off into the darkness.

"This feeling you have," my doppelganger called. "This new-found love for humanity. It's not going to last."

"That's just my self-doubt talking. My unwillingness to be happy."

"Won't last," he said, and I woke with those words in my ears. Took me a long, uneasy moment to recognize that all was well with my family and me, after which I tried to write down as much of the dream as I could remember. That accomplished, I scrambled the letters in my figment's name to find nothing much for "Bill Angler." Still, "William Angler" could be deciphered as "Animal Grew Ill," and "Ankh-eyed Bill Angler" decrypted neatly as "Gabriel Kennedy Hall."

sloane

Headfirst into a thresher is not how I want to die. Turn my face into tapas? Fuck no. That's got to be down there with the worst. I wouldn't do it to my most hated enemy and I'd sure as hell never do it to myself. I'm way too vain, messed-up loser though I am. Think about it. Headfirst. Thresher. How hopeless do you have to be?

In military jargon, a suicide gets termed a "non-hostile gunshot wound." This one had "farm-related fatal accident" getting tossed around for a couple of hours, but that dried up when people realized there was nothing accidental about it.

The bottom feeder who did it was still in his twenties, time spent in cryonic storage aside. The heir to a software empire, smart as all get-out and not bad-looking, either. Still with so much to live for, you'd think. Wife and kids, a bright new world full of opportunity. No, into the thresher he leapt.

Here's how they're reporting it on the Echo (with other news channels following the leader): It's a tragedy. This poor man. He simply couldn't take it. With the specter of war hanging over us, he made a desperate choice and threw himself into harm's way. Though we must stay prepared for an attack from those who would seek to impose their will upon us, we mustn't forget that negotiations are ongoing. We mustn't lose hope, nor allow the fear to grow so thick it overwhelms.

Here's what really happened: They thawed this yutz out and told him he'd been conscripted to five years of labor. Welcome to the future, yutzy. If you want us to thaw your family out, you'll play ball. If you'd rather try your luck somewhere else, you can join up with the President, but he's a bit of a nutjob, hiding in his evil underground lair. Want to go to Europe? Sure, if the people there have time for you, and by the way, they're not even human. Want to live by yourself in the wilderness? Good luck with that. Whatever you decide, you're not taking your family with you. They'll be staying right here. So how about giving it a shot with us? What do you say?

So he tried. Then he cracked. He'd already been through so much from the plague, he didn't have the wherewithal to buck up and stick around. Most of the thawed are made of stronger stuff, but I can't exactly blame this one for buckling under the pressure.

Hal's buddy saw it happen. Shinawatra, what's his name, the one they call Kody. These days, he's been sporting a meh-stache. That's a mustache that doesn't grow in right and you wonder why it's there. Been talking with him lately, even though I'm not supposed to. Not safe for Hal's spies to congregate, but I met him anyway in Grendel's Den. Shot a little pool and he talked about the old days before I was born. The last days with all their civil unrest, shortages, riots and bombings.

"It sounds like you're describing hell on earth."

"No, you don't understand," he said. "It could have been so much worse."

He's convinced that everything's going to right itself here. People are resilient, the occasional thresher tragedy aside. They look out for each other. They'll only put up with so much. It's just a matter of time until someone puts Ning in his place. Maybe the President, too.

"That's pretty rosy," I teased him. "How the hell did Hal ever put up with you?"

"Thursday? Deep down he's an optimist at heart."

"Maybe way deep down." I scanned the crowd again to see if we were being watched. Also scanning for DLR, the way Hal taught me. That's what he calls *doesn't look right,* subtle indications that something's out of place. All I saw were drunks. "So why do you call him Thursday?"

"The hair," he confided. Different colors for different days in Thai culture. Orange is Thursday. Simple as that. He went on about how the tradition started in the Ayutthaya period, but my eyes glazed over. "It's become an inside joke for me," he said, "because he never asks and I can tell he doesn't know."

Doubt that. Hal knows everything.

We drank and talked about how honored we were that he trusted us, even though we both knew he really didn't.

I've been drinking a lot lately. That and linking to bouncy, catchy, crappy songs. Helps get me through the grind. Not just me, I'm seeing a lot of thawed hitting the bottle, and I'm going to be seeing a lot more. When the next story breaks.

Bridge and I used to mess with our sisters. "Why are you hitting yourself?" was the biggest of the old standbys, but the runner-up was the one about your hand being bigger than your face. You go, "You know, if your hand's bigger than your face, you have cancer." They hold out their hand to measure. You smack their hand up into their face. Funny shit. Well, that game's about to get less funny because we've got an unusual number of thawed coming to doctors with tumors. Oral cancer, skin cancer, acoustic neuroma—things you don't want. It's not just Claire who's suffering.

Ning's doctors are starting to sweat. There's something wrong here, some carcinogen getting people sick, and no one knows what it is. Until they do, they're keeping it real quiet. But they won't be able to keep up the silence for long.

This disease is beatable. We've got medicines to mitigate, and we can beat it at its source with smart dust, tiny specks of silicon nanotech that hunt out cancerous cells. Not fun, painful as fuck, but doable. But like I say, the city's not really set up for this. Limited supplies. Piss-poor oncology. We can take care of a few patients at a time, but what if everyone in the town gets cancer? We're looking at a "who lives and who dies" situation, and it could get real ugly real quick.

isaac

I don't know who these men are but what they're proposing is monstrous. I've tried reasoning and can only conclude I am up against the unreasonable. You and I both know that civilized people talk; they don't resort to violence. But my words have no influence and I'm running out of options.

They've given me a moment to think. Everyone else is held at gunpoint. They took us by surprise. They are soldiers, English speaking, carrying assault rifles and covered from head to toe in body armor. I've counted six of them, and there may be more. Their leader may be a former United States Marine. I've heard him invoke a variation of the Rifleman's creed: "Until victory is ours and there is no enemy."

It's unclear whom these mercenaries work for, but they share the goals of grudge-holding madmen. Strangelove patriots. They insist that China must never be a world power again. We've been told that we are free to leave. We are free to take those few we have already thawed, but they will pull the plug on everyone else. This is systematic mass murder, Lazarus. Genocide.

I have become the negotiator for the Chinese, where it should be Li Quan Yin. They will not listen to her. Only I can make a difference. What do I have to negotiate with except an appeal to basic humanity? The soldiers hide behind a veneer of civility, but it goes no deeper.

"This is a shit assignment," said the leader. He won't say who assigned it.

So don't follow it.

"You don't like it? Join the fucking club. Orders are orders, buddy, and I'm already cutting you the biggest break I can, letting you go. Don't make me regret it."

The links are down, all frequencies jammed. Even if I could call for help, no one would come in time. I am put on edge by how stark Champagne's fear is. It's wild in her eyes, though unable to dim her beauty or cloud her heart. I see something deeper when she's looking at me. She needs me to make the right decision. There is no one else. Not even you, Lazarus. You're just a memory. I've idealized you the way I've done with so many others. My greatest flaw. In the final analysis, I'm all alone. As are we all.

This negotiation has very little give and take. Decapitating China is nonnegotiable, but because the soldier in charge does not relish this task, perhaps he will allow me to save one of the sleepers. Surely, a single act of mercy would do no harm. What about two? I raised the number one by one, but could not shame him into agreeing to more than six. And so my repeated attempts at appealing to common decency have won us the right to drag half a dozen cryostats outside to safety before the extermination begins. But which ones?

I have been charged with deciding which of thousands of lives are worth saving. That is a vile and impossible choice. Who lives? Who dies? Unconscionable.

I could save the innocent. Six: a fitting number. Once upon a time, I had six of my own. Hessa, Mu'tazz, Rashid, Haji, Ngozi and Dalila. How I miss them.

With the anguish, certainty draws near. Were my children with me now, they would have me take courage as I taught them. There is no call for fear. They would tell me to breathe. They would tell me to focus. They would tell me that six is not enough.

I would be a fool not to listen. I have been a fool for far too long. There is a call that must be answered. Though I live in a wicked world, I need not be swayed by it.

This is the day I make amends.

halloween

Mal's alert went straight to my adrenal gland. New-parent fatigue instantly obliterated—I became wide awake, muscles pumping into full sprint, rounding anyone I could into a transport plane and taking off for Beijing.

An electromagnetic pulse had made the links useless there. No information coming from China at all. The last image Malachi got was of a squad of soldiers approaching the Great People's Hall—he caught a glimpse through Champagne's link, and then the pulse wiped everything out.

"Satellites?"

"I'm still locked out of the sky," he told me. "I can hack back in, but it'll take some time. Less if I don't bother to cover my tracks."

"I don't care about tracks—just get me all the information you can."

When we reached China, our hearts sank at the sight of the Hall half in rubble and fires burning out of control. The target of a bomb attack. We'd come ready for anything, knowing that a negotiation or an armed rescue attempt would be best-case scenarios. This was the worst.

My team—comprised entirely of Vashti and Champagne's daughters—scrambled to put out the flames and hunt for survivors. I directed traffic, rifle at the ready in case any hostiles had survived. I needn't have bothered. Between the chemical foam, the thermal-imaging body search, and the excavation of corpses, concrete, plastic, glass and steel, we turned up only one living, breathing soul. Not an enemy. And not one of us. Isaac and Champagne had been ripped apart.

They didn't deserve this. It sickened me to see them that way. Even though we had never liked each other as kids, we had since become friends. More than friends: We'd bonded as survivors, sharing a mutual respect, if only for having made it this long. I'd gone around the sun with them. We had grown up and raised our children. We'd struggled with our mistakes. And now they both lay at my feet, lifeless and violated. Discarded like so much refuse. I stared into their empty eyes. And even though I knew it wouldn't happen, part of me expected them to blink or start laughing, holding their sides as they laughed at accomplishing the best practical joke of all time. It would be lighthearted revenge on their macabre-minded friend. Revenge for the times I'd insulted them back in school, for all our petty rivalries, for how seriously we took ourselves. But their wounds were real and fatal, and there was no denying them.

Amidst the shock and the tears and the outrage, Champagne's daughters achieved a rescue. Bridge and Tomi pulled a man out from beneath a pile of concrete. He'd survived the blast with nothing worse than a concussion and broken bones.

Once we got him talking, we learned he was Zhang Zhao, one of the Chinese posthumans. He'd turned his back on the recovery of his countrymen, only to realize he had nowhere else to go. After wandering about, he'd gone to a temple to look for guidance, but finding nothing there but an overwhelming sense of obligation, he'd decided to return to the work he'd abandoned. He arrived in time to see mercenaries enter the Hall. He tried to link us, but had no success and so he planned a rescue. But by the time he moved to push his way in, Isaac had begun a maneuver of his own.

He witnessed Isaac wrenching a weapon away from one, only to be shot in the back by another. Still, his courageous act had inspired the others to overpower their captors as well. Champagne had fought with skill and fury, her assault rifle thundering the commander down as Zhao had tried to beckon her and his countrymen to make for the exit. To his dismay, he saw the mortally wounded commander stirring (top-of-the-line RNA interference meds shutting down his pain receptors and keeping him out of shock, later forensics would reveal), reaching for a detonator in his belt. The blast flung Zhao back and out of the building, but collapsed the roof on everyone else.

We disabled the electromag pulse and linked for help. We found the transport the mercenaries had used, but nothing indicated who'd hired them. His access to the satellites temporarily restored, Malachi was able to reassure us that no more hostiles were on the way. But the origin of these who'd killed my friends remained a mystery.

Ning and President Coleman both denied involvement. They sent condolences. Ning used his Chinese heritage as a blanket denial, and promised to erect a statue in Isaac and Champagne's honor for setting his city off on the right path. The President talked about how a tragedy such as this cannot be allowed, and how under his unified leadership, this brand of lawlessness would never go unanswered. Each pointed the finger at the other, and at the end there was no proving anything.

All I knew for certain: my friends were dead, Zhao alive, the Hall half-destroyed and—somewhat miraculously—almost six hundred cryostats remained intact. With the fires put out and the damage repaired, the men, women and children inside could still be revived someday. The soldiers who'd come to China had meant to slaughter every last one, but in an act of self-sacrifice, my friends had stood up for those who couldn't stand up for themselves.

They died heroes. Honest-to-goodness heroes. Now I imagine I could try to cast myself in that light, and pound my chest about how I wanted to get justice for them. But I won't do that. I'm really not that good a person. Justice wasn't what I wanted.

I wanted vengeance.

sloane

Nothing brings family together like a funeral. My mom murdered and Uncle Isaac, too. Had to fly home like a swallow back to Capistrano. My other mom meets me and we hug, trying to console each other, but it doesn't take. Everything is surreal. This is the single saddest moment in my life, and I don't know what I'm supposed to be feeling. I should be grieving, but how do you do it? I've never tried before. It just feels like sick to me. The more I think about what happened, the less I want to be here. Saying goodbye to people who won't ever come back is a waste of time. It won't make me feel better. I could spend this time going after the butchers who made it happen.

Surviving mom (that's what my brain starts to call Vashti) doesn't really do comfort. That was more dead mom's turf. Whenever I skinned a knee or broke a bone, dead mom came to the rescue. Surviving mom has to stretch now, do something she's never really tried. That's why she calls for backup, having me sit down with Dr. Danny for grief counseling. I could give a fuck about Dr. Danny. Sorry son of a bitch won't stop sneezing throughout the interview, which makes it easy to ignore his psychobabble about shock (*haachoo, 'scuse me*), denial (*sniff*), anger (*waa-achoo!*) and some other one I forget. Don't tell me I have to find meaning to my suffering. There's no meaning in this shit.

Dead mom used to plant fruits and vegetables in methodical rows and then go crazy with the wildflowers. Artistic gardening, a splash of color to please the eye. On my way to change into funeral black, I find my sister, Olivia, ripping up weeds. Uncharacteristic for her because she so rarely goes outside these days. Or Outside, for that matter. Spends all her time mucking around in the IVR, maintaining it for idiots who like their experiences artificial because they're too scared to face the world. Dead mom got IVR-addicted for a while until we snapped her out of it.

In desperate need of a tan and a heaping spoonful of shut-the-fuck-up, Olivia makes the mistake of telling me how she's going to create virtual shrines for the dead. Yeah, go back Inside, you IVR nerd. Fake bullshit for real people, fuck off. Real people shouldn't lead fake lives.

Except for Brigit, that's probably the best conversation I have with any of my sisters. They're all weepy and useless from funeral to wake—even Tomi, whom I've learned to respect. Brigit gets me. There's nothing better than payback. She agrees, only she doesn't see how we can do anything. C'mon, Bridge. Enough of this fucking grief orgy. We can feel lost and powerless after business is taken care of. Her hesitation pisses me off. I resolve to get completely drunk.

Several drinks later and I'm watching Pandora show off the newborn. Here, hold my squalling breed creature. No, I'm not ready to have kids. Even so, I think I'm jealous. Wait. Yup, jealous. Hal's a family man again and I can tell he'll get it right this time. He may be distant, but with Pan and his kid, what can't be denied is he loves them and would lay down his life for them, even if he won't ever spend his Sunday afternoons fawning over baby photos. Not that Pan could fawn over baby photos, being blind and all. Though that might change. One of the Gedaechtnis scientists has put her on gene therapy, trying for optic-nerve regeneration.

When I talk to Hal, he's uneasy about the spread of cancer in New Cambridge. He wants me out of there. That's my choice, not his, and never mind that, what are we going to do about the killers? He tells me *we* aren't going to do anything, and that's just crap, because she was his friend but my mother. Don't you dare cut me out.

He won't take me seriously. He thinks I'll get in the way. Says we'll talk about this when I'm sober. It gets worse from there. I don't bother stopping myself and say lots of things I'll later regret, the way you're not supposed to. But it's a funeral and I'm grieving, so everything's excusable.

Fantasia puts an arm around me to steer me away before I can say anything else, which surprises me because she's barely said two words to me the entire time I've known her. At first I'm pissed because it's a violation of my personal space and she should know better since she hates to be touched. Pretty soon, though, we're talking, and she's telling me about her memories of my moms and Isaac, and I don't know if she's trying to make me feel better or just herself. Either way, I'm cool with it because there's something dangerous about her and Hal and Lodune that I like. That I'm drawn to. It's how I want to be. Screw that, it's how I'm going to be. Even if it costs me everything.

fantasia

Relieved to be back at zoo. Took over from assistants Vashti provided. Chimps treated satisfactorily in my absence. Should release them into wild now that their part is complete. Unsure how they would fare without me. Must attempt it for their sake.

No more control group. All patched. Looking out for each other. Less fuss for me.

Recent murders reinforce hypothesis. More faith than ever in my convictions. More faith than ever in myself. Not Whore of Babylon. Nor perfectly sane, but sane enough to bring liberation, not slavery. Synthesis of N and D.

Viral cocktail taking command of cells, inserting material via infection. Sore throats. Sneezing. Air droplets from each cough and sneeze my vector. Fine delivery system for contaminants. Works well with humans. Against enhanced immune systems, stronger mechanism required. Made concentrated dose, dermally active, greased it on fingertips and passed it through skin-to-skin contact. Untested. Might be too strong. Risk seems worthwhile because target will be traveling to not one but both major American population centers.

Good luck, Sloane.

sloane

I've got a plan. The plan is to pick up that guy, bring him to this secluded location, ply him with these drugs, get the information with this tool, then dump the body here. That's how I find out who killed my mom.

That guy: One of Ning's soldiers. One of Lodune's friends. The jarheads who watch me whenever I walk by. I scan the pack like a hyena looking for the weakest, slowest gazelle. Physically, I can't make that distinction, because they're all magnificent specimens, but mentally, there's a big difference from one to the next. I settle on Johansson. He's got a loose tongue. Get him talking and he forgets to shut up.

This secluded location: The apartment complex where my sister Izzy got raped. Reconstruction's still not done there. After the unpleasantness, the construction team abandoned it in favor of other sites.

These drugs: All the Wretched XS I've got from Claire, and a few stiff drinks to get things started.

This tool: An old school Hissatsu knife. The one Tomi gave me for my birthday two years back. Sharp enough to take care of business and then finish the job. Hissatsu means "coup de grâce" in Japanese. I don't care how tough you are, a stab in the heart is a deathblow.

Here: Down in the underground tunnels. Sub-Harvard. I know that maze as well as anyone now, and I've got the perfect dumping ground picked out. They won't find him for weeks.

That's the plan. What actually happens: I flirt like a politician whoring for votes, but I've got this stupid cold I picked up from Dr. Danny. It makes me breathless and lispy. I try to suppress it, but eventually have to go with it, because it turns out breathless and lispy is what works for Johansson. Big strong soldier of fortune likes women who sound vulnerable—who knew?

We steal away to my ambush. Drunk and stoned, he's even more of a Chatty Cathy than I'd hoped. He won't shut up. He loves me. He loves everyone. We do it. He starts crying about how beautiful everything is. Jesus fucking Christ. His fingernails are too sharp—not half as sharp as my Hissatsu. But I don't even have to use it. He tells me everything right when I ask. I don't have to hurt him or kill him. My instinct says do it anyway, so I don't, which is really better in the long run because his mysterious disappearance would just get people talking. This way I'm mostly under the radar.

I learned: Lodune killed my mom and Lodune was working for the President. Which means: I have bad taste in men and I'm going to assassinate the President. I'd been plotting against Ning, so it's not too drastic an adjustment. Just have to set my sights a little more west.

What works out perfectly is Ning has a mission for me, one he's been talking about for days. Go to the President's Mount Weather compound in Bluemont, Virginia. Go and bring back some of Ning's people. Apparently, the Prez has taken some spies captive. An exchange will take place and I get to go along for escort duty. There's a catch, I'm sure of it, but I haven't figured out what it is.

Doesn't matter. The pendulum's been pushed and now it's got to swing back. I'll be Booth to his Lincoln.

halloween

The call was unexpected and brief.

"What can I do for you, Mr. President?"

"It's really what I can do for you," he began.

He told me that Ning had clearly gone mad with power, and as such he had no choice but to remove the man from office. He had plans to make a military move against New Cambridge, and wanted to alert me ahead of time.

"That's between you and him."

"Not entirely."

He warned me that in the conflict ahead there would be refugees. Already a growing number of Americans (those supporting Ning and those opposing him) had expressed an interest in fleeing the theater of conflict, ideally to Europe.

"You want us to take people in."

"You misunderstand me," he said, lips pursed grimly. "With so many refugees wanting to come to your shores, I'd advise you to be judicious about who you accept."

He warned me that Ning, the man he'd accused as the architect of the Beijing massacre, had an interest in sending agents to Europe in the guise of immigrants. We could be murdered next, and would be welcoming those men in at our peril.

We talked it over and he repeated it. "I'd be very careful who I accept."

I thanked him, said I'd think about it and ended the call. It left an odd taste in my mouth. *Are you trying to help me? Or put fear in me? Why are you telling me this?*

sloane

I'm at Mount Weather and the weather's bad enough to bring out the earthworms and the slugs. Wind roaring, the unwelcoming rain pouring down in bursts. Good thing we brought umbrellas. I'm with three Green Mountain Boys and our contribution to the hostage exchange: the senior senator from Texas, recently thawed from the Amarillo facility. We're crowded under the awning of one of the aboveground FEMA offices, blinking through the downpour to see a welcoming committee coming our way.

Flanked by Gauss rifle–toting minders who might be Secret Servicemen, our tour guide is the acting Assistant Press Secretary, an ex–New Cambridgian I recognize from when she waited tables at Harvest. Used to be a movie star back before the plague. There's the perfunctory greeting, the obligatory frisking, the inevitable joke about the rain, then a march around the bunkers, past the razor-wire fence, toward the water-purification tower, then abruptly down into the belly of the beast—the underground city where the real action is.

They've got streets, a maglev transit system, generators, shops and offices for every cabinet in the United States. A mini White House, a mini Congress and a war room with tactical maps flashing across giant screens. Impressive shit. The First Lady comes to greet us, but doesn't stay. Military personnel are thick as ticks on a deer—they've thawed out more soldiers than I would have guessed, and I wonder if the reason I'm here is so they can demonstrate power. They've got to suspect I still talk to Hal—maybe they want to make him think twice about doing something rash. That probably won't work with him. And definitely won't with me.

We make the exchange at the end, six hostages escorted off the maglev train. They don't look mistreated. Don't look very much like hostages at all. As it turns out, three are CDC health workers who've never even been to New Cambridge. They're coming back with us to investigate the spread of cancer. Look at the big humanitarian gesture from the President, so praiseworthy considering how close we are to war.

Of course, no trip would be complete without a little acknowledgment from the man of the house. That's what I expect of him. Common courtesy. So we can make small talk, share an insincere handshake, arrange a small photo op. Just the moment I need to drive a stake through President Fuckface's heart. My Hissatsu is as sharp as despair and they took it from me in the frisk, but my hairpin remains. Two inches long, inconspicuous, the tip coated with a synthetic botulin I've been saving for a rainy day. Jab him and his nerves will stop. Between the respiratory failure and the heart attack he's sure to get (weak ticker, die quicker), there's no saving this man, no way, no how. After the kill, I won't leave here alive, but that was never my plan to begin with.

The last stop on the tour has my guide asking us to wait at a security station while an aide fetches my target. I'm smiling as polite as you please, trying to eat my nervousness and suck sweat back in through my pores. I have to be patient and wait for the whites of his eyes. Get him there. Or in the neck. Hell, anywhere I can break the skin. During the handshake even. Quick and it's done.

I'm dizzy and my aim is for shit but I can do this.

When the aide comes back, she comes back alone, apologetic that the President isn't with her.

"Believe me, I know how busy he is. I won't take much of his time," I tell her. I've planned for this. I know just what she's going to say next and I have the answer for it. Every bone in my body says I can talk my way in.

Except I'm wrong about what she says. Embarrassed to have to tell me this, she explains how with my constant sniffling and occasional sneeze, it's clear that I'm under the weather. "Technically, we're all under the weather, since it's Mount Weather," she simpers, "but you might be contagious, and he's concerned about catching your cold."

I swallow my phlegm and try to muster up a healthy glow, but nothing I do or say does me the slightest good. It's the plague culture. No one wants to catch anything.

It's so unfair. I almost never get sick. Goddamn Dr. Danny. No choice here, I have to abort, go back home and try again later, or not at all.

What does it matter?

No matter what I do, I'm never going to break this curse. I've failed again. I have the worst fucking luck in the world.

halloween

I'd started to piece it together. The nature of the conflict between Mount Weather and New Cambridge. Why the President had warned me not to take in refugees. How the massacre in Beijing could be used as an object lesson.

President John Henry Coleman and Richard Ning had struck a deal, and they'd struck it a long time ago. There was no clash between them; there was simply an arrangement. With each demonizing the other and posing a credible military threat, the citizens caught in the middle had little choice but to fall into line. Opposing your government isn't easy when a madman appears to be threatening it. When your very existence appears nonessential to that madman (as Beijing would suggest), you need a strong government to protect you. If that protection means losing your liberties in the process, better your liberties than your life. The choice of the lesser evil. This is how "the old way of doing business" could return, with those at the top of the food chain exploiting everyone beneath them, and those at the bottom too frightened to express their discontent. *And why'd he warn me about taking in refugees? Because he doesn't want anyone siphoning off their populace. He wants them not to have anywhere else to go.*

The two men had allegedly worked together before the plague, never proven, but they'd apparently been discreet business partners and, arguably, war profiteers. Malachi dug back into the newsfeeds to draw my attention to an article in the *Washington Post*. Ning had been accused of blatantly overcharging the military through one of his many companies, but the President's Justice Department had been reluctant to pursue, ultimately dismissing the case for lack of evidence before Ning could ever be brought before a grand jury. You couldn't prove collusion, but the inference could be made.

By the same token, I couldn't prove they'd pooled their resources to slaughter those Chinese citizens and two of my oldest friends. And yet I knew they'd done it. If I took them out, blood for blood, would it do any good? What backlash would it bring? Wouldn't others just crawl up from the sewer to take their places? The Great Law of Unintended Consequences was staring me in the face once again, and the sense of futility that accompanied it dragged me back to a dark and negative space. Real or imagined, the thing in my dreams had said my good feelings for my fellow man would die, and the prediction had largely come true. The thirst for revenge burned within me. But . . .

Is it my place to play God? To assume the mantle of executioner once again? What good will it do in the long run? Will it put those I love at risk?

If we'd had the legal authority to try these men, that would have been ideal, but then nothing about this world was ideal. We were stuck with the cards we'd been dealt.

"Get Sloane off the links," said the voice in my ear. Just audio on an anonymous channel, but I recognized the speaker. Onetime lottery winner, Mr. Lucky.

"What's this about?"

"All the links in New Cambridge."

"What's wrong with them?"

Under the guise of improving the connections, he'd jacked up their output to unsafe levels. They were spitting out too much radiation, sparking tumors through eyepieces and earpieces. Long ago, cellular phones were mistakenly thought to cause cancer; this act of violence was the culmination of those paranoid, century-old fears.

It was the sort of sabotage Mr. Lucky alone could get away with. While others held a background in business, law, politics, medicine or entertainment, he'd been trained as a communications engineer.

"Now, because she's like you, with your heightened immune system, I figured she'd stay healthy, but I've seen her sick lately. You should get her to stop using the links and you should get her out of the city. It's not safe anyway."

"Thanks for the tip. Why the sudden change of heart?"

"Because she's not my enemy. She's a pawn, just like you are."

"I'm no pawn."

"Yeah, you are. Don't pretend. You were specifically bred to bring back the most powerful men on the planet."

And that's whom he'd sworn to destroy, the survivors. It sounded like the ranting of a sociopath, but the more I listened, the more sympathetic I became to his point of view. From his perspective, billions had gone the way of all flesh simply because they weren't rich enough or well connected enough. Aside from him, everyone we'd thawed had earned a chance at resurrection by exploiting others, or by currying favor with those who did. Billions annihilated because they were poor. Look how few minorities made it to this day. The future belonged not to the meek, but to rich white men who cared only about themselves. By what right should they live? Why should they be rewarded for their crimes?

"I can't kill all of them, but I can make their lives miserable. They don't have enough doctors. I can make them suffer for what they've done," he said.

"That won't bring your wife back."

"Nothing can. That's my point."

"You think this is unfair. I know a little about unfair myself. Enough to know you might be right. But you can't stand in judgment of all these people."

"Why not?"

"For one thing, they're not all guilty. There are children."

His voice cracked with grief. "Do you have any idea how badly Jenny and I wanted kids? We don't get to bring our children into the world but these bastards do? Ruthless, privileged, criminal, selfish bastards?"

I told him about Kody. How he was just a chauffeur. How he didn't deserve the misery Lucky wanted to inflict.

"That's unfortunate," Lucky admitted, "but I'm working for the greater good."

"Revenge?"

"Justice. You know it's justice. After what these people did to your friends in Beijing? Are you really going to tell me it's not?"

"I don't think any of us are in the position to say what justice is," I told him.

"Let he who is without sin cast the first stone?" he mocked. "I know what's wrong and what's right, and to say I shouldn't even the score is high-minded, idealistic bullshit. I expected better of you."

I felt my jaw tighten. "I'm not saying you're wrong about who deserves what, but I'm not going to let you give people cancer and get away with it."

"The links are just the beginning," he assured me. "I've got much more in store and you're really in no position to stop me. Just get Sloane out of here. Get her out now. You're the only one who's shown me kindness, and for that I owe as much to keep someone in your family safe."

"You can't do this. I'm begging you to reconsider."

"I'm sorry, we're done talking," he said, and the link dropped the call. I didn't try to get him back. No point in it.

Twice before I'd had to hunt those who'd moved to do society harm. When the whole of civilization consisted of just my friends, I'd used a gun to put down Mercutio. Years later, I'd done it with Penny. I'd no wish to do it again.

"Malachi?"

"Yes?"

"Can you get a lock?"

There are many types of bad apples. Bitter, sour, chalky, over-ripe, stale, mealy, spoiled, insect-riddled, rotten. When Vashti had first started thawing, she'd empowered me to make threat assessments, separating the good from the bad. The good apples got left alone. The bad apples got seeded.

Mr. Lucky had been a mystery man. I'd thought it better to err on the side of bad apple. Expect the dark side of human nature; you're less likely to be surprised or hurt.

"Are you sure, Hal?"

"Applesauce."

At my command, a satellite signal reached a subdermal explosive a continent away. The microbomb detonated at the base of his skull where the spinal column attaches, a mercy killing. He'd said I was in no position to stop him, but he couldn't have been more wrong.

I'd thought to do this with the hospital siege, though Malachi wisely had talked me out of it. Not with children as hostages. Too much danger of someone getting hurt. Nor did I want to trauma-tize anyone with the sight of a decapitation. Bad risks. I'd have taken those risks in Beijing, if only I could, but the soldiers who'd done the butchery hadn't come from New Cambridge, and Vashti and I had never had a chance to seed them.

I had sympathy for Mr. Lucky. He'd been right about some things. Not all but some. Justified in his anger. And yet I'd taken his life. I had to do it, didn't I?

Maybe I should have just alerted the Assembly. Maybe I should have done nothing at all. Stay out of harm's way. It had made sense at the time. You put rabid dogs down, no matter how sad their story, no matter how right or wrong their cause.

The more I thought about it, the worse I felt. I'd empathized with him. Pitied him. How could I put him down and let the others live?

Didn't seem right. And in the end, I couldn't let it stand.

"Malachi, two more."

One after the other, in New Cambridge and Mount Weather, both Richard Ning and the President of the United States went pop.

PART THREE

patchwork

•

(to rain in hell)

We'd nicknamed one of the Nymphenburg conference rooms "Camelot" because of its stainless-steel round table. No corners, no one in a privileged position. By the time I reached the room, Vashti and Pandora had already taken seats, with Fantasia leaning against the back of a chair. I closed the door behind me, remained standing and broke the news about what I'd done.

"We may be getting some calls."

"We're already getting them," Vashti said, a look of alarm simmering in her eyes. "No accusations yet, but surely that's just a matter of time. I thought we agreed you were going to discuss this with us before you actually pulled the trigger."

"We agreed that ultimately it would be my choice to do it. And my responsibility," I said.

"You couldn't spare a little fair warning?"

"No, it's his decision," Pandora said. "We all agreed on that."

"What exactly are you three talking about?" asked Fantasia, who'd been holed up in Washington State while we'd planned all our contingencies. I explained it to her, and she found it grimly amusing. "Kill the leader of the free world?"

I laid out my evidence for his involvement in Beijing, and she just shrugged. "You give up the moral high ground the moment you put bombs in people's heads," she noted.

"I remember making that argument once upon a time," grumbled Pan.

"But I don't care much about moral high ground," Fan continued. "Just risk. Sounds like a crazy risk to me. The sort of thing I'd do if I were off my meds. Now we have to worry about what their forensics will turn up. Can it be traced back here?"

"Potentially, but so far they don't know anything," Vashti said.

"The mechanisms are built to disintegrate on trigger, making forensics difficult," I explained. "Difficult, but not impossible."

"No, not impossible," Vashti overlapped. "Anyway, they'll search their own houses first. When they come knocking here, we'll deny, keeping them in the dark as long as we feasibly can."

"Who'll take the reins in New Cambridge?" Pandora gave a squint of concentration, much as she would upon thinking several chess moves ahead—an impressive feat, sighted or blind.

"It might legitimately go back to the Assembly," I said, "but more likely, a strongman will seize control. Someone with the support of Ning's soldiers."

"Or the Green Mountain Boys," she suggested.

"Ax and his men, if they want it, sure."

"What about the widow?"

"She's well liked by the town, but I don't think she has the muscle."

"Speaking of which, how many innocents get to die while that muscle fights for control?" Vashti asked.

"Unknowable. Shall we measure it against how many would have died with Ning in power?"

"I'd be more concerned about who's taking over the presidency," said Fan. "Doesn't he have the football that launches all the nukes?"

I told her how Isaac and I had spent years hunting for and disabling command-and-control centers in the United States and around the world. We'd surely not found them all, but we had made a sizable dent. Either way, a nuclear response struck me as exceedingly unlikely. Though not outside the realm of possibility, especially in the wake of Beijing.

"What do we know about the V.P.?" Pan asked.

"Socially moderate. Fiscally conservative. He said maybe three things during Coleman's first term. Your basic nonfactor. Nothing to hide, but nothing to hang his hat on."

"Spoke to him briefly during the funeral when he called to send his condolences," Vashti said. "Seemed nice enough. Couldn't tell if he was genuine."

"I guess we'll find out."

"What can we do to lend a helping hand and maybe at the same time cover our asses?" Pandora wanted to know.

We discussed it and didn't come up with any easy answers.

"Let's sit tight and see how everything shakes out."

We got Sloane out and Kody, too. Neither was eager to leave, but with the instability spreading rapidly, it seemed only prudent. While the Assembly conducted an investigation and pretended to carry on business as usual, the alliance between Ning's troops and the Green Mountain Boys started to come apart at the seams.

One faction took over the supply depot, under the contention of protecting it from potential looters. The other faction countered by taking armed positions around the Assembly. Meanwhile, Mr. Lucky's body was discovered in his apartment, along with enough poison to kill the city many times over. They also found a journal entitled, "In the Event of My Death," which detailed his grievances, and thus made it much easier for investigators to determine how the links were misaligned and carcinogenic. Of course, they got clued in to Mr. Lucky through an anonymous tip—one that I put out there, which they'd yet to trace back to me.

It wasn't long before everyone started comparing notes. What did Mr. Lucky, Ning and the President have in common? What could connect them either in the cause or means of their deaths? Mount Weather cut their communication with us down to nothing. An eerie silence while they conducted their investigation. We'd little choice but to sit and wait for the hammer to drop, continuing our efforts to thaw the cryonically preserved Europeans, while helping to support a slowly recovering China. That being Zhang Zhao and all the Good Samaritan peacekeepers who'd volunteered to help stand watch over what was left of the Great Hall of the People, carrying on the work that Isaac and Champagne had started.

We brought out the German Chancellor and tried to unify Munich around her, though when she insisted on strict regulatory control over all companies based on German soil, Gedaechtnis balked. The traditional jockeying between governments and corporations: *Who gets to be whose puppet?* A failed attempt to resurrect the E.U. And then the French petition: understandable but exasperating.

We, the undersigned, recognize the severity of this catastrophe and appreciate the urgent need for food, shelter, medicine, counseling and other essential services. Nonetheless, we remain greatly concerned about the emptying of the Louvre, and believe the recovery of the greatest cultural artifacts of this or any age should be made a priority. We would petition your help in this enterprise. The lift in spirits to all men, women and children would be incalculable and precisely what we need in these trying times.

I agreed to help, but of course it was we PH who retained possession of many of these treasures. Upon fleeing New Cambridge, Champagne had scurried them back to Nymphenburg. She'd considered us far better stewards than any other, and I had to agree, loathe to return works of art to any public museum for fear of genuine burglars taking them. Without order in a society, without long-term stability, theft seemed too great a risk.

For Europe, my nieces assumed the responsibilities Champagne used to hold: planning, community building, uncorking decades-aged wine for all to enjoy, etc. Beyond security, I took up the role of supply manager, but left the negotiation to others, as I lacked Isaac's gift for diplomacy.

Unfortunate, as it was a gift I could have used.

Mount Weather held; New Cambridge began to eat itself.

Ning's men and the Green Mountain Boys fell into a sequence of murder and reprisal. One-upmanship. One man beaten to death. Two hanged from streetlights. Five dropped in a hail of bullets. And in the cross fire: innocent men and women.

They tried to cover it up, but with the links recalibrated and everyone using them again, there was no hiding the truth. Too many amateur journalists documenting the horror with their feeds. A broadcast society. The Assembly did their level best to reestablish a sense of order, but they had no real power in the face of armed gunmen with grievances to air. The Ax sat down with Ning's widow, a public show of unity, and the next day violence erupted again.

Both sides fought over supplies, territory and people, trained medical personnel most of all. When a group of doctors chose not to treat anyone until a workable cease-fire could be put in place, their spokesman turned up missing. That rallied more citizens to support the protest, but when the second and third disappeared, fear took hold and the movement fell apart.

Many citizens fled the city to live in the surrounding area instead. Isolation seemed safer. Some appealed to us for help, wanting safe passage to Europe—the great exodus. But whether it was meant as pure manipulation or not, the President had made me think twice about giving people refuge. It came down to a question of trust. Until we could secure our own borders, we couldn't afford to bring in anyone who might think to do us harm. Of the trustworthy, we let in as many as we could support with our limited supplies. But our refusal to help the rest caused a schism in the religious subset who'd wanted to deify us. Did we lack the power or simply the will? Perhaps we weren't divine at all.

Pandora fielded a call from the newly sworn-in President, the former V.P. He wasted no time accusing us of assassinating his predecessor.

"What you don't see with your eyes, don't invent with your tongue," she told him, neither a Brazilian nor Portuguese expression, but rather a Yiddish one her mother had taught her. "You think this has anything to do with us? Bring proof."

Two days later, he did.

Though able to hack his way in, Malachi had been unable to erase his footprints. Our enemies simply followed the routing and traced the satellite signal right back to its source: an AI built by Gedaechtnis and in service of posthumans. Armed with know-how, a good hunch and a satscan decrypter, whomever Mount Weather had working intelligence had proved cleverer than we'd hoped.

The flat denial we'd proffered couldn't last under the light of evidence, so we switched tactics, buying time with the promise of an internal investigation.

I'd already decided to take the blame. Or credit, depending on your point of view. The only question: Fall on my sword or brandish it? Better to admit it and go on the run? Or better to admit it and threaten more targeted killings if they misbehaved again?

Pandora wouldn't hear of it. To exile myself or put myself at risk? Not when my family needed me. Not when my baby daughter needed a dad. Never! We'd have to find another way. But I didn't see many options and it wasn't her decision to make.

Nor was it mine, as it turned out.

Before we could agree on a strategy, Malachi took the initiative, contacting Mount Weather himself. He confessed to triggering the explosives, claiming he'd done it entirely of his own volition. His motive? He said he'd calculated the three greatest threats to world peace and had stepped up to eliminate them. Stripping his confession of all emotion, he presented himself to Mount Weather as precisely what so many humans had feared intelligent machines would evolve into: a rogue AI, conscienceless, sociopathic, superior.

"It is a far, far better thing I do than I have ever done before? This isn't *A Tale of Two Cities*," I snapped, when Mal finished his pronouncement and closed the link to Mount Weather.

"It's better this way," he said.

"It was my decision. You gave me every chance not to do it. You shouldn't be the one to take the fall."

"You're not the only one who can be self-sacrificing," he replied. "Besides, compared to me, you've barely lived."

Though we were roughly the same age, he'd spent his time in a virtual universe where he was fully capable of multitasking many experiences at once. Bodiless, his consciousness stretched. He was the Ghost in the Machine. Whenever you talked to him, you couldn't be sure he wasn't also talking to someone else. Or helping Pandora to see. Or scuba-diving with IVR sharks. Or living in ancient Rome.

I could see him through my link's eyepiece, smiling wryly at me, wraithlike, with clothes and skin the color of an overcast sky. Before I ever learned his name, I'd called him the Gray Kid. Upon leaving Idlewild, and seeing what was real and what wasn't, I'd blamed him for many things. I'd thought to delete him, only to decide against it. Now he'd come to save me. A true friend.

"You haven't thought this through," I said. "They might believe you pulled the trigger, but they'll still want to know how bombs got into their people."

"As we speak, it's being taken care of."

While I'd been talking with Malachi, Vashti had placed a call to Mount Weather. She'd spoken with the powers that be, apologizing for the cabal she'd just uncovered. She told them how while she'd been running the hospital in New Cambridge, microbombs had been surgically implanted in selected individuals retrieved from cryonic storage. Though this sort of radical security measure had been discussed, Vashti had rejected it as morally reprehensible. Only now had she discovered how the plan had gone forward without her knowledge. Right under her nose. The architects of this outrage: Isaac Abdelrazek and his digitized accomplice, Malachi.

In reality, it was much the opposite. Vash and I had devised the tactical measure, keeping Isaac and Cham in the dark because we knew they'd never have gone along with it. I'd insisted on bringing Pan into the loop; she'd argued against us; I'd convinced her with a promise to select for this procedure only the thawed we considered extreme risks. And I'd kept my word, though in fairness my paranoia interprets "extreme risk" more liberally than most.

Unlikely that Isaac would be responsible; he'd stayed clear of the hospital and left all surgical procedures to others. Also, the idea that he'd collaborate with Malachi was absurd; the two rarely spoke. But there was no way for anyone at Mount Weather to disprove Vashti's alleged sequence of events.

They asked who else in New Cambridge had an implanted bomb. Was there any danger of the explosives detonating accidentally? What did we intend to do about Malachi? She answered the questions she could, assuring them that Malachi would be deactivated for the sake of public safety, and promising to do all she could to rectify the situation and restore trust.

I found her afterward, stopping her in a hallway. "You've slandered our friend."

"And?"

"And you expect me to go along with it."

"You want to contradict me? What will that accomplish?"

"I told you: It was my call, and I'm the one who should take the blame for it."

"Bullshit. You've far more value to me here. I don't need you as a scapegoat when there's someone else who serves that purpose better."

"This ruins his reputation."

"So? He's dead; his reputation doesn't matter anymore."

"It's unfair to him."

She dismissed that with a shrug. "Be pragmatic. Think of us."

"Here's pragmatic: Our supporters see Isaac as a hero for what he did in Beijing. As a symbol. Tarnishing him like this erodes support."

"Not at all. That's why I didn't implicate Champagne. She can play victim and hero. To say nothing of all the innocent Chinese."

"How much of this has to do with him taking Cham away from you?"

"Yes, I'm letting petty jealousy determine my policy decisions," she mocked. "You know me so well."

"Better than you think."

"Look," she said, raising her voice slightly before gritting her teeth and regaining control. "I understand you're angry, and I'm not saying I wasn't hurt by them running off together, but this isn't about me. This is about what's best for all of us."

Silence between us until I said, "What makes you think they'll even believe you?"

"He's black. He's Muslim. I'm making the case to an over-whelmingly white audience. As scapegoats go, it's not the tough-est sell."

"That doesn't make it right."

"I won't argue with you there. But it's not about right. It's about survival."

Pan and Isaac had been the best of friends. When I found her later, she was tormented by what Vashti had done, but said she knew how Isaac would feel.

"He'd accept this. He'd want to protect us."

She was right. He'd cared about us just as much as I did, per-haps more. This was never going to sit well with any of us, but the damage to Isaac's character had already been done. Vashti had carved him up, but I had offered the knife. His debasement had come as a direct consequence of the actions I'd taken.

Worst of all, a sinking feeling of all for nothing. I thought: *Our enemies might accept Isaac as a sacrifice and Malachi, too, but acceptance is one thing and retaliation another. Who's to say they won't want to exact a further price?*

Among the Egyptian gods, it was ibis-headed Thoth who had the power to resolve disputes. Perhaps that's why Isaac had felt an affin-ity toward him as a child. He'd spent much of his IVR time in a customized version of Khmunu, the fabled settlement known as "the City of Hares" and "the City of Eight," which the ancient

Egyptians had dedicated to Thoth. When I went to visit the shrine dedicated to my fallen friend, the resemblance to Khmunu was only fitting.

I stood in the cradle of civilization, the Nile visible in the distance, sun and moon both overhead, Isaac's architecture dotting the horizon, and before me, statues of the man himself, his children, and an inverted pyramid, the broad base aboveground, the point buried deep in the sand. The upside-down configuration reflected his utilitarian point of view; the widest section at top symbolizing the most good done for the most people. And inside: a testament to his life. No mention of his death.

Olivia had done a good job commemorating him. I made a mental note to tell her so after I unplugged. Her mother's shrine remained a work in progress; she was too close to it, and doing Champagne justice would be harder for her.

"Not bad," said a voice at my back.

Behind me stood a bald man dressed in white, half-German and half-Persian. My old rival, Lazarus Weiss. Mal's AI simulation of him, at least.

"Not bad at all," I agreed.

Back when I was young, I'd been naïve and foolish enough to see Laz as my enemy because he'd struck me as a conformist while I'd fancied myself a nonconformist, and because the girl I'd fancied fancied him. How innocent I was to think that was an enemy. I'd found more than enough real enemies since.

"We've been waiting for you," he smiled.

He led me to another domain, one I remembered fondly from my youth. Twain's hadn't changed since I'd last set foot in it. For those of us who had attended Idlewild, Twain's was such an institution that updating it would have been an act of sacrilege. My old hangout: a run-of-the-mill diner with torn leatherette seats. We made our way to one of the booths by the back. Laz slid in next to Simone, slipping an arm around her. Tyler scooched over to make room for me next to him.

Three dead schoolmates resurrected in digital form. Pandora and Malachi had spent countless hours coding the virtual Simone—they'd taken every experience she'd had here in the IVR and measured her vital signs in the real world, correlating the two. From this data, they constructed a "best guess" personality composite, giving "life" to the illusion with the same advanced technology that Malachi himself enjoyed. The end result was reasonably close to the Simone I'd known, not perfect, but real enough. Lazarus and Tyler had been Malachi's follow-up projects. Given enough time, he intended to do the same for Isaac and Champagne.

We exchanged condolences. Remembered the dead. Then to business. Six surprises along the way.

One: I didn't feel the slightest twinge of jealousy seeing Lazarus and Simone together. Dead and gone, I'd lost those feelings a long time ago.

Two: There were moments I felt close to them, and moments I felt like they were another species entirely. They'd bonded together here, lived through things I never had. They had their own shorthand now, inside jokes I didn't know. That made me feel like I'd missed something important, but I had to let it go. No point staying mad at ghosts.

Three: In my younger days, I'd mythologized my generation, seeing us not just as a dysfunctional family, but also as a kind of pantheon: Isaac as a god of civilization, Mercutio as a god of mischief, Fantasia as our chaos goddess, myself as the god of death, and so on. But for these three, the labels no longer applied. Lazarus was no longer the head of our pantheon; he'd become no more important than any other. Simone was no longer the embodiment of intellect; she had a lightness to her, a carefree quality that might have been wisdom. My old friend Tyler was no longer the god of war; he'd gone from a force of pure competition to someone who had nothing to prove.

Four: My friends had taken over one of Pandora's pet projects: reviving the Webbies. Sometimes called Websicles, and really a bastardization of WBE, Whole Brain Emulation, these men and women had preferred a cheaper alternative to cryonic storage. Digital preservation. The Webbies had paid to have every neuron of their brains mapped in the hope that some later survivor would download that topography and translate it into a new artificially intelligent consciousness. Essentially they wanted to become like Malachi, living in an IVR environment but retaining the complexities of their flesh-and-blood personalities. Laz told me how close they'd come to accomplishing this. Another few months and the system would surge with life.

Five: No one blamed me for Isaac and Champagne. "They lived over twice as long as we did," said Simone. In fact, no one blamed me for anything. "You couldn't possibly have stopped Mercutio any sooner than you did," Ty said. "Take yourself off the cross."

Six: When I asked them to make a sacrifice, they laughed and assured me they were way ahead of me. They owed so much to Malachi. They'd already started a plan to save him, giving up pieces of themselves so he could survive. Mal was an enormous, sprawling program, but so were they. He could scatter himself into them, hide code within code, and our enemies might never find him. He could wait, dormant, a sleeper to be revived many years from now, once the strong feelings my assassinations had provoked wilted into quieter, weaker concerns. I wondered how long that would take. And who would rule the world on that distant day.

With the plan moving into place, we continued to talk. Even

though I had so much yet to do, we shot the breeze for almost an hour. Hanging out in Twain's, making the moment last. Nothing more than that. My rival, my first love, and my friend; it felt so good, all of us sitting together, getting along so well. Just like it never was.

The following day, back in the real world, fact finders from Mount Weather flew in to oversee the deactivation. We greeted them cordially and watched them the way wild animals watch hunters. The right questions got asked; I fielded them all. They were computer experts and sharp; I was sharper. By the end, they'd declared Malachi neutralized, and he was, though not as permanently as they would have liked.

"I miss him," Pandora would later say. "He was more than a friend. He was so much a part of me." We'd had no choice but to transfer the duties Mal had done for her (acting as her eyes, first and foremost) to another AI, the one that had served as Pan's Nanny back when we'd gone to Idlewild. The replacement proved suitable, but it just wasn't the same.

One of the fact finders broke ranks and befriended Vashti. He turned out to be a descendant of Jonas Salk, one of her heroes. More than that: Salk had been her most salient inspiration as she'd struggled with a cure for Black Ep. This Salk apologized for the unfortunate circumstance of his visit, lamenting how his government had come to be at odds with the greatest medical mind in human history. That kind of language endeared him to Vashti right off the bat, though it wasn't empty flattery. Vashti had in fact triumphed over a microbe that looked certain to obliterate the human race; no one could take that away from her, and she'd yet to truly receive her due.

"It's just not right that you're being vilified," he told us. "Whatever you've done or they think you've done, you're heroes to me. And I'm not the only one who thinks so."

"How many like-minded individuals do you have over there?" Vashti asked, when I could have told her ahead of time the answer was not enough.

We managed to get a few useful tidbits out of Salk. He proved able to confirm my fears about how bad New Cambridge was getting. Mount Weather had been watching that power struggle carefully, content to let the various factions whittle each other down before swooping in to claim their prize. How long until the annexation? Given the rate of attrition over there, the call could come at any time.

I found the contrast interesting. America had become a land of turmoil, one city self-destructing, coming apart at the seams, and the other city apathetic, perfectly willing to let the carnage continue until they could safely reunify the nation. But here in Munich, the days were relatively calm. More than that, they'd become increasingly hopeful.

From my time in New Cambridge, I'd learned that when faced with a disaster such as this, people's behavior tended to polarize. Surviving Black Ep could bring out the best or it could bring out the worst. Some would grow eager to help their fellow man, while others would seek only to exploit. We'd had our share of both before, but the newly thawed Europeans (who, though frozen in Munich, hailed from nations across the continent and the U.K.) seemed far more willing to go the extra mile for one another, with even bitter corporate rivals putting aside their differences to focus on making their community that much better.

There was no "little red hen" phenomenon of everyone expecting someone else to do the job. Those who resisted hard work were gently chastised by their peers and soon came around. Even though there was always something to be done, we had no shortage of volunteers. It begged the question of what was going right here that had gone wrong thousands of miles to the west.

Had they seen the strife in America and China as cautionary tales? Had it pushed them to ensure that those past mistakes would not be made here? Fear can be an excellent motivator. Or was there something about the Europeans that kept them unified where the Americans had fallen back on a more dog-eat-dog mentality? That struck me as unlikely, given the oceans of blood that had been shed on European soil.

It wasn't until I mentioned this to Fantasia that I learned why we were having such an easy run.

"That's my doing," she said.

"What, your wishing it into existence?"

"Why wish when you can make it happen?"

I checked her eyes for any sign of humor, madness or chemical enhancement. She held my gaze, something she wouldn't often do back in the days before her brush with sanity. Eye contact used to make her uncomfortable, physical contact even more so. Now I was the one growing uncomfortable.

"I'm serious, Hal."

I beckoned her with my fingers, the universal sign for *keep it coming, tell me more.*

"Remember when I visited you in New Cambridge? When I saw what you were trying to do? What did I tell you?"

"You said it wouldn't work."

"And it didn't. Because you were trying to make people behave with laws. That won't work. The problem's deeper than that, more ingrained. It's not in our laws; it's in our blood."

"What is?"

"Selfishness. Hierarchy. He has to lose so I can win. Form cliques and persecute outsiders. All that crap. In the blood."

"This is why you've been studying chimps?"

"Bingo."

"The dark side of primate behavior?"

"What if I told you my chimps didn't have that anymore? No alphas, no betas. What if they welcomed each other, looked out for each other, worked together, shared their treats? What if every time they had a disagreement they resolved it peacefully? What if every time they did something nice for each other, they felt euphoric, safe and loved?"

It started to click. Alarmed, I felt my pulse pound. "What did you do?"

Upon abandoning Idlewild, she'd gone on a quest to "kill her mind." And in a sense she had, discovering the right medications to take the edge off her chemical imbalance. This part of her past I knew, but now I learned the lesson she'd drawn from it. Encouraged by her success, she next set her sights on the rest of the world. What had gone wrong with us? How had we fallen to this dismal point? What could be done to prevent it from ever happening again?

Others had gone down this path before. One of these, Dr. Caspar Erlich, had been a genetic engineer and "end of the world" theorist. Convinced that evolution had not only made us the dominant species, but had also sown the seeds of destruction into our DNA, Erlich spent his life postulating ways to defuse what he termed "genetic time bombs," the pieces of code that might lead to our ruin. Black Ep had claimed him before he could put his last theory to the test; Fantasia had taken up the calling and finished what he'd started.

"It was different years ago," Fan explained. "Not that we were different so much. Just the technology. A person could murder another person, or a family, or maybe even a whole village before anyone could stop him. Today, with the right tech and the will to use it, there's no stopping anything. Unleash a weapon, watch it spin out of control, and kill the whole damn species. That's what happened with Black Ep, don't you think? Stupid to let it happen again."

"You haven't answered my question," I said.

"Look at it this way. The 'me first' and 'I'm better' animal instincts got us through the first four billion years, but throw deadly tech into the mix and they fuck us over in the end. So those guiding instincts—the software that runs the hardware—need an update for the next four billion years. A 'patch.' That's what I've delivered."

"A patch for people? Not chimps?"

"Tested it on chimps. Tweaked it. Moved on to humans."

"And that's why everyone's getting along here?"

"It's the first point of contagion: European humans. Oh, also posthumans."

For a long moment I just stared at her. She glanced down at how my hands had balled into fists. I watched a grin spread across her face.

"I'd be mad, too," she said. "You think I should've told you up front, but I'm telling you now. You're the first one, you know. Our little secret."

"Tell me exactly what you did, Fan."

"I've created a virus and sent it round the world. It's making the rounds in Europe and America, and China's next. The virus is just a delivery system, highly infectious but harmless, sore throat, sneezing, that sort of thing. But it carries new genes packed in a plasmid together with a transcribing enzyme. The enzyme goes after your mRNA, making proteins that in turn go after your

DNA. All in all, it strengthens the correlation between altruism and pleasure. Takes a few weeks to get going, but once it kicks in, it's really great. Do something nice for someone and you feel good in return."

"The warm fuzzies?"

"Dopamine and oxytocin, mostly."

"Do you have any idea how dangerous it is to play fast and loose with someone's genetic structure?"

"Believe me, I know what I'm doing."

"Am I infected?"

"Got a sore throat?"

"Yes."

"Then I'd say the odds are pretty strong. Given enough time, you'll feel as good as you've ever felt before," she said. "Don't worry—I've got an antidote."

"I'm not seeing the humor in this." I'd gone from hoping this might be an elaborate fantasy of hers to wondering how much damage she'd caused. Her lucidity was no longer in question; her competence was. A little knowledge is a dangerous thing indeed, and when it comes to biohacking, even a lot of knowledge may not be enough. Don't fuck with anyone's DNA unless your understanding is dead-solid perfect. And up to that point, when I thought of Fantasia, *perfect* was never a word that leapt to mind.

"Have a little faith in me, why don't you?"

When I told her she'd been reckless, she said, "Well, it's not like putting bombs in people." Except, effectively, that's exactly what it was.

She showed me her data, first for the patch, then for the antidote. Most of it was beyond me. I'm better at hacking computers than the human body. But what I did understand seemed to add up. She'd put years into it. Erlich had put in many more. Between them, they'd given rise to something wonderful and terrible.

"Whatever this experiment is capable of, I don't want it in me."

"So? Take the antidote," she said, snapping open a little black bag to offer me a syringe. "You have a choice."

She'd punched extra emphasis on the word *you*. "The others don't?"

"You, me, Vashti and Pandora. We have a choice. We'll be more contented if we let the patch take hold, but we can take the antidote or give it to anyone we want."

"And everyone else?"

She cupped her hand to her ear, pretending to listen to the city. "I don't hear any arguments. No shouting or screaming. You said yourself there's a difference between here and the U.S. Why not give it a chance to work?"

"You know, it would be one thing if you'd made it available to those who want it, but you've taken away the choice."

"Everyone has to get it. Otherwise, what's the point?"

"Everyone, but not our little clique?"

"Not the people I trust. We're not half as likely to destroy the world."

I smiled; the smile tasted bitter.

"What's so funny?" she asked, hands at her hips, a familiar stance for her.

I said, "You talk about people forming cliques and discriminating against those who don't belong to them. Haven't you just done that?"

"Hal"—she grinned—"in the long run that won't matter, because the patch is going to work, and when we all see how well it works, we're all going to want it. So there's only going to be one clique—and we'll all be in it."

I shook my head—*don't count on that.*

"Except maybe for you. You'd be miserable if you couldn't be miserable," she conceded. "But that's all right. If anyone's going to play designated driver, I'm happy it's you. Now come on. Help me break the news to Vashti."

Recognizing it was only a matter of time before Vashti noticed a new pathogen on the loose, Fantasia had vowed to cut her off at the pass. But she wanted me there as a buffer against Vashti's vitriol. Though I found I was a bit too angry myself to mitigate faultlessly, I did manage to keep either of them from coming to blows.

"Criminally irresponsible, underhanded, treacherous and untested!"

"You don't think I tested it?"

"On humans—I don't care if it works on chimps or not!"

"I'm testing it now, okay? Better late than never."

Vash looked apoplectic, fixing her with a stare that might have turned a lesser woman to stone.

"I know what I'm doing," Fan said, and smiled. "I'm not stupid. Yeah, I have a history. But you're discounting my gifts. I might be just as brilliant as you are."

I told Vashti that, if nothing else, Fan was thinking out of the box.

"Shove the box, for all we know she's afflicted us with the next Black Ep," came the ill-tempered response. "In fact, I'll bet Black Ep originated through the same kind of arrogance she's demonstrated here."

"You think it's arrogant to try and make a better world?"

"If you believe you're smarter than evolution, I do. Instead of natural selection, survival of the fittest, what will this lead to? Survival of the friendly?"

"How about humility? Unselfishness? Empathy? Not that we won't argue or get angry. We will, but we'll work it out. And not that we won't fight when we have to," Fan said, explaining how her patched chimps had not cleaved to pacifism when a helicopter pilot had killed one of their number, instead banding together against a common foe.

"You act like there's nothing wrong with this," I said.

A happy glint twinkled in her eyes and she bounced up on her toes to tell us that while behavior modification had been proposed before, most had overlooked the carrot in favor of the stick. What she'd done was all carrot.

"We'll come to learn that looking out for each other is not only nutritious for the species but delicious to the individual," she said. And I realized how thoroughly this creation of hers played into the psychotic conflict of her childhood: nutritious vs. delicious, the struggle between healthfulness and desire. At last she'd squared the circle. She claimed sanity now, and while the uncontrolled delusive thoughts had perhaps left her, their impact remained like a departed sleeper's impression in an unmade bed.

Vashti put aside the "you've put us at risk" argument to trot out "flooding unsuspecting people with chemicals is unethical," nearly murdering me when I pointed out that she and Champagne had done as much to their girls. Which allowed Fan to reveal that she'd used Sloane as a carrier to infect the U.S., but not before she defended her actions like so: "There's nothing unethical about what I've done. It's socialization. We encourage people to contribute to society for the common good, to get along, live by the Golden Rule—all I've done is implant that chemically."

And then the question of free will reared its head. Assuming Fan's cure-all actually did what she'd designed it to do, would it be right to forsake free will for an indoctrination that could be beneficial to everyone?

I accepted my role as peacemaker, and did all I could to maintain calm. In the old days I might not have cared. But now with only four of my generation left, and two of them at odds, I felt a profound need to keep us from fracturing any further.

Despite my efforts, the division didn't end. However, it did move. Vashti's safety concerns remained (and so she poured herself into Fan's data), but her moral objections became less strident. I could tell she saw value in the patch as a means of controlling others—especially those who'd ungratefully conspired against us after all we'd done for them. By spreading the virus and withholding the antidote, we might find safety. There is no safety without control. And perhaps we'd find something more. We might inherit a happy proletariat. Despite how she'd committed herself to helping her fellow man, Vash wasn't even remotely egoless or self-effacing. Rulership appealed to her. Watching the wheels turn in her head, I couldn't help but remember her costume choice at the last party I'd thrown: Alexander the Great.

By way of contrast, Fantasia saw our embrace of the patch as inevitable—having self-experimented, she'd become convinced that even if we had an antidote, we'd never use it. We'd see how much better it was not to defend ourselves from the chemical utopia. The last party I threw, she'd come as a fairy princess. The patch was her *happily ever after.*

In listening to my own body and mind, except for the cold/flu symptoms (which cleared up fairly quickly), I didn't feel an effect from the patch. Even so, I got on the antidote, and so did Pan, with Hope receiving it via breast milk during her daily feedings.

Over the next several days, I studied those around me to try and measure what, if anything, Fan's efforts were accomplishing. Nothing definitive. No magical transformation. Just a steadily emerging sense of camaraderie.

And then, something odd: the Storyteller. Out of love or lust, she followed Dr. Danny to Munich. Here she carried on the same pattern of reading to children she quietly loathed. Though never voiced, her disdain for and discomfort around children had made her something of a private joke. Imagine my surprise to find her passing out hugs as well as stories, a genuine show of affection as she finally bonded with her young charges, the future of Europe. When I asked her about it, she smiled and admitted her previous "mixed feelings" about her audience. "But one day it just clicked."

When I sank back into a state of lucid dreaming, Bill Angler was waiting for me. I hadn't seen him in a little while. He told me as much and I said I hadn't missed him.

"You don't have to like me," he said, flashing me a humorless smile. "You just have to understand more of us are on the way."

"So you keep telling me. When can we expect you?"

"That's what I want to talk to you about."

He told me how the patch would inhibit the speed at which his civilization could make itself known to mine. Each wave of ambassadors took time to send, and the ones currently on the way would be unable to reveal themselves to those who'd been infected. That's why I hadn't heard from Angler in a while; only the antidote allowed him to return. Without help, the Free would have no choice but to compensate for the changed brain chemistry, spawning new representatives to send through the vastness of space. The adjustment would set them back years. And since they were out to help us, we'd all suffer from that delay. It would help the Free significantly, if only I would put a stop to Fantasia's plan.

"That's the best reason I've heard *not* to stop the patch," I replied.

"There's no call for us to be enemies. There's so much we can learn from each other." He extended his arm to me—a gesture of supplication? Or maybe he wanted a handshake. If that's what it was, I just left him hanging.

"Ignorance is bliss," I remembered saying before waking up.

More dreams chased by more sleepless nights. This was the place for it, I expected, Nymphenburg's history intertwined as it was with Bavaria's eccentric Ludwig II, better known as the Dream King.

Between my insomnia, the baby's fussiness and Pan's migraines, Team Halloween made quite a trio. About that last: Watkins, the Gedaechtnis scientist who'd started Mercutio off in the wrong direction, had made Pan's sight his top priority. His redemption meant exactly nothing to me, but his plan had made sense and there was nothing I wouldn't do to help restore Pan's vision. Especially since my son had cost her it. The regeneration was working—she could now distinguish between extremes of light and dark—though the process was painful, inflicting headaches (she made a joke of calling them "blinding headaches") that would force her to retreat for hours.

On one of those rare nights when the pain wasn't so bad, she and I were awake, and Hope was soundly snoozing, she told me she'd had a dream not so different from the kind that had been plaguing me.

"I can't remember it completely," she said, "but I know there were clouds. Someone talking to me. And a feeling like I was talking to myself."

"Sounds like a spillover from one of my dreams."

"Maybe so. Like when you're in a restaurant and someone at another table says something and soon you're talking about it at your table, too. Even though you didn't really hear it clearly the first time."

"That's probably it," I said. "I mean, I've told you so much about this nonsense, it's only natural for you to dream about it, too."

"Unless it's not nonsense," she said.

"Don't even joke about that."

"I'm not saying that's what happened. Just leaving open the possibility."

"Well, don't."

"You sound threatened and you don't have to be."

I sighed. "They're flights of fancy, complete with magical thinking and anthropomorphized microbes. You shouldn't encourage them."

"All right."

"Besides, what if it was true? There are enough fucktards on this planet."

"If it was true, they wouldn't be fucktards."

"Oh, no? Created Black Ep? Killed billions?"

"Billions of fucktards, no?" Pandora teased. "You'd think you'd like them."

I had to smile at that, and from there we got into a debate about the possibility of extraterrestrial life, and why with such an enormous universe it seemed so empty. Every search for life—sweeping the moon and Mars, and listening for signals with SETI—had turned up nothing. With so many places where life could exist, why hadn't we discovered it? Was life unique to Earth? Or was it plentiful but doomed?

"Fan's right about one thing," I said. "The aggressive rise to the top of the food chain. Then where can you turn that aggression except against each other? If life does exist out there, it probably blows itself up the moment it develops the kind of armaments we've invented. Once you *can* create a doomsday scenario, you do."

"And that's why you think these are just dreams?"

"That's some of it."

"But maybe life doesn't destroy itself. Maybe it finds a way to evolve past that."

"You're making Fan's argument."

"I just don't believe things are as dark as you say."

"Well, I don't see how they can't be. Survival of the fittest leads to aggression."

"You mean adaptation."

"That's aggression. Competition. All life-forms compete for resources; the ones that are best suited to get them leave behind the most offspring. So when you've got limited resources up for grabs, the best grabbers win."

"You fight your neighbors to get what you need."

"Exactly, Nature rewards the winners and the losers die out. Evolve for millions of years, and those patterns get hard to break."

"But it's not just aggression," she insisted. "Nature also rewards compassion. Taking care of others. It's not just about the individual surviving, Hal—it's the family, the species, the whole gene pool."

"That's the altruism Fan wants to tickle."

"Tell me it's not a big part of who we are."

"It goes hand in hand with aggression," I admitted, "though it's not as deeply ingrained. Aggression comes first because that's where survival comes from."

She bit her lip, hunting for hypotheticals. "Imagine a planet that's so big the resources never run out."

"If the resources never run out, there's no need to evolve. What's the biological imperative to better yourself if everything you need is always there?"

"Maybe there's a place where competition for resources doesn't require aggression, or where natural selection as we know it doesn't apply."

"Doesn't seem likely. You're basing an argument on wish fulfillment. On faith."

"Then I guess we're back to Fan's argument again—better living through chemistry."

"I don't know. Vashti's right, I think. If this patch works, it flies in the face of natural selection. It's antievolutionary."

"I'd say it's just an evolution of evolution. Like birth control."

"Birth control? How so?"

"You say it's antievolutionary; that's what contraception looks like, too—at first. But really it raises the standard of life, so it's beneficial to the genes."

I noticed myself chuckling.

"What's so funny?"

"You, arguing for birth control when the world's so empty."

"And when we just had a baby," she said, laughing too. "Maybe I'm just arguing to argue. Blame it on the bad dream."

We went back to bed, and she fell asleep in the crook of my arm. I tried to sleep, too, but the conversation kept echoing in my head, plus the fact that she'd dreamt something that might give substance to the shadow of Bill Angler and his fellow Free. Self-indulgent madness, I decided. I couldn't afford it. In the struggle to push those thoughts away, words crept in, a famous quote from the ancestor of the man who'd come to ensure Malachi's destruction: "I have had dreams and I have had nightmares, but I have conquered my nightmares because of my dreams."

Predawn, I woke, convinced by a squirming in my gut that something was terribly wrong. Upon making certain that Pan and Hope were still sleeping and in no danger, I dressed and left, off to query the security system.

Minutes later, I emerged, unlocking one of the balcony doors at the rear of the palace to step out into the cool, moonless night.

A favorite song twisted through my memory, competing for my attention; I ignored it to keep my ears sharp.

Did a twig snap?

Nymphenburg had been built for aesthetics, and while the inside had achieved fame as an overly elaborate white-and-gold baroque paradise filled with mythological frescoes, the lush outside had become equally admired for its lawns, gardens, statues and fountains. From my vantage point by the back, the grounds sprawled out before me, leading off to the distant woods.

Nymphenburg. Where my son had died. As such, I'd mythicized it as an evil place. But the raw beauty before me here, the landscape at night, no one could deny.

Nymphenburg, I'd saved from destruction once. Since then, I'd studied it the way a Zen monk studies a koan. Playing it out in my head time and again, I'd gotten to know its ins and outs, a fair idea of how to storm it and how best to weather that storm.

Motion detectors and heat sensors both on the blink tonight. Three guesses why. Off by the fountain, my eyes picked up the faintest haze, a wet shimmer in the air.

That's fitting, I thought.

Stealth tech. Displaced light, refracting. I'd encountered it before.

Clicked the trigger concealed in my hand. Out spiked the electromagnetic wave. On the lawn, by the fountain, and on the walkways: dozens of stealth-suited soldiers, armed for battle, visible now, their equipment fritzing out. Looking up at me like children caught in an act of mischief. And me looking down at them, as if they were the last of the damned.

Don't underestimate a paranoid. Not when he's been burned before. Not when he has something to protect.

They'd love to shoot me now, I remember thinking, *but I'm too ready. Too on the ball. They've got the best RNA interference money can buy, but it's nothing compared to my zanshin. I've got alertness on my side, pure action, what warriors call the remaining mind.*

Deuce and Penny had given me a lot to think about; I'd anticipated an attack on this soil for seven years. And knowing the types we'd be thawing, knowing what they'd be capable of . . .

The next trigger I hit sent the sprinklers into action; hydrating my uninvited guests while the ground hummed with current. They flash-fried, wrong place, wrong time, like vampires caught out after sunrise. Whomever they were—private army, U.S. Special Forces, a Concerned Citizens Against Halloween action group—I cooked them from the inside out, until their hearts and minds became useless melted tissue.

That was it. Trap sprung. There was no battle, nothing competitive nor spirited. They'd asked for death; I'd accommodated them. I simply killed them where they stood.

Electrocution is not pleasant. I'd had a taste of it once. They'd gotten much more, which was merciful. I'd made it quick.

While I'd been dispatching the main force at the back, my nieces had been mopping up the soldiers at the flank. Slow Bridge and Tomi sniping from the palace rooftop, bullets cracking through body armor to fragment into the flesh. I circled around to add support, but incoming fire forced me to duck for cover behind a statue: above my head a bearded, sparely dressed man raised an unconscious infant up to his mouth, about to take a bite out of it. Saturn devouring one of his children, perhaps. One of the creepier statues in Nymphenburg, taking bullets meant for me.

Chipped fragments rained down, the shooters pinning me there until one of them could sweep around to take an unobstructed shot. Retreating straight back made the most sense, but if I could predict the direction from which they'd come, I could pop them before . . .

A chemical agent put an end to those thoughts. Had to push off and run just as the grenade went boom, misting the statue with blister gas. I rolled to the side, whipped my head back to see baby and babyeater disintegrating, fought the urge to take a wild potshot at my enemies and kept on the move instead. Better for me to find new cover and keep drawing their fire. Pull their attention from the snipers on the roof.

That tactic paid off. Flawless sharpshooting from my nieces. The only critique I could make: They were taking it personally. But who could blame them? These were the same sorts who had murdered Isaac and Champagne. Brutal though it was, the girls found it cathartic. Especially Sloane, who broke down afterward, sobbing uncontrollably. The first tears she'd shed for her mother.

For an instant, that night, I became a teenager again, surrendering to a crushing sense of déjà vu. I was playing war games in the IVR. Strategizing against my friends. But instead of commanding nightgaunts, it had been my nieces. Against a real enemy. And the stakes had been so much higher than pride.

As one we swept the theater of war, making sure we'd zapped them all. When we'd neutralized the blister gas and verified that no other nasty surprises had been left behind for us, I gave the all-clear and told them how proud I was. They were dazed, I think, but behind the shock there shined trust and a sense of family I'd been fighting for many years. It reacquainted me with how much they looked up to me. How they saw me as a role model. It's funny how I forget things like that.

The other denizens of Nymphenburg crept out cautiously, eyes blinking, as if they'd just woken from a long sleep. A good thing, because we needed their help. Each pulling his or her weight, we all worked together on the immediate task: getting the bodies to the morgue before they could start rotting in the sun.

. . .

We contacted Mount Weather and accused them of sending fifty men to their doom. Also, attempted murder. They categorically denied it but refused to go through the farce of being overly solicitous of our condition. The inevitable attempt to pass off blame on another party came, but only in a halfhearted fashion.

We tried to predict their next move. Maybe the way in which we utterly defeated their attempted coup (or was it just an attempted assassination?) would set them back. Maybe it would make them think twice before trying something like that again. Maybe it would convince them that the cost would always be higher than the potential gain. Or maybe it would encourage them to hit us with everything they had.

We braced for another attack. . . .

They kept us waiting. I raised the prospect of going on the offensive, but Vashti and Pan talked me out of it. "Let's see how things play out," Vash said. I didn't like it. But she had a good reason.

She'd been testing the locals, taking measure of the patch. Every test that she performed of those who'd been infected suggested new neural pathways forming. New activity in the hypothalamus and the amygdala. Increased levels of dopamine, oxytocin and the other pleasure-and-trust-producing chemicals in the brain. And so far no side effects.

Encouragingly, the biological changes were leading to behavioral changes. The promising signs we'd seen previously were bearing fruit. The first example being the kind of unity we saw after the attack, the degree to which the European people supported us, stepping forward to take the initiative, volunteering to do whatever it took to keep us safe and free. There was something stirring about it.

I saw it manifest in so many little ways, each portending larger change. For example, noise. Noise had been one of the constant hassles I'd had to address in New Cambridge: One group would throw a party too late at night, blasting music at much too loud a decibel level; the neighbors would complain, and if we didn't respond quickly enough, a feud was certain to break out. Bad feelings, sometimes a fistfight. Once even a stabbing. But while the patched Europeans liked to drink and party as much as the Americans, they always policed themselves. If one house began making too much noise, its neighbors would come over, talk it out, and the volume would drop. They'd work it out together. Displays of consideration and empathy that the unpatched showed only on occasion, the patched would do each and every time. Without even having to be asked.

The flood of chemicals seemed to give courage to the cowardly and a broader perspective to the self-obsessed. I kept watching for flaws to appear. Would the patched fall into groupthink, losing their individuality? Would the desire to resolve conflicts lead to stagnation or unreasonable compromises? Would Munich become a city of zombies, sheep and fools? But every time I saw a danger sign, the smoke never led to fire. In fact, every objection Vashti, Pan or I posed withered when confronted with the facts on the ground. One after another our worries were proved baseless. The patch worked. Not perfectly, but better than any of us had dared to hope.

Could that be happening overseas? And if so, were we not better off allowing it to run its course instead of taking the fight to Mount Weather's door? Could peace be won chemically?

We hid the patch even from our own. The secret stayed only with Pandora, Vashti, Fantasia and yours truly. Vashti's daughters were left in the dark, their mother's choice. We didn't want chatter. No chatter meant less potential for advance warning. Let it work on our enemies as long as it could before discovery. "What about free will?" Exactly, what about it?

We expected the doctors under their control would turn up the patch's existence sooner or later, but took our chances on later. Perhaps by then the genetic changes would be so pronounced, they'd prefer having it and would be sympathetic to its creation and dissemination. That was Vashti's argument. She'd made a complete one-eighty, hopping aboard the train Fan had pulled out of the station. This she did not out of a professed desire to evolve evolution or improve the lot of all mankind. Fearing for our safety, she did it purely for tactical purposes, a need to clamp collars around our enemies' necks.

With surreptitious use of the antidote, she'd shielded one of her daughters from the patch. Not the ones she'd historically bumped heads with—Brigit, Sloane, Izzy, Katrina. Those four began to transform just like the human population. Effectively, she'd created a subject and a control group of posthumans. Morally reprehensible? Possibly. Only I'd never seen the patched girls happier. Flushed with joy (or, more accurately, with fantastic drugs), they turned more caring, less selfish, better balanced. Model citizens, you could argue, and all without removing the essence of who they were.

All this while my last deep-cover spy in the New Cambridge area kept me as up to date as he could afford to without putting his life at gratuitous risk. Mars had fled the city, hiding out in the suburbs instead. I'd lost contact with him for weeks; I was relieved to hear he still lived. I thought it best to extract him, but heard rumors of Mount Weather's new willingness to scramble fighters; they'd shoot down any unauthorized transcontinental flight approaching American shores. The risk was too great. Instead, I told him to stay out of the city itself until things settled down. (After all, we already had an agent over there, and the agent was in viral form.)

Despite having only a peripheral vantage point, Mars was able to bring me up-to-date: Charles "the Ax" Axakowsky had rallied his Green Mountain Boys to win the day from the last holdouts of Ning's private army. But the cost had been high. The city had all but degenerated into a state of barbarism. Mars expressed serious doubt as to whether it might ever pull itself out of the depths to which it had sunk.

For a long while we played a waiting game, us watching for the American cities to make a move, Ax doing all he could to keep New Cambridge from splitting apart, and Mount Weather as silent as the dead. Were they plotting their next step or waiting for us to take the lead? With the patch systematically snaking its way through the general population, we became uneasy spectators in the race between Man's desire to resolve differences through violence, and his inherent need to make positive emotional bonds. Thanks to Fantasia, that latter was getting unprecedented biochemical support.

Watching. Waiting. That was a stressful time.

But before long, those of us who'd doubted Fan felt foolish—history would bear out the fact that the patch had brought us through a dark time, ushering in the Age of Compassion, a stretch of global peace and harmony that had eluded the species since the dawn of history.

The first moment of détente, the first crack in the ice, so to speak, was delivered by the Ax, who asked us for support against Mount Weather. He pledged complete transparency and openness. He'd committed himself to "building a future we can all be proud of." Patched, we'd no doubt of it. What he asked for we readily gave him. Despite the threat of getting shot out of the sky, I led a team to New Cambridge. And Mount Weather never struck. Instead of sending troops, they sent delegates to discuss a peaceful settlement. Patched, every last one of them.

When I look back on how Mount Weather made their first entreaty, I like to think of it as this: They sent us a Hallmark card with a sad-eyed cartoon hound dog on the front with the words "Sorry We Tried To Kill You" above his head and beneath his drooping jowls. And inside the card: the same dog wagging his tail, with the words "Doggone It, Can't We Be Friends?" That's not quite how it went, but the sentiment was just the same.

Over the next year, the new President and Ax would form a united country. America would be whole again. And across the ocean, a United Europe and China would each emerge as a power. The three would come to a meeting of the minds and make peaceful coexistence a reality. Next, I watched the United Nations rise from the dead, the fulfillment of one of Isaac's dearest dreams. Though lacking many of the diplomatic credentials of his predecessors, the newly elected U.N. Secretary General, Kriengsak Tangmatitham, benefited from a reputation for evenhandedness. Despite "only" having been a chauffeur and despite masquerading as Suchart Shinawatra. That didn't matter anymore; Kody could use his real name.

The first resolution he oversaw wiped the slate clean, electing not to sanction those who'd committed recent crimes—Mount Weather, the Green Mountain Boys and us posthumans. Most of those who'd been blamed for the carnage were already dead, and there seemed far greater benefit in forgiveness and moving forward.

The kind of exploitation Ning had fought for dissolved away. Those still in cryonic sleep were extracted, liberated from Black Ep and afforded the same rights as everyone else. Some thawed proved difficult at first, but sooner or later Fan's virus would catch up with them and set them right. There was no need for any Doctrine, not per se. Not when people were willing to share the workload on unpleasant tasks. Not when complaints were so few and helping hands so many. Not when everyone behaved as they should.

I spent most of my time walking around in a state of open-mouthed disbelief.

To think that Fantasia had done this? My crazy friend Fan? The teenager who'd rocked back and forth and rambled senselessly? The girl I'd pitied? Fuck me if she hadn't saved humans from humans, engineering a remedy to all the world's poisons.

That's not exactly right. There are things the patch didn't do.

It didn't stop criminality. Not altogether. However, it put a huge dent in it. Why take advantage of people when you feel better looking out for them? Why resort to theft when society truly wants to meet all your needs?

It didn't stop stupid decision-making. Still no shortage of that. But it made the vast majority of those stupid mistakes well intentioned.

It didn't stop magical thinking. It put no end to faith-based reasoning. Nor did it unify everyone under the same religion. Rather, it made everyone more tolerant of others' beliefs.

It didn't create universal vegetarianism, but it encouraged it. Those who did hunt did so for food, not sport. Compassion with the prey made it so no one would take a life lightly.

It didn't put an end to jealousy, deceit or hard feelings, but it pushed people to talk their problems out and be a little less cruel than they otherwise would.

One thing it did do, Fantasia had warned us about ahead of time. It contributed to a lot of consensual sex. Question: What do you get when sharing pleasure with someone gives even greater chemical highs and even greater feelings of trust? Answer: A puritan's nightmare. Along with common chimpanzees, bonobos are our closest genetic relatives, but for years they were barred from zoos for fear that their constant sex play might offend delicate visitors. Fan joked that she'd unleashed everyone's inner bonobo.

Better to be fucking than fucking each other over.

And even though I'd an antidote to the patch, its very existence had a profound effect on me. Because I didn't have to share the planet with quite so many dreadful people. When everyone around you seems committed to not being a total bastard in the short time they have between cradle and coffin, your outlook can only improve. I found myself laughing more. Relaxing. Enjoying life.

How could Pandora and I possibly object to this? Maybe the patched were doing good deeds "for the wrong reasons." Out of a desire to feel bliss instead of a genuine moral imperative. So what? Results are results. Happiness is happiness.

Better living through chemistry indeed. Drug 'em all.

Naturally, the world's medical professionals figured out what had happened, but by the time everyone realized they'd been patched, almost no one wanted to go back to the way it was before. You could count those people on one hand. The overwhelming consensus: "Yes, someone unleashed this, but so long as it's safe and it makes things better, you'd have to be a masochist not to want it."

No stranger to self-medicating, Fantasia wasted no time patching herself, dropping off the antidote as soon as she could. Why not?

But she'd been wrong about all of us getting patched. Vashti wanted to keep her objectivity. She liked her genetic structure just fine, thank you. Taking the patch meant losing control. She didn't want that. However, it didn't stop her from cutting her daughters off from the antidote one by one, taking care to see that the transformation agreed with them. In all cases, it did. Medically astute Tomi was the only one Vash spared. She brought her into the fold, exposing the origin of the patch and the existence of the antidote. It was a safe choice. She stayed silent and, like her mother, unpatched.

That left Pandora and yours truly. And our child. What would it be for Team Halloween? Evolve or no?

We talked about it.

We didn't need it.

We had each other.

At long last, humankind was on the way to pulling itself up by its bootstraps. Vashti and her daughters would be as much a part of it as they wished, having a subtle hand in world affairs. Increasingly the daughters would take the lead there. Vashti herself would find meaning in putting more and more of her time into finding a cure for the disease that had felled Isaac's children, what we'd called "The End of The World." Beating it might pay Isaac back for all he'd done, and for what she'd done to his good name. If anyone could beat it, she could. Fantasia would live life to the fullest, at peace finally, satisfied in the knowledge of what she'd done.

And we? We could go away. Wherever we wanted. For as long as we wanted. Call it a vacation from all we'd done and seen. Nothing holding us back now. No debts to repay. A chance to start anew.

The world would go on without us.

epilogue

.

(years later)

Monarch butterflies are indigenous to North America but can thrive wherever the climate's good and there's plenty of milkweed to eat. They got introduced to Australia almost a century ago, where swan plant milkweed grows in abundance. Now they're everywhere you look.

We're transplants ourselves. Having a picnic in the Royal Botanic Gardens. Just a short walk from the Opera House and the most pristine blue water you could ever ask for. Later we're going into the outback in search of marsupials. Actually, the whole country qualifies as outback—it's yet to be repopulated. We have it all to ourselves.

Came Down Under on a whim. Hope's whim. She liked her stuffed kangaroo so much, she wanted to know where it came from. She's been hopping about like a kangaroo for hours, tugging at my arm to get me to stay on the lookout. Will do. Also I have to watch for koalas. She says they look grumpy and we have to cheer them up. Kids.

We make our own schedule now. I'd almost forgotten what that was like.

I'll admit I don't know much about happy and well-adjusted children, but that's what Hope seems to be. Endless curiosity, endless enthusiasm. Maybe a little cynicism. We told her she was the best kid in the world yesterday, and she rolled her eyes and replied, "That's what *every* mom and dad says." Ha. Subversive books. She reads anything and everything. That's all Pan's doing. Started her off on a good habit—the moment she could read to our daughter, she did. Now Hope reads to us.

By the way, twenty-twenty vision, my Pandora. No migraine in years.

Always amazes me how things can heal. Gaps in my memory won't come back, but her green eyes look as brilliant as ever. And that's the way I want it.

It's funny. So many people wander through their lives never knowing why they're here, but Pan and I, we found out. We were designed for a reason. To cure Black Ep and bring the human race back from the brink. Since birth—even before then—we'd had that responsibility hanging over our heads. We've felt the weight of that burden, had to carry it for years. But now it's done. Whatever you want to call it—our obligation, our life's work, our destiny—it's been fulfilled. We're finally free.

That's a thorny word for me, *free*. I don't know exactly what it means. My waking life tells me it's about being able to do what I want. Having alternatives. The first of which is not selecting the one that closes all the others. Never have I felt less like wanting to die. But my dreams tell me the word means something else entirely. . . .

We've made certain not to discuss it around Hope. If she has a dream on her own, we'll have to keep an eye out. Until then, I'm seeing it as nothing more than stress and an overactive imagination.

That doesn't stop me from wanting to pop into the local observatory to see if the telescope still works. Ah, forget it. What would I look for anyway? If the Free do exist and they want to come, let them. I'll deal with them then.

I don't mean to be glib. Real contact with the Free would be a turning point for humanity. A defining moment. For good or ill, it would be the most significant event in our history. But how can I prove they're real? In the face of an unknowable world, what can I really do?

Whoops, thought we had a koala sighting. False alarm. Hope's yelling her head off and pulling us toward what I'm reasonably sure is a wombat. Not too close, Hope, those things bite. We'll find a koala soon enough.

Interesting claim about the koala. The eucalyptus leaves it likes to munch get it stoned out of its furry little mind. The junkie of the animal kingdom. Spends most of its time doing nothing but eating and resting. Which makes the psychotropic, calming effect of the eucalyptus a good thing because, cute as the koala is, it's surprisingly aggressive by nature. Makes you wonder what would happen if the drug ever stopped working.

The thing about the patch is it only works for so long. The human body just isn't meant to work that way. After a few years of bliss, people are finding the effects are starting to wear off. And after rising to such dizzying heights, slipping back down to the way things were before fills every patched man, woman and child with an unreasonable terror. Reality looms bleaker than ever before.

Fantasia, Vashti and Tomi are holed up in Nymphenburg, feverishly working on a patch for the patch. They have a plan to compensate for the miscalculation. Unfortunately, time's ticking fast. The demand for dopamine and oxytocin is spreading the world over. In the meantime people are using whatever they can find to take the edge off their pain. That means overdoses. The new way of life that so many have cleaved to is gradually being replaced with a need to get high at any cost. They ate from the apple and here comes the fall.

The Age of Compassion lasted not quite five years.

I try not to talk too much to the rest of the world, but the sense I'm getting is that things might be worse than they've ever been.

Hope has just discovered a swarm of monarchs. They're fluttering around her, orbiting her as if she were the sun. There's no other moment than this one right here. Pandora and I are lost in the magic of her smile.

I have enormous faith in the abilities of my peers. They have a good chance of fixing things. If they fail, maybe we'll help. Maybe we won't. I'm okay if the world comes crashing down around everyone's ears.

And why shouldn't I be?

I'm with the people I love. That's good enough for me.

ACKNOWLEDGMENTS

The first debt of thanks goes to my hardworking editors: Susan Allison and Jennifer Hershey at Putnam, and Simon Taylor at Transworld (U.K.). *Everfree* has been enriched by their insight, patience and support.

I'm also grateful to Matthew Guma, Richard Pine, Lori Andiman, and everyone at InkWell Management.

David Koral copyedited the manuscript. Andrea Ho designed the U.S. edition jacket and Gretchen Achilles rendered the internal design.

Cheers to Andy Zawacki of the Cryonics Institute for taking time to answer my questions. While I've postulated a future where Black Ep sends the price of successful cryopreservation skyrocketing, the cost isn't so prohibitive today. For more information, try www.cryonics.org.

Pamela Ku provided a wealth of information about China and Chinese culture, and many members of the Cornell Thai Association wrote to answer my questions about Thailand. Special thanks to Tichakorn Wongpiromsarn and Matipon Tangmatitham.

Those of you who know how I write know how important music is to my creative process. I'm so happy to have an excerpt from "Scarred but Smarter" as the epigraph, as that song and "Fly Me Courageous" served as major inspirations for this trilogy. drivin' n' cryin' is a terrific band, and I'm very grateful to front man Kevn Kinney.

Doselle Young and Janine Ellen Young went above and beyond for *Everfree:* tremendously charitable with their time, helping me see a path through the initial scenes when writer's block had me spinning my wheels. Without their suggestions, I'd have spun for much longer. Deep thanks for getting me moving.

Erik Baard took a look at the early pages and reassured me that I hadn't gone mad. Very encouraging, and his notes proved valuable.

Walt McGraw's insightful feedback helped flesh out New Cambridge and its inhabitants. He recommended I read *The Natural History of the Rich,* by Richard Conniff, which proved to be an excellent resource.

John Scalzi has this weird mutant power where I feel really positive about the writing process whenever I talk with him. That definitely helped.

Enormously constructive conversations with Christopher Wood about evolution and human nature helped sew up the Patchwork section.

Uncle Jerry read the first draft and sparked to it, giving me smart, avuncular counsel, for which I apparently now owe him a villa.

As always, Dave Parks gave incredible advice. He's got great sensibilities, and I can't say enough about how much I value his perspective.

Additional support, encouragement, assistance and/or inspiration sprang from Nick Bortman, Andrew Chaikin, Marilyn Clair, Damned If I Don't Productions, Mike Dix, Harry Druyan, Les and Vicki Druyan, Jessica Flood, Chris Genoa, Brian Gilmore, Dan Gilmore, Dan Goldman, Rich Green, Sharon Greene, Guy Guthridge, Mozetta Hilliard, Jared Hoffman, Annah Hutchings, Nathan Jarvis, David Klein, Joanne Lamoureux, Louise Marley, Zack Marley, Joel McKuin, Maurice and Renee Minnis, Roger L. Payne, G. J. Pruss, Shayni Rae, Robby Ringer, Sam Sagan,

Sasha Sagan, Shari Smiley, Martha Soukup, Jessica Wade and Lyall Watson.

Thanks are overdue to the late, great Roger Zelazny. His *Amber* series is wonderfully thought-provoking, and I've no doubt that it served as a strong subconscious influence on these books.

I'm grateful to the fans of my writing, and especially the ones who stopped by www.nicksagan.com and took the time out to send me a note. Writers often feel isolated, and your support goes a long way toward keeping those demons at bay.

I think the world of Ann Druyan, and am honored by her continued confidence in me. Thanks for everything, Annie.

Clinnette Minnis is one of the best writers I know, and it's my great fortune to have her on my side. She's lived and breathed this trilogy just as I have over the past four years, and her contributions to its success have been tremendous.

Linda Salzman Sagan has always encouraged me, both as a fellow writer and as my mother. She's endlessly supportive, and I'm lucky to have her in my life. I hope she knows how much I love her.

With deep affection, I remember the starlight conversations my father and I would have about the universe and those who inhabit it. From the time I was very young, he inspired me to look at the big picture and ask the kinds of questions that really matter. Who are we? Where are we going? Are we alone? What does it all mean? To a large extent, *Everfree* is a natural extension of those questions and the conversations we used to have. He was more of an optimist, and I a pessimist, and that tug of war informs these books. My sensibilities may be darker than most, but his sense of wonder is with me still.

NICK SAGAN is the author of the novels *Idlewild*, *Edenborn* and *Everfree*. He is the son of astronomer Carl Sagan and artist/writer Linda Salzman. His greeting—"Hello from the children of planet Earth"—was recorded and placed aboard NASA's *Voyager I* and *Voyager II* spacecraft, which are now the most distant human-made objects in the universe. The writer of numerous screenplays and television episodes, Sagan graduated summa cum laude from UCLA Film School. Visit his Web site at www.nicksagan.com.